A Working Man's Apocrypha

A Working Man's Apocrypha

SHORT STORIES

WILLIAM LUVAAS

University of Oklahoma Press : Norman

The author wishes to thank the National Endowment for the Arts
for its generous support of this story collection.

Library of Congress Cataloging-in-Publication Data

Luvaas, William, 1945–
    A working man's apocrypha : short stories / William Luvaas.
        p. cm.
    ISBN 978-0-8061-3837-4 (alk. paper)
    I. Title.
    PS3562.U86W67 2007
    813'.54--dc22   2007000363

The paper in this book meets the guidelines for permanence and durability of the
Committee on Production Guidelines for Book Longevity of the Council on Library
Resources, Inc. ∞

Copyright ©2007 by the University of Oklahoma Press, Norman, Publishing Division of
the University. All rights reserved. Manufactured in the U.S.A.

1 2 3 4 5 6 7 8 9 10

For my mother

CONTENTS

Original Sin   3
The Sexual Revolution   18
Carpentry   28
Trespass   41
The Woman Who Was Allergic to Herself   54
A Working Man's Apocrypha   71
Yesterday After the Storm . . .   89
Season of Limb Fall   108
Hilltop (An American Story)   126
Silver Thaw   141
Let It Snow   150
Rain   161
To the Death   176
How I Died   188
Acknowledgments   207

A Working Man's Apocrypha

Original Sin

My aunt Louise wore three feathers in her hair that summer I went to live with her. "Red-tailed hawk," she said, though the feathers were tawny brown and glistened evilly from the black bun where she stuck them, conjuring in a boy's mind the commandment *Thou shalt not commit adultery,* barked sternly by our old minister back home. I couldn't say why it should, any more than I understood the commandment's meaning.

Aunt Louise committed *adulthood.* Mother had warned me of that often enough, but was helpless before the necessity of bequeathing me to her. Mother had become paler and thinner through the spring, so listless she often refused to eat. By May, I cooked what few meals were taken in our house, hardly eating myself. Nobody mentioned the dreaded word, but somehow I picked it out of thin air—the smell of her vomit in the morning, hollows where her eyes had been, prescriptions I fetched from the pharmacy (cocooned in the pharmacist's silence, the sly consolation of his eyes): *cancer.* I knew.

My boyhood, which never had much of a flight without a father to navigate it, crashed hard that spring and remained down. Innocence was soon to follow.

Actually, Aunt Louise fit more naturally into the realm of childhood than adulthood: hawk feathers and pink tennis shoes, her habit of taking Ralph, a raggedy-eared tabby cat, to bed with her, beginning each day in her bedroom next to mine profanely expelling him. "Ungrateful little *shit*," she'd scream. I rubbed the word's hard underside against my palate, learning it was possible—as Mother had taught me it was not—to use profanity without conjuring a vivid image of the word uttered. Likely Mother had little practice.

But I stood transfixed, ears pinned to the sides of my head, the first time I heard Louise use the "F-word." It was a word I had never actually heard uttered—certainly not in my mother's house. I couldn't get enough of it. I practiced firing it at knickknacks in my room like a Remington hollow-point. I never missed. It made my ears burn to think of Mother lying in a hospital bed in Portland while I practiced the F-word in Seattle, but I was as helpless before it as some are before a slot machine. Any boy raised to believe humans are featureless beneath their clothing is at the mercy of every obscenity.

The obscenity facing Mother that summer was too filthy even for Aunt Louise's seasoned lips. I knew well enough that, without drastic cause, mothers like mine do not bequeath their adolescent sons to Aunts like Louise. Surely, Mother would have kept me among her own people if there had been any. But she, too, was an only child, her parents dead. So in desperation, days before she checked in for her operation, she turned to Louise, who had always had a soft spot for mother and me.

"You are going to stay with your father's sister a time," Mother told me that last day, exhausted from the effort of sitting up in a chair, her hands icy wafers, sandwiching mine between. Their cold terrified me, as did the pulsing blue veins, like angleworms, that had appeared overnight in the hollow above her nose. "You may see some strange things, Tommy. Louise's hygiene isn't up to what you are accustomed to, she keeps odd hours, and she smokes too much." Mother's fingers clutched my elbow, her eyes the ethereal blue of a saint with only one foot in this world. "Remember what I've taught you. Trust in your own good judgment." She smiled at me with lips alkaline pale and chafed. It occurred to me then that she expected me to see strange things—that she counted on it, as she had once counted on my learning to swim at summer camp.

Aunt Louise lived alone in a narrow house on a back street of Seattle. The kitchen was flooded with light that poured in through huge casement windows and bathed the tile floor like clean white water. But the front of the house was dark and cluttered, shut away from prying eyes, heavy curtains always drawn. It seemed odd to me: my "liberal-minded" aunt, who voted for Kefauver and believed in premarital sex, living in a junk shop full of old-fashioned furniture my Mother would have thrown out. Books, written in French or windy, strident English that reminded me of an equinoctial storm, lay on their bellies over rug and davenport, their spines broken. "Existentialists," she called them.

Her neighbors she dubbed "dirty-minded little conformists," saying, "They'd burn me at the stake if it were legal." She dismissed them with a wave of her hand, fixing restless black eyes on me. "Whatever you do, Tommy, promise me you won't become a cruddy little go-along."

I shook my head vigorously, staring at the red rind about her cigarette filter, piled atop other cigarette butts spilling from the ashtray.

Mother said Louise was smart enough to teach college but lacked ambition. She worked as a supermarket cashier, didn't have much to say about college, and wasn't interested in anything that hadn't fallen into disrepute or disrepair or that wasn't threatened with extinction. Openhearted, she talked to anyone: the mailman, Fuller Brush salesmen, Paul Harvey on the radio (shrieking, "Piss-pot conservative!" from the kitchen sink, refuting his every point as if he stood there in the room beside her). She talked nonstop to me: the Brooklyn Dodgers, the Three Stooges, the Korean War. The war worried me. After all, my dad had died in the last war. In just six years I would be old enough for the draft. Louise assured me that modern wars don't last that long. "This nuclear business has put an end to that."

Somewhere along the line Aunt Louise had picked up a southern accent, along with the tight little bun, feathers, and purple sack dresses. She loved Elvis, knew his ring size and brand of deodorant, and every record in the order he'd recorded it. She embroidered his slick-haired silhouette on pillow cases and sang "Hound Dog" in the shower, but confessed to me her suspicion he wasn't much in bed. "Vain men make lousy lovers." Winking in that broad way she had of making me feel privy to something generally unknown.

About the house, she wore a sleeveless smock without any shape but what she gave it. I was just becoming aware of such things: my aunt's sharp breasts and bony hips. I would lean to the side—as if to catch sight of a bird passing outside—and steal, through an armhole, a peek of a creamy breast. Once she caught me at it.

"Look at you! You're red as a beefsteak tomato." She laughed. "Hey, it's healthy to be curious. Look!—nothing to hide." Louise gripped the hem of her smock as if to lift it.

"No, Ma'am!" I cried. "I don't . . . I mean . . ."

"I got your number. On the sly." She winked and ruffled my hair.

I pulled away, my cheeks burning chili hot, and went straight outside. Not to my friend Jeff's next door (who wasn't allowed on Louise's property because she said he possessed "a low moral temperament"), but to the nearby hills, from whose tops I caught flint blue glimpses of Puget Sound. Late that afternoon, I returned through a cold drizzle, clothes damp, a chill working into my bones, and moved stealthily through the gloomy living room, planning to go straight upstairs without speaking to Louise. It wasn't my fault she didn't wear proper underthings or that she undressed—as Jeff assured me she did—without closing her drapes. ("Come see for yourself. It's better than *Playboy*.") I tiptoed past bookshelves, and lion-footed overstuffed chairs, certain I could make it to my room unnoticed and somehow survive the night without supper. But a voice snagged me from the shadows.

"I was worried about you."

Louise was folded deep into the couch, barely visible, swaddled in the burgundy glow from the drapes.

"Holy shit! You scared me."

"Better don't talk like that when you go home. I'll catch hell for teaching you profanity."

"You say it all the time."

"I'm free to say whatever I please, buster." She made a rustling sound, sitting up on the couch. "Your mama wrote."

"To me?"

"Listen, Tommy, you might have to stay a little longer."

I shrugged, pretending not to care. "She got out of the hospital last week."

"They've checked her back in. Nothing serious, honey. Routine." Her eyes slid away like they did when she discussed Elvis's religious beliefs or Kefauver's wife.

I sensed fog creeping up from the Sound along empty streets, ambushing buildings, filling nether regions of my aunt's long, tall house.

"You got to have faith, Tommy. You know I think churches are turkey piss, but I believe in rightness. I believe in faith."

"Will they open her up again?"

"Not very far." Her eyes flashed at me. "Just a little."

I envisioned a zipper in my mother's stomach that they could open and close at will. The idea scandalized me as nothing Louise said ever could.

We ate lavishly that night: corn waffles, rice with milk and sugar, Chet's turkey potpies; our favorites. We felt like being kind to ourselves.

Next morning, when I shuffled from my bedroom to pee, I discovered Louise had left the bathroom door ajar. Another kindness? I stopped short, staring at my aunt afloat in the tub, lazily steaming water lapping blue-green at the rim, her eyes gazing blankly upward, knobby knees breaking the surface, long black hair snaking down her stomach, clinging to her secret parts. For an instant I thought she was dead. Though I knew artificial respiration from Scouts, how could I possibly perform mouth-to-mouth on my naked aunt in the bathtub? Better to pretend I hadn't seen her. I had started to tiptoe away, mortified with guilt, when her corpse spoke behind me.

"You can use the toilet, honey. I won't peek."

Afterward, neither of us mentioned the incident. At breakfast I kept my eyes focused on hawk feathers, leaning at acute angles from her bun, like TV antennas clinging to tenement roofs. This was another lesson of that summer: If two people ignore a thing it's as if it never occurred. The world is not as black and white a place as I was raised to believe.

On that basis, I accepted Jeff's offer to stay the night at his house. Louise thought it a splendid idea. "We could use time off from each other, don't you think?"

Later that night, when she returned from work, Louise sniffed us out as we peeked into her bedroom window from Jeff's window next door, facing hers on the second floor. Her bedroom light snapped on, adding density to the hazy emptiness between houses. Louise stood at the window, looking directly across at Venetian blinds behind which we huddled. Instinctively, I ducked. "She can't see nothing," Jeff huffed. "Who cares anyways?"

My aunt toyed a moment with a blouse button, then drew the shades. I breathed relief. And disappointment.

Jeff groaned. "You never told me she had a guy over there. She only closes up when she's doing it."

His imputation made me mad. "My Aunt Louise lives alone, jerk."

He looked me over with a sly tilt of the head. "I guess you don't know much down in Oregon."

I punched his shoulder, bereft of the good judgment my mother had assured me would guide a son through such predicaments. Jeff was all over me, pummeling viciously at my head, chest, groin. I swooned beneath green currents, nausea clinging like seaweed to my stomach. Jeff pinned me down with his knees and breathed sourly in my face, teeth rooted in collars of yellow tartar, then cursed and rolled away in disgust. And I rolled up in my sleeping bag on the floor, tight as a mummy, amid a faint aura of dirty socks. Next morning the events of the previous night went unmentioned. Forgotten, as if they had never happened at all.

―――――

Later at Louise's I met Uncle Sam. He told me to call him "uncle," anyhow, in a tone that brooked no disagreement. Biceps sagged down his arms like the contented bellies of Dylan Thomas's uncles after a Christmas feed. A trellis of roses twined up the left forearm, enclosing in its lattice: *Don't Tread On Me!* Then I realized the rose vines were really snakes. Grinning a gold tooth, Sammy demonstrated how, in the crook of his right elbow, a hula-skirted girl wiggled her belly when he pumped his arm.

"He's a big ol' shipwrecked dummy," Louise said, flopping arms over his shoulders and resting her chin on the bald center strip of his head. "His ship is in port for the week. We hoped you wouldn't mind if he came on board as our guest."

They watched, awaiting my decision. I wasn't stupid. I knew that, shipwrecked or not, men weren't supposed to cohabit with women who weren't their wives. Besides, tattooed sailors did not shack up with eggheads like Aunt Louise. I longed to return home, where women closed bathroom doors and uncles were truly uncles. It was all happening too fast: curse words, nudity, adults seeking my permission to sleep together in the house where I was a summer guest.

I nodded okay. Then Uncle Sam demonstrated the manly art of arm wrestling while Louise made ham and eggs. Years later, I would empathize with Sam's shipwrecked nature and wonder whether every port of call in his sailor's life offered some challenge akin to the nephew who lived with his aunt while his mother was dying in a Portland hospital. A faltering, white-skinned, long-eyed, hay-feverish boy who, raised on simple virtues, took every word you said quite literally. Possibly in another port—Lake Charles, Louisiana or Houston, Texas—a wife hounded him to settle down and his own son grew sullen, as mistrustful as I was of his itinerant sailor father.

Sam tried to instill in me his enthusiasm for tattoos and fighter planes, and pointed out the naked woman on a Camel pack. (I couldn't find her, looking as I was for Aunt Louise afloat in the tub.) His sluggish blue eyes had a red crease through each pupil. Blood blisters, he explained, from some barroom brawl. He was as proud of those wounds as he wasn't of his war record. That troubled me.

Sam took me fishing on the pier: a highway of wooden planks on pilings against which the black sea frothed and snarled. I loved to watch the waves seethe white over layered barnacles and mussels on the timbers and spill slimy green off seaweed. One day, standing beside Sam on the pier, I told how my father had died on a troop transport, torpedoed off the Philippines before he reached the fighting. Sam stood indifferently watching the gulls, his bamboo pole drooping, line bellying close to the water. He seemed unaware of it, other than to check occasionally to see if he had lost his bait. I knew he had been a bombardier, flying missions over Pacific atolls. (He rattled off odd, tongue-tickling names: Saipan, Morotai, Pelelieu.) I envisioned him squatting in the bomb bay of a B-52, knees to chest, cradling each bomb lovingly in his hands before letting it drop into jungles below, squinting aim through the red cross hairs on his eyeballs. Avenging my father. It was the thing I found to like in him.

"I saw the whole shootin' match, right on into Okinawa," he said at last. "Personally, I liquidated sixty-thousand Nips. You know what that does to a man? You know what he dreams about at night?"

"The Japs killed lots of people. They killed my dad."

"Yeah, sure. Sure they did." He patted a shirt pocket for the Alka-Seltzer he took for his ulcer, screwing eyes tight as if swallowing molten lead.

"Don't you use any water?" I asked him.

"Tommy, I'm real sorry about your dad. Still, it don't matter who they are. Nips, Russians . . . don't matter." The line click-clicking as he reeled in. "It's all human beings the same."

"The Japs killed my dad."

He looked at me, eyes gone vague and polished. Moisture burst from his lips. "What do you know about my dreams?" Wheeling on a duo of old-timers strolling the pier. "What do you know? Legionnaire bastards!" Sea gulls squealed away from his shout.

The men stood gawking at him. One led the other away by an elbow, throwing back nervous glances. Sam feinted toward them, and they leapt forward in a bowlegged, geriatric sprint.

"What do any of them know about my dreams?"

A black man, fishing over the rail nearby, shook his head at me as if I were at fault somehow. When I wanted only to escape. Not understanding why Louise sent me off to carry Sam's bait bucket. Disgusted to think of him sharing my aunt's bed. They tried to fool me by turning up the radio, but behind liquid rhythms of jazz, secret rhythms were at work. Every now and again a cry broke through—a wail half-heard on the verge of sleep, so I couldn't be sure it didn't originate in my own unconscious.

Louise took me aside one day, eyes darting about the precincts of my room, smiling at a drawing I had done of a *Tyrannosaurus rex*. She put an arm around my shoulders and nuzzled my head, an affection I had learned to tolerate.

"Goodness sake, you're nearly tall as me."

I knew she hadn't come to discuss my height.

"Listen, honeybunch. If this was an ideal world, wouldn't be a thing you couldn't tell your mother. But it isn't. There's things she doesn't need to know about. Things a woman of her high character wouldn't appreciate. You understand?"

"I know you have sex with Sammy," I said.

Her head shook confusion. I wondered why she could not smile without lipstick leaking onto her teeth.

"We don't all share the same convictions. Some of us need some comforting. You might learn that yourself one day. Mama doesn't need to know about Uncle Sam." Her voice gone cold and mercantile. "Maybe she doesn't get so lonely." She gripped my head in the crook of her arm, grinding her chin into my scalp. I struggled free from her smell of stale deodorant and perspiration.

"Is Mother dying?" I asked.

Louise flinched. "What makes you ask such a thing?"

"You won't let me read her letter."

"It wasn't hers, honey. It was the doctor's."

"She's dying, isn't she?"

"I don't believe it a minute. You'll be going home soon. You'll remember the good times we had and how you went fishing with Sammy. How about later we go to Discovery Park and ride the roller coaster? And maybe you can win a blue bear at the dime toss to send home to her. Think she'd like a blue bear?"

"I'm almost grown up," I snapped. "I seen you naked in the bathtub. I've done things you wouldn't even guess."

She stared. "Well I . . ."

"You don't honor that at all."

"I was thinking about your mother. And you, Tom."

"I believe she wants it to go back like it used to be before they opened her up, when I lived at home and came to visit for a week in the summer. And me, that's all I want."

"Me too. I'd like that." She hugged me again, the sharp point of a breast inflaming me with mixed emotions. I wanted to tell her how I'd defended her that night at Jeff's. There was too much world to hold up at once. I didn't yet know the cleansing power of tears. I felt them dammed, cloistered inside of me, felt their pressure at my temples and at the back of my throat, felt them leak cautiously into my eyes and survey the landscape. But didn't let them come. Tears are final. No one needed to teach me that. They come when we have surrendered to grief and there is no turning back. I was not willing to surrender Mother, or Aunt Louise. I wanted them both.

The argument started before supper. Uncle Sam boisterous all afternoon, drinking hard from a bottle in a brown paper bag, winking at me when I looked up from baseball cards spread across the dining room rug. (I had two Hank Aarons but needed a Pee Wee Reese.) Drinking buddy, claimant to his lewd jokes. I wished he would go down to Silky's on the corner. Instead, he sprawled in blue jeans and buttonless work shirt on a kitchen chair, speaking to no one in particular about a scar across his belly.

"Friggin' American Legion think war's a dance around a cathouse. See that!" Opening his shirt to display a glazed pink weal slashing left to right (opposite what I imagined Mother's to be).

"We've heard the story, Sammy. You're talking to yourself," Louise said.

"A Legionnaire done that. I carried my guts half a block before they got me down."

"It isn't the right time and place, Sammy."

"You know what it feels like?" he asked me. "Slimy and soft, like wet silk. Heavy. You wouldn't believe."

I leapt up from my cards and charged upstairs to the bathroom with a hand over my mouth, afraid I was going to be sick.

"Shuddup!" Louise shouted. "Just shuddup your idiot mouth. His mother is dying . . ." Her words trailing off.

Sammy came blubbering behind me. "Sorry, kid. Didn't mean no harm." I hid behind the bathroom door. He stumbled. Seeing my chance, I leapt past him like a cat and was gone down the stairs and out of the house.

Thinking I might hitchhike to the hospital back home, I wandered the streets, until fog moved uphill along the wide avenues from the sound and scrubbed the facades of shingled houses. Cold in my sweatshirt, I started back to Louise's.

The house was quiet. Yet there was breathing, as though the walls themselves were alive. The chill followed me inside. Front room clutter had spread into the kitchen—but violently. An overturned chair, Louise's blouse with two buttons missing. Silence was shattered by a single cry. Upstairs. A wavering, ululant groan, going on and on, with whimpering spasms between: the sound a woman might make with her throat locked in the hands of a beefy man.

I moved fast. Grabbed the largest butcher knife from the kitchen drawer, rivets of the wooden handle pressed cold against my palm, thick blade flat against my thigh, as I took the stairs two at a time.

Louise was smart enough to leave the bedroom door ajar, so I understood that first time—the bathroom—had been practice for what she had sensed coming. A woman's intuition, Mother called it. I knelt behind the door, eyes adjusting to the greater darkness within. Sammy straddled her, as I expected he would. Bedcovers torn aside in brutal, heedless assault. His bare back faced me, quilted with hair.

He made a sound low in his throat and cast his eyes toward the ceiling. His hands slipped from her neck and gripped her shoulders, shaking. Regretting, perhaps, what he had done. I remembered reading in a Dick Tracy comic how a knife thrust six inches beneath the shoulder blade, just to the side of the spinal column, would plunge straight into the heart. The question was whether to go stealthily or to rush forward all at once like a football fullback and plunge the knife into him. I decided on the second.

He was talking again—that sotted, rambling patter of obscenity and regret. I plunged forward, knife raised over my head in both hands, a war cry in my throat.

Perhaps it was Louise's eyes that made me hesitate. Not dead but alive, and gleaming as I had never seen them. Giving Uncle Sam time to pivot and catch the knife blade in his bare fist. Louise curled against the headboard, knees instinctively coiled to chest. Her eyes blinked in a feverish attempt to recognize me. "No," she moaned. "Oh no."

Sammy slid the knife from his buckled, bleeding fingers. "Your daddy must've been a Legionnaire," he said.

"I th-thought you choked her," I stammered.

Blood dripped from his clenched fist onto the sheet. *Sure to stain*, was all I could think. Perhaps Louise thought the same. She stared dumbly. Then leapt up. Firming a hand in the matted dent of Sammy's back, she guided him downstairs to the kitchen.

I followed, gaping at those two naked adults. The wiry yet bearish man clutching one fragile hand in the other, relinquishing it to her—dripping red over the sink—his mouth opening in a mute cry. I couldn't comprehend what had happened or how I could have done such a thing. Couldn't understand it at all. Louise ripped a flowered towel down the middle and wrapped it around his palm, split ends tied in a knot over the wound: what I recognized as a tourniquet, from Scouts.

"It's deep, Sammy," she said. "We better call a doctor."

He sucked air out of his cheeks and ran the good hand back over his scalp. His eyes rolled at me, each pupil creased, a tiny fold of red.

My mouth worked to tell him I was sorry.

"Does it hurt?" I managed.

"Only when I think about it." He winked.

"We need a doctor," Louise insisted.

At that instant the phone rang. Louise seized it.

"Dr. Bailey!" She laughed surprise. "Yes, yes, he's right here with me."

She discovered me then—her free hand pestering the air with gestures of concealment —the corner of her lip spasming reflexive smiles, as when she imitated Elvis's "Hound Dog."

"Yes, I understand." Her eyes closed, the heavy lids. "Ohhhh," she groaned. "Oh, damn it all to holy hell."

I watched, trying to concentrate, to focus: her deflated nipples dark as coffee, puffy body sagging toward middle age. Not shocking or dirty, in the way Jeff next door had it. Merely unexpected. Even Mother, I thought, if one saw her like the day she was born . . . Then, before tears gripped me, it occurred to me that I could flee. Before it was too late. Before Aunt Louise sent the house of cards tumbling with a whack of the hand. But she had already let the phone slide into its berth, snatched up her torn blouse from the floor and slipped it over her shoulders, as if considering her informality inappropriate to the task at hand.

Sammy had vanished. That blouse with its missing buttons the only evidence he had been there at all.

"He'll be back," she said huskily, slipping an arm around me. "Like reincarnation. Do you know about reincarnation? Our ship departs, but it returns. I want you to believe that, Tommy. No one ever leaves for good and final."

That night she took me into her bed and held me close, explained that some lessons come when one is too young to receive them. Death always arrives too young. Nestled against the loaf of her belly, I understood my Aunt Louise was a living metaphor. In her person, she had condensed life and offered it to me as a gift. Perhaps that is why mother had sent me to her, knowing her own chances. Strong diseases require strong remedies. All night I lay awake while her chest rose and fell.

"Mama's dead," I said when Louise woke beside me next morning.

Ill-humored to find me in her bed, eyes gritty with sleep, she shooed me out as she did Ralph, but gently.

"How would you like to live with me?" she asked later. "Maybe we could adopt each other." She promised to tell me how Mama passed away—as soon as she could do so without breaking down.

"There will have to be rules," she told me, after grief had come like a prodigal father returned from a long absence. Taunted and reduced me to bone in clean, pure sunshine. And when it left I was weak and new footed, making my way through a bleak but acceptable terrain.

"No more sleeping in my bed; you're too old for that. You make breakfast, I'll make dinner. You can do housework when you can't stand the mess any longer. Do your homework every night. And in cases where her judgment and mine conflict, you will honor your mother. First and foremost, you will always be her son."

The Sexual Revolution

Mrs. Bloomenthal lived directly across from the twins while they were growing up on Purdy Street. No one in the neighborhood knew more about her than that she worked part time as a legal secretary and that Mr. Bloomenthal was no longer around, thus—in days before divorce was as common as now—was presumed dead. Once, Holly called Mrs. Bloomenthal "widow" behind her back.

"'Widow' isn't a word for children," Mother chided in her gentle manner. For a suspended moment her pale yellowish eyes went blank as if she had no great conviction in what she said but felt obliged to say it anyway.

"Why not?" Holly's twin brother How asked (Howard! but the name had been nicked short to How as Holly's had to Hol). It was not unusual for him to ask the question foremost on his sister's mind, or vice versa.

"Because it's not," Mom snapped. In those days that was answer enough.

Secretly, the twins called Mrs. Bloomenthal "widow" anyway, and the term took on vaguely erotic qualities it wouldn't have possessed had it been allowed to remain in the open. "Gopher," "jigsaw," many words might take on similar qualities if you locked them up. Behind backs, too, the twins debated whether Mrs. Bloomenthal wore a bra. A "thingy" they called it, both to themselves and publicly. For here, truly, was a seditious word that ten-year-olds in the late fifties had no business using. Or if they did, only with explosive giggles. The word would ricochet off their soft palates, sounding something like a lamb bleat.

One day after school in the fall, Mother was out shopping and the twins arrived home to a note on the front door saying they must go across the street to Mrs. Bloomenthal's until she returned. On this day the bra debate was to become a matter of contention between them. No small matter, for How and Hol were like taut piano wires side by side: a vibration begun in one invariably translated to the other. It wasn't uncommon in those days before puberty betrayed them that they read each other's thoughts. Or one would have a sudden vivid intuition regarding the other as twins often do. Hol actually saw the golf ball sailing through the branchless blue sky of her mind above the country club parking lot the day it came speeding towards Howie's head. She tackled him an instant before it hit. Dad said to quit horsing around, for Pete's sake, tilting his chin upward as the ball popped explosively off the asphalt not five feet from where he stood, popped twice more before crashing through a station wagon windshield.

However convenient at times, this telepathic coziness could be confusing, as when they shared mutual crushes on one or another of the tan blonds arriving in town from California. First a girl, then a boy, depending on which of the twins initiated the affair. Mom fretted when the twins brought their latest infatuation home and began squabbling over which of them would serve Kool Aid or form an alliance with their new friend in a game of Monopoly.

"They're just kids, I wouldn't worry about it," Howard overheard Dad saying one night as he passed his parents' bedroom on his way to the bathroom.

"What did they say?" Hol demanded the moment her brother returned to the twins' bedroom, sitting upright in the top bunk.

"Mom said we're abnormal."

"Sure, dumb-cough, we're twins. Twins are s'posed to be abnormal."

"Not like that. Bad abnormal."

"Mrs. Bloomenthal is abnormal. She mixes sand and cat poop in a cardboard box in her kitchen."

"I think Mom thinks we're queers."

Hol was silent a minute. How sensed her overhead in the dark as he settled into the lower deck. But could make out only a vague downward bellying of the grid of metal bands supporting her mattress, reflecting the night light in the hallway. Sometimes he dreamt that the brassy bands snapped one by one and his sister's body plummeted down atop him, mattress and all. The dream carried mixed emotional messages: the simple physical terror of suffocation, complicated first by outrage, then near tenderness as he envisioned his sister carrying on for both of them. A brother/sister hybrid. That was comforting. She'd always been the better speller, while he was better in math (their telepathy didn't extend to academics). Together they would make a formidable brain. But now he planted foot soles in her bottom and pushed upward until his legs were stiff. Letting Hol drop, he watched the grid expand and contract. The bunk bed jiggled as if shaken by an earthquake.

"What's a queer?" Holly asked when she had settled.

"You know . . . if you're a boy they want to see your wong."

"Big deal."

"It'th a man who talkth like thith and likes to touch men'th privatth." Mr. Kips, the scoutmaster, used the term "privates" for the baggage hanging between your legs, so How saw no harm in saying it himself. Holly protested.

"You shouldn't of said that. I'm gonna tell Mommy what you said." After a moment she reconsidered. "Ugh! that's disgusting. I don't believe she really said that. Mom must've meant *you*."

"I'm not any queer." It amazed How, too, that Mom could think such a thing of her own kids. Though, actually, now that he considered it, she didn't say they were "queers," she said it was "queer." Mrs. Bloomenthal was queer. The word, like so many others, had a double meaning—like "dip" or "jerk."

"You are so," Hol was giggling. "If you play with yourth maybe you want to play with somebody elth'th."

"Liar. You liar." He blushed fiercely. How did she know he did that? He always waited until after she was asleep.

"Tommy Olthon," she lisped. "You want to play with Tommy Olthon'th privath."

"Dumb-cough!" he snapped. It wasn't fair. Tommy was a friend. You didn't say things like that about your friends. You could like a friend if you wanted to; there was nothing wrong with that. "Maybe *you* do. Tommy's your boyfriend," he countered angrily, just as Dad yelled from across the hall.

"Hey, you two, knock it off in there."

"Sally Paterson . . . Lizzie Coltrane!" he tortured his sister over Cheerios next morning. Sally was a fragile, wispy angel, with an olive complexion offsetting platinum blond hair, who had stolen his heart a year ago. Then his sister's. If he thought about it, it was probably Hol's jealous bickering that had driven Sally away. There were others he could mention to prove Mom's point. Instead, he didn't share the banana he had peeled with his sister as he usually did. But ate it all himself.

Riding home on the bus that afternoon from school, they sat sullenly side by side, sensing by means of that telepathy which became clairvoyance when jointly focused that the debate over widow Bloomenthal was to reach a head that very day. They arrived home to Mom's note on the door.

"I don't want to go over there. The old witch will just make us pick apples."

"Widow Broom-en-witch," said How. "She's weird."

"She probably eats a hundred apples every day."

"After their husband dies, widows can't fart anymore. That's how you can always pick a widow out of the normal women," How said, glad the feud with his sister was over.

"We have to go over," Holly said.

Sure enough, Mrs. Bloomenthal met them cheerily at the door and suggested they go out back and pick apples before it rained. "Wouldn't that be nice? Show me a boy who doesn't like candied apples." She smiled and stooped down over them.

How many teeth does she have? Hol was thinking, causing her brother to wonder at the same moment. Probably twice the average amount, How thought back, all jammed together. Glossy white. She probably polishes them every morning with baking soda and a chammy cloth. Her chin came to a disquieting point, making her whole face seem plaque-shaped, features pasted on where engraved lettering might be. There was a name for that shape, Holly knew from mathematics but couldn't remember it (though Howie could), but would have been able to spell it if she could. Besides being not exactly ugly, only queer, widow Bloomenthal was God-knows-how-old. Thirty-five, thought Howie. More like fifty, Hol rejoined. A living mummy's tomb. But the real trouble—both realized at once—was she didn't have any children. That made them feel sorry for her. No wonder she picked so many apples.

Besides, and worst of all, her house had an odd fermented odor. Though it was spotlessly clean. Dad, who was a lawyer, would say, "She has a strong case in that department." Even her shoes were stylish enough. Still, she was peculiar. It was partly this bra business and, of course, her pentagonal face and agelessness. How concluded she was the combined age of everyone in their family divided by two. A formula that added dignity in his eyes. Besides, if you did plastic surgery on her chin and maybe found a way to keep her nose from reminding you of Queen Elizabeth, she would be actually okay looking, if not exactly pretty. She had pliant, sad brown eyes.

In weight, she was only the formula of Tommy Olson plus the twins divided by two. Not much for a woman. Skinny almost.

Holly thought her brother dumb about the bra business. Who cared? She might remind him of the USSR and Mom's fear that atomic bombs would soon be landing in their backyard, but all he could think about was whether witch Bloomenthal wore a dumb thingy.

Mrs. B's backyard was enclosed by a white picket fence. There were two apple trees, a peach, a cherry, many varieties of old-lady bushes and flowers with names that sounded like cold medicine, and a ground cover creeping over rocks in one corner like a sticky green spider web sucking the nutrition out of everything. The wind had picked up. Overhead, clouds thickened like puddles at the bus stop after passing cars stirred up mud in them, growing darker and darker.

"I believe it's fixing," Mrs. Bloomenthal said, "fast a-fixing." It was her plan to place Hol picking at top of the step ladder, herself on the second rung, and How on terra firma. In a chain of moving hands, they passed golden delicious apples to him and he arranged them in the bucket, careful not to bruise them (Mrs. B spoke of apples as if they were delicate newborn babies). It was this arrangement, along with Mrs. Bloomenthal's loose-fitting shorty blouse, that led to How's discovery—as the widow stretched up to grip an apple or to caution, "Easy, dear, don't reach too high," the blouse hem rising along with her arm.

Holly knew in advance what her brother would report—knew by the way he craned his neck sideways to peek, upper lip hunched moronically, like Elvis Presley's—and wished to drop an apple down on his dumb-cough head. Knew by the way his agitated thoughts bombarded her across linked circuitry that something new and terrible was happening to her twin. Howard was breaking off, becoming something she couldn't follow and wouldn't wish to lead. Always before she had been a willing accomplice to How's antics, but in this she refused. Howard stood before her more naked than he'd ever been in those growing up years they had showered together. Nude.

She wanted to warn Mrs. Bloomenthal somehow that her brother was peeking up her blouse. But how would she? She wasn't ready to cross the line to betrayal. She felt sudden unexpected kinship with this woman whose face, glowing softly in gathering dusk, had shed its witchiness and become the face nearly of a friend. A person with whom—if your twin brother suddenly died or changed so you no longer knew him—you might share your secrets as you'd once shared them with him. Compromising, Holly thrust a finger downward in a way that caused Mrs. B to cry out in alarm, "What is it, dear? The ladder?"

Howard straightened quickly up when she glanced down, looking as though he had been swallowing apples rather than placing them in the bucket. However, the second time, when Holly dropped an apple to the ground in vexation, Mrs. Bloomenthal caught him in the act: head cocked, eyes walling, but hair remaining arrogantly in place like Richard Nixon's always did.

Holly froze, fearing Mrs. B would scream, or slap him across the cheek, or leap from the ladder and run to the house, locking them outside in the sprinkling rain like twin imps. Howard himself felt in advance her five fingers formed in a solid stinging fan that remolded his smirk into something respectable. But remarkably she smiled and patted the top of his head. "I think we'd better keep our eyes on our work," she scolded. "Oh! it's raining."

"She was," he whispered later on the porch as they sat sorting apples by size into a trio of boxes, "stark raving naked underneath. Honest!"

"Dirty-minded," Holly hissed back in his ear, keeping an eye on Mrs. B.

"Honest. Like twin dogs' noses on her chest."

"What, dear?" Mrs. Bloomenthal stretched over to pluck out an apple How had misplaced in the medium box, resorting it into the small with spidery fingers.

"Nothing, Ma'am." He hadn't meant her to overhear.

"Disgusting," Holly snapped, narrowing eyes that were cold and vulpine in the gathering gloom. Beyond, rain pelted dark rhododendron leaves. Widow Bloomenthal glanced back and forth between them with what must be called irony (a word How could not have spelled but Hol could).

"Oh, I know what goes on between brothers and sisters. I had a brother myself once. We two shared everything; there was no such thing as a secret between us. Until one day, right out of nowhere, he rebelled against it. I didn't know why. I just credited it to the nature of males. One day they decide they want to keep things to themselves."

Her eyes were fixed on Howard, knowing and full of the dark ripe brown of forgiveness. But he stared at her pointy chin and could see nothing but breasts. While Holly wondered: Will this happen to me? One day, picking apples, my brother will go weird and yucky, then my eyes will get sad. I will grow up to be a widow with hairs on my chin, never again knowing a boy I can trust with my secrets.

All this seemed preparation for what was to arrive that very next week. What Mom called, "the most important event of your life since you were born." A trauma actually. A mysterious onslaught from within that required Hol to wear thick absorbent padding under her clothes and to walk with the plodding steps of an old-fashioned knight. How did you share the same room with your nosy brother when that was happening to you?

At once, in a single day, Dad's basement den was transformed to a boy's bedroom. Nothing to it. The pipe rack and leather recliner and bookshelves were moved to a corner of the living room, the desk, with its locked drawers, went to the attic, the ersatz knotty pine paneling and deer antlers remained, along with the wagon wheel overhead fixture. Howard said they made him feel at home. The bunk bed was divided in two: half to her room, half to his. Dad spoke about outfitting another den in the attic some day, but never did.

It was as if one moment they were twins, the next they were just brother and sister with separate bedrooms and separate identities. Holly with the first experience of her life she could not find a way to share with her brother (or the second, if you counted Mrs. Bloomenthal's bra).

She dreamt of the widow that first night alone in her new/old bedroom that seemed already to be shedding the smell of a boy's sour socks and musty baseball glove. In her dream, Mrs. B's backyard was as lush as any jungle. Lianas crept up gnarled apple tree limbs, vipers coiled in thick emerald ground cover, Mrs. Bloomenthal herself, stripped to the waist, guarded the garden gates, seizing a double-bladed sword in a backhand tennis grip. Her eyes glowing like obsidian flakes. When Holly approached with her apple basket, the widow sliced at the air, throwing out sparks and hissing blue flames to bar her path. Holly dropped her basket and fled, spilling apples over the ground, knowing she would never pick them again.

For his part, How didn't seem to mind the new arrangement. He spent endless hours holed up in the basement, where stacks of Marvel comics under his bed were reinforced with Dad's old *Playboys* salvaged from the trash. Joined down there by his new friends, indifferent now to Holly's blond junior surfers. She sometimes heard their raucous voices drifting up through hot air vents. Mom, in her way, wondered if it was "healthy" for a growing boy to spend so much time in the basement. "Look at me!" Dad insisted (for their parents' discussions had come out of the closet), "I guess it didn't do me any harm."

Actually, Holly, too, was involved with her own sex mainly now: other girls whose likeness to her was not superficial, as it was with

How—a deceptive similarity that tells nothing of what is beneath—but a likeness of gender and growing interests and destiny. "You can't trust appearances" had become her favorite phrase in those days. Coming from a twin, it made an impression on people. Such great changes, coming all at once, were disruptive to the family. Although "wholesome" Mother said, smiling upon her children over their Quaker oats in the morning.

When rarely it occurred to her, Holly realized she no longer knew what her brother was thinking. She wondered if Howard was troubled also by a cloying sense of loss. But could not tell. Couldn't even bring herself to ask.

Carpentry

Sinclair asked if I knew carpentry.

"I've built a fence or two."

"Plumb and level carpentry?"

"Not much," I admitted. "Guess I can swing a hammer."

He looked me over as if he doubted it. At the time I was cutting shingle bolts in the woods. I knew checker wedge, froe and sledge, could drive a pickup anywhere loggers had been, come rain or shit salad. But business was slow. "No one's building houses," Mr. Angellino down at the mill said. "Pretty soon no one will be cutting trees either, what with this spotted-owl monkey business."

The owl didn't trouble me; I just needed steady work.

"You have experience, I have the contact," I told Sinclair. "We could partner up." What I didn't tell him was I only saw the job advertised on the A and P bulletin board. He might as well think it was a friend of mine.

The notice asked for skilled carpenters. A man named Norton answered the phone, said he'd bought land and a couple of cabins out on the ridge. He planned to build workshops, barns, a shooting range, and he wanted estimates. That's where Sinclair came in; I've never estimated a carpenter job in my life.

Sinclair was a burly man. His forearms didn't taper one bit at the wrist, covered in a pelt of rusty fuzz. My guess is he was nappy that way chin to toe if you cared to look. Bald up top of his big billiard ball head. One hot day, straddling rafters with our shirts off, I suggested he might transplant chest hair up to his chrome dome. Sinclair had neat white teeth when he smiled, tiny bird's eggs in a beard's nest of orange scruff.

"You think so?"

"Just joking, Phil."

He stared off at the tree line a second. Then, quick for a man his size, yanked the framing hammer from his belt and slammed the rafter I was straddling. Vibration hit my testicles like electric shock. I glowed up there maybe five minutes and was still climbing ladders bowlegged next day. Sinclair wasn't your joking kind of man.

"I'm offering fifty-fifty partnership," I told him.

"Lopsided for a novice who doesn't know piss-all about carpentry," he said.

"My business contact."

"Seventy-thirty. I'll teach you how to pound a nail."

What choice did I have? Slow economy and a wife and daughter to support. I look at her as my daughter anyhow, though technically Annie is Jack Nicholson's—Becky's first husband's—kid. She calls him Jack Nicholson anyway. "He kept playing joker, so I took a walk," is how she tells it. Joker is a role I don't want any part of.

We shook hands and I told Sinclair, "The economy's got me in a bad place." He grinned. I knew right then there would be trouble. But it generally comes from a direction you never expected.

It was Becky's idea to move to the ranch. Truth is, she was bored in town, kept talking about finding a job. Norton said we could live in the main cabin rent-free in exchange for fixing it up. Something I could do in my spare time, chance to try my hand at finish work. There was no electricity. We used hurricane lamps and kerosene wickers. The cabin was cozy, paneled in redwood. One glance at that place—charred redwood stumps big enough to build a house atop amid thickets of huckleberry, manzanita and coyote bush—and you knew there had been one hell of a devastation way back when. Ten trees to a city block. It pleased me fine to be out of the logging business. Besides the cabin was romantic. Every marriage needs a booster shot now and then to keep up its immunity. We were into three years already without one.

We began with the workshop: ninety feet long and thirty wide, shed roof, loft, concrete slab floor where Norton could park his vintage cars. He had a vision of the place. Regular redwood stump resort. Though, myself, I couldn't see it.

After a week, Sinclair asked to stay out there with us while his wife and daughter were south visiting her mother. "It's not the cooking," he said; "I do half the cooking myself, anyway. But I can't stand sitting down to dinner alone."

Wasn't what I had in mind: ol' vulture dome sharing my second honeymoon. But Becky felt sorry for him. Motherly sort of thing. Or maybe she liked the idea of company. That's when I began seeing another side to Sinclair, something you wouldn't expect of a man his size. Type who talks easier to women than to his own sex.

I noticed right off he liked talking to Becky. I just counted it to him missing his wife. Jealousy didn't cross my mind. Though Becky began wearing cutoffs and halter tops about the house. Nothing out of her normal range of apparel, just to the outside edge.

I overheard them laughing in the kitchen one morning as I came in from the can, Becky in whooping hoots that sounded like a schoolgirl's imitation of a jay. Sinclair's hands waved clownish at his sides, while Becky swabbed soap suds from his beard with a towel, and he eyeballed down her nightgown.

"Little give, little take, it all comes out even in the end," he was saying.

"Not everyone sees it that way," Becky said.

"You scrubbing plates with your whiskers again, Phil?" I asked.

He looked up, startled. Becky waved me off, taking a final dab with the rag and leaning forward to peck his forehead. "We're doing just fine."

Sinclair gave me a slice of his teeth. Morning light accentuated gaps between them; could have been a savage stepped out of *National Geographic* that lay in stacks about the place. "Just like racism or nuclear energy, it takes time for stupidity to die out. Right, Ace?"

"Depends on what stupidity you mean," I said.

Becky laughed her careless laugh. "I never did expect to hear a man call it 'stupid.'"

"What's stupid?"

"Well, isn't it?" Sinclair ignored me. "Where's it written that men fix cars and women clean house and watch the kids? The ten commandments of sexual behavior, right."

"What's sex got to do with it?"

"How about carpentry? I don't see many women out on the job with you guys." Becky slid eyes at him in a teasing way.

"Come join us! Hey! I subscribe to full and universal equality between the sexes."

Seemed a funny word to me, "subscribe," like you might receive it in the mail. It didn't phase Beck.

"That's two of us then." She cut eyes at me. "Not like some I might mention."

"Guess I walked sideways into a conversation where I don't belong," I said.

"The original sideways man. You ready to do some serious damage this morning, Ace?" Sinclair stood over the sink with suds dripping from his big hands.

"Like I said, my name's Jimmy, Jim, James. You might call your dog 'Ace.'" Something in the way my wife regarded me put me off. "So what's the joke? I guess my daughter will wish me a proper good morning, anyhow."

Annette wandered in from the living room in her white PJs with the bucking broncos. (That was a mistaken diagnosis. The doctor said Becky was carrying a boy, and her aunt who worked in children's discount clothing sent boxes full of little boy outfits. The compromise was she wore boy about the house; out in public she went girl.) She was sleep-grouchy and slanty-eyed, reaching for me to pick her up.

"Mornin', Tex." I kissed behind a sticky ear. Her hair smelled shampoo sweet.

"There's a earwig in my slipper," Annie grumped, wearing only the one.

Sinclair's mouth fell open; he wide-eyed her in funny-paper horror. "Get out the Raid!" He stumped toward her bedroom, Lux bottle at the ready, his thumb over the cap. Annette giggled and squirmed in my arms, afraid he'd tickle her. He did that plenty, pinning her on the sofa, while she screamed laughter. I wanted to put a stop to that, but Becky told me to piss off. "Annie likes him," she said. He claimed she reminded him of his own daughter, and Annie was no end of curiosity about the girl.

I stepped out front of him. "I'll take care of it, Phil."

"Hey, I've faced some pretty mean earwigs in my time."

"I'll bet. But it's my cabin here."

"So that's how it is." He straightened to his full height.

Becky frowned. "Is this a fucking earwig killing contest?"

"Pincers. They got pincers." Annie wiggled for me to put her down.

"They crawl into your brain and eat your thoughts," Sinclair hissed, "then your eyeballs."

"You're sick," Becky laughed.

We were crowding into Annie's doorway—two men and a small girl between—eye-balling for that slipper. I decided he wouldn't get there first. But I no more than grabbed the slipper when Sinclair snatched it away in his teeth and went romping into the living room,

Annie chasing behind. They squealed laughter, while I searched under the rug for earwigs.

When I came out, Becky sat at table thumbing through a *National Geographic*. Sun rays lit her bare crossed legs and accentuated old acne scars that marred a German Madonna sort of pretty: sharp features, eyes set deep, seeming judgmental when she didn't intend it. Some women would curse her hair—limp, all-purpose brown (auburn, with sunlight shining through)—but Becky didn't give a damn about your cover-girl image. Some men read recklessness into that. Maybe Sinclair. Slim hipped and large busted, an inch taller than me myself. Chin uptilted to suggest she'd rather be someplace else.

"Dubrovnik, that's a funny name," she said.

"Yugoslavia—on the coast," Sinclair said.

"We got ourselves a regular Mr. Know-It-All."

"I went there on my honeymoon. Blue water, white beaches . . . it's dreamland." He sat on the couch, flushed from exertion.

"I guess you miss your wife," Becky said.

"Now that's true, the way he mopes about this cabin every night. You ought to sit down and write her a letter some time."

He didn't react like I expected, just stared at the *Geographic*, eyes gone flat, the window reflected in miniature off his domed skull. "I'm the kind of person, out of sight, out of mind," he said. "When I'm there, I'm all there. When I'm not, I'm not."

Becky shrugged. "It's a philosophy I guess."

"There's all kinds of philosophies in this world," I said.

"But I like to think somebody is thinking about me." Becky tittered in her give-a-damn way, staring into the magazine.

"Guess you got it made then. Right, Ace?"

"What I wonder is, I wonder what your wife thinks about it."

"Hey, out of sight . . . Who knows?" He laughed.

"Or your little girl."

I glanced at Annie rocking on the couch, twin ponytails bobbing, cheeks so smooth the light shined off of them. You didn't imagine she would inherit her mother's gravelly complexion. She burped a giggle when Sinclair looked down at her. "My little girl! Guess who's my little girl now?" He went for her; she shrieked delight.

"Hold on right there," I snapped. "There's things we got to get straight here."

"Don't be an asshole," Becky said. "He misses his kid."

"He just sat here telling us he don't miss nobody."

"People have their own ways of feeling."

"You want my opinion, he doesn't give a shit about anybody in this world. Not one soul."

"It's like a bug up your ass, isn't it, Jimmy? Like maybe we'd be out here at all without him."

"It's *my* job, you understand? *My* cabin—"

"Don't say *her*! Don't you say *Annie*." Becky stabbed a finger at her daughter perched on Sinclair's stomach (like they were on the far side of a one-way mirror and couldn't hear us). "She's one thing isn't yours. Don't say *me* neither."

"Balls is what I say." I started for the kitchen. "You want some eggs, Annie babe?"

Becky dropped the magazine, eyes wide as a trucker's headlights out on the freeway. "Major moment in the history of Albion Ridge, everybody. King James enters the kitchen."

My wife leaned around the partition to gawk at me—engulfed by the raw taco smell of cupboards I was building out of redwood quarter-inch ply. Beautiful work. Although Sinclair predicted they would warp. Fuck him. Fuck 'em all. I was trying to remember how to scramble eggs.

"Is there anything you know how to do?" Sinclair frowned, holding the chisel he had copped from my tool belt up to sunlight, which glinted from gouges where I'd snagged nails. Sinclair turned it over in his meaty hands. Grisly-chested sonnabitch. All morning, as we decked the roof, he had whistled that Beatles' song "Mr. Nowhere Man." I used to like that song.

"Anything at all, Ace?"

I glanced down at Norton, below, inspecting the slab we had poured the day before. He seemed to like the way it tapered towards a drain in the center. I was hoping he hadn't overheard.

"You do good work," he called up.

"Top notch." Sinclair grinned over my chisel.

Norton squinted. Maybe he saw the roof already on, clerestories up, gun lathe and workbench in place. He wore a fringed buckskin shirt, blond hair tied back in a ponytail: Last of the Mohicans sort of thing. Early American features and a week's beard stubble, like he couldn't find hot water to shave that morning or he stepped off the cover of *Rolling Stone*. Norton built muzzle-loading rifles from scratch, what time he could spare from buying stocks and Bentley cars. Still, somehow, he reminded me of myself: piece from here, piece there, like clothes swirled together in a dryer. I liked the impression he had of me as journeyman carpenter. We were already discussing other building projects on the ranch. I didn't need Sinclair mucking that up.

I reached for the chisel. "There's a sharp one in my tool box."

"Use it! Check this out," Sinclair called to Norton, shying the chisel end over end. It hit and skittered across clay-pack fifty feet below.

"Why'd you do that?" I whispered.

"A man ought to know who's working for him."

Norton picked it up and ran a thumb along the blade with the casual affection of a man who knows tools.

"Gouged it."

"Gouged already." Sinclair aimed his hammer butt at me.

Norton shrugged. "I have a grinding wheel in town. I'll re-edge it and bring it out next time I come."

"Appreciate that," I said.

There's two kinds of men. One takes what comes his way and figures, I can live with it. The other never finds enough fault to satisfy his craving. Norton was the first kind, Sinclair the second. Me, I fit somewhere in between.

At noon, Becky brought out sandwiches, her legs exposed X-ray fashion beneath a rayon see-through skirt. Me thinking: it's a morning done; I'll just finish up the sheet of ply I'm tacking down and eat lunch. Annette peeking at me over the top rung of the ladder across decking already in place.

"Don't you fall," Becky warned her.

Maybe it was Norton and Becky looking on below made me nervous. Or the skirt. Or Sinclair grinning down from the sloping roof like a sailor on a rocking ship, one knee bent, the other leg extended, hands on his hips. My first nail caught thin air beside a rafter. Sinclair saw the ply dimple but not pull down.

"Strike one," he shouted. "Clean miss."

He handed me a second nail.

I'll admit I was angry. What I had in mind: it's his chrome dome glinting in the sunlight, instead of an inferior 8d Japanese galvanized. I'd often fantasized that Easter egg cracking under impact of twenty ounces of case-hardened steel swung full bore. Nervous about fudging that second nail, I tapped it half-ass instead of bearing down.

"Bent it!" Sinclair flung his big head off toward the trees like an umpire. Plain gleeful. "How many times have I told you: drive a nail decisively or you'll bend it."

"Daddy bent the nail," Annette reported to them below.

"I know, honey. We saw."

"*Federal fucking case.*" I looked from ol' God in Heaven to Annie's worried face, settling finally on Norton. A vagueness to his eyes; like the family money, you didn't know what was behind it.

"Making him nervous," he mumbled.

I let the froth settle in my gut. "Hey, I guess I can drive a nail. Okay! All right?"

Sinclair crossed his arms, lip pulling away from teeth like old putty. "Lunch is waiting, Ace."

I didn't even see the hammer go. Just a quick snap off the wrist. What I saw was right off the Simpsons on TV. Sinclair's eyes widened, he staggered back, big moon head bunching on the neck, then snapping forward as the hammer cracked off his forehead in an explosion of blood. His hands jerked upward trying to get there. But he went down before they could, slamming dead weight on decking with the dull, terrible thud of a heavyweight going down on the canvas. The roof trembled for seconds after.

I can't say it surprised me. Although I never hit anyone with a hammer before. But surprises started coming in fast.

After a minute—Annette screaming bloody murder, me thinking him a goner with his skull broke and my whole sorry life flashing out ahead of me like it was me dying instead of him, and who knows what all happening below—Sinclair raised his head from the deck. His face red as a July Fourth raspberry down the roof angle.

"Mother of Jesus! I thought you killed me."

"Holy shit, Phil, I'm sorry. I didn't—"

"Don't worry about it." Closing his eyes, small teeth clenched together like a double string of costume pearls, he touched a hand to his forehead. It came away bloody.

I helped him sit up.

"Is he dead?" Becky asked in a crackly voice below. I realized she couldn't see us. "Jimmy . . . you killed him?"

"He's dead, Mommy," Annette screamed. "Phil is all bloody. Daddy killed him with the hammer."

"Hush up," I snapped.

"I have a tendency to faint at sight of blood," Sinclair mumbled, copper green creeping about his jawline. He wiped the bloody hand on his pants in a prissy way, not looking at it. I pulled off my T-shirt and pressed it to the wound to staunch the bleeding.

"Thanks." He seemed to mean it.

"Jimmy, what's happening up there?"

"Jim?" echoed Norton.

All the commotion seemed uncalled for—Annie shrieking he's dead over and over—while up top Sinclair and I had begun negotiations on how to get him down. He grit his teeth and gripped my arm, beard clotted with jellied blood dribbling down his cheeks. There was power there, a small kernel of hate back in his eyes to tell me he could break my neck anytime he's ready.

Surprise number two: Down at the hospital emergency, where we took him to stitch the wound, we learned Sinclair's skull wasn't broke, just a mild concussion.

Number three: Norton didn't fire me. Only wanted a guarantee I'd stop throwing hammers. No problem.

Unable to negotiate ladders, Sinclair hung out below while I finished the roof—slipping me the good word on the q.t. when I fucked up, so as not to embarrass me before Norton. Seems like we had reached an understanding. Blood will do that. Annie wouldn't let me touch her since the hammer business, but Becky assured me she would get over it. Nights when we put her to bed, she asked, "Is Phil dead, Mommy?"

"Don't be silly. He's right out sitting in the living room," Becky told her. But Annette regarded me like she wasn't sure.

We were talking one evening over a beer, Phil and me, Becky making a cheery rattle of dishes in the sink and Annie in bed. Going over plans for the pole barn I intended to build, using redwood saplings growing on the property.

"For footers, I'll dig holes and plant the poles in concrete."

"Termite resistant, dry rot resistant, rust resistant." Phil pointed to the south side of the stall area. "I'd do a dutch door for manure removal, like the door to the tack room."

"Beautiful. I'm thinking cedar siding."

"It's cheaper. Unless Norton wants to take down trees."

"Let them stand. He's a rich man."

"Save a redwood, right?"

Sinclair no longer complained of headaches and dizzy spells. In their place had come a faraway gleam in his eye like he had travel on his mind.

Becky came in to sponge the table, leaning down far enough you could see she didn't wear a bra. Taunting is how it struck me. Like there was something unsettled and she wanted to see it done. Sinclair watched her dark braid swing like a pendulum between beer bottles, gone quiet. Suddenly he reached out and imprisoned the scrubbing hand. All three of us stared at his sunburnt fingers, fat as sausages, atop Becky's pale slender ones. Me thinking: let him make his move, I made mine. Becky bug-eyeing flesh on Phil's forehead, puckered in a wicked Y, held together by eight metal staples. Tittering as she does when she's nervous.

But wasn't the hand Sinclair wanted, only the sponge. He extracted it across the web of her thumb and wiped the table himself.

"Male talk here," he said.

"BFD." Her eyes scalded him. Then me.

She turned up the radio. Throwing a hip into music, skirt clinging to her legs in the lamplight. Bumps and grinds, halter strap slipped down one shoulder, lips miming words of a song. Phil watched sullenly, rolling the beer bottle between his hands.

"My old lady didn't go south to visit her mother," he said. "She left me. She's down in Frisco with her sister."

"Jesus, Phil! I didn't know. Your kid?"

"Your wife knows. I told her the morning you coldcocked me."

"Really, I didn't."

"That's why I'm here. Trying to hold it together."

"Jes'christ, I nearly took you out. Nothing personal."

"Sure it was. Hey, I was an asshole. I watched it happening and told myself, 'Phil, you're an A-hole.' Didn't matter. I was trying to hit the pavement running. You woke me up. I appreciate that." Touching the stapled Y on his forehead as if to make sure he was awake. In the lamplight, the deep-in-the-eye hatred had softened.

It all fell into place then, the way he'd been with Annie—everything. We fell silent and watched Becky: slit-eyed, nostrils flaring like the gaping eye sockets of a trout caught in a weir. I wanted to call her a filthy name, wanted to slap her, let her know she had it wrong. *I'm right here*, she seemed to mock as she danced, *right out here in the open.*

"Sometimes you don't know what's living in your own house," Phil muttered, "until it stands up and announces itself." He leapt up like someone thumped him on the shoulder, stumbling over a chair toward her. For a moment I wasn't certain: his teeth clenched, Becky's eyes startled wide, skirt frozen like ivy twining up her legs. Then he threw his pelvis at her in an awkward, slew-footed mock dance, swiveling on the ball joints of his hips like a fat man in an aerobics class. Clapping hands over his head and hooting, forehead staples reflecting lamp light. Becky boogying around him. Me whooping. Like it had all gone and done and spent itself in us, leaving behind crackling glass underfoot, like a barroom floor after revelers have gone home.

Trespass

The man sat out by the front gate in the scrappy shade of an olive tree. I recognized him as the lanky itinerant fellow we see walking local roads, thin as a garter snake, skin dry and scaly slick. I watched him for a time from the house and decided he was harmless. Still, it troubled me to have him occupying a shadow of my time and space. I thought I might let the dogs out to chase him off, as I did once when I saw him peeking over blooming honeysuckle along my front fence: elongated skull stubbled in peach fuzz, hard lines etched either side of his mouth, like a drifter in a Dorothea Lange photograph. Casing the place for a spot to bed down possibly, muttering to himself. Now I hesitated, debating the miser in myself. No harm done. Besides, I wondered what he wanted: sitting cross-legged, staring at the ground between his splayed feet. Resting in the shade of a hot afternoon? Grubby T-shirt and workman's brown khakis, knapsack sagging down his back. I slid eyes from one wavy antique glass pane to another of my mullioned front-door window and watched him start up taller as if refracted by water. But soon tired of the game and returned to my desk.

He was still there an hour later, stooped over. He might have been asleep sitting up. His visit had become occupancy. I marched outside, setting the dogs loose, yipping and raising holy howling hell, flinging themselves at the chain-link fence. "Technically," I called, "you are on my property, bud."

He looked not at me or the dogs, rather cocked his head as if some far off voice called his name, then peered down at baked earth as if to note what I was claiming. Heat waves coiled off the ground either side of him. Finally, when I reached the gate, he did look at me—eyes glazed to a translucent blue like that trapped in thick ice, ghost blue, charged neither with fear nor curiosity, coldly watching. The dogs were inconsolable. Ignoring my "Enough," they growled low in their throats and bowed the fence outward. He sat unperturbed. The usual half-inch stubble over his cheeks thickened to a grizzled beard, beside him the ragged sleeping bag he clutched underarm while migrating local roads. He gestured at a hose lying in the grass at my feet.

"Could I have me a drinkwater?"

"You sat here all this time wanting a drink of water?"

His finger trailed the hose length back to the spigot as if to illustrate. Poor bastard. Wandering back roads day in and out must be thirsty business. Like Cain, it occurred to me, trekking without rest, harassed by dogs, property owners, stinging insects. How does a man reach such a state? What curse or loss dogged him? "I'll shove the hose out and turn it on," I said. "You don't want to get too near the dogs." In response, he bent forward and hung a boot heel over the back of his neck, yoga fashion. Dogs stumbled over themselves in outrage. Some smell, maybe, something evil or menacing that clung to his skin. I thought I smelled it myself. I slid the hose end out to him and turned on the spigot. He poked it in his mouth without breaking pose. His cheeks bulged, then deflated as he swallowed, bulged-deflated for a full minute. I wouldn't have thought it possible. Then he expelled hose and water from his mouth in a fire hose gush and collapsed forward, heel sliding down his back.

"Jesus Christ, man, you were thirsty."

The foot came whumping down on the ground. He leapt to his

feet and bowed, then flopped down again indifferently, like the Straw Man from the *Wizard of Oz*. Or a kinky yogi.

"Anything else I can do for you?"

"Hushup." He slammed the heel of a hand on the ground—incredibly, the earth lurched under my feet as if hollow—then he spun about on a fist planted in the dirt and slithered forward on his belly quick as a snake to the fence and dogs pawing and growling beyond, noses snuffling through fence links, wanting at him. Butch seized chain links in his big incisors and shook. The visitor snarled back a wretched pit bull growl, half his teeth missing. They backed away, whining. He sat up, dusted his hands off, and grinned at me.

"I'd prefer you didn't mess with my dogs. Anything else you want besides water?" He looked off, pondering, nodding his head. Began to count off on filthy fingers, pointed over his shoulder from pickup truck to farmhouse to the garden hose spewing precious water down the drive. "Evarthin except but your skin."

"Lunatic." When I stood from closing the spigot, he was leaning back against the fence, the big Akita male, Butch, licking his beard through chain links, just as he does mine mornings, half draped over my lap. "Tickledy-tickledy-tickledy." He laughed.

"I don't give money, all right! If that's what it is."

"Little one'll slit y'r gizzle." Pointing at Millie. "I see her eat a squirrel oncet."

"Because once you start where does it stop?" I'd hoped it wouldn't be an issue out here, away from walking blankets on city streets, spewing malty breath in your face, demanding spare change. "You recognize misfortune in the world—" gesturing vaguely at him "—I'm aware of it. I like to think I give back in my work." Troubled me I should be justifying myself to a trespassing stranger. But he paid no attention.

"I'd take me a shower as down payment." His grin was dental disaster. Even the dogs shied from it.

"You want to cart your rear end off my place?"

He rolled over on one buttock and peered down at the other. Millie licking him now, too. Regular love feast. "Wun't masturbate neether."

I'll admit I'm no good at this. I don't like people messing with my dogs, my place, or my head. Talk of masturbating in my bathroom flat pisses me off. I turned the hose on him, backed him off my property with the high pressure nozzle: elbows protecting his face, T-shirt jacked up over his taut, filthy belly, water cutting trails through grime. And hoped I'd seen the last of him. A kink in the weave is all. Nothing indigenous.

My wife didn't need to know about it. Then I realized she did. Jan and I teach different schedules. Potentially, she could arrive home to him sitting there. No problem, she said, she would call 911 on her cell. No authorities, I insisted, citing slow response time, all the forms that need filling out. In truth, it worried me that he might press assault charges for the hose incident. I advised Jan to drive over to Mick's or Sandy's and get someone to come home with her. "I doubt he's dangerous really."

"Oh no. He just wants to masturbate in our bathroom."

"Actually, he said he didn't. Crazy . . . okay. I'll give him that."

Another factor: I'd fallen behind on upkeep after an El Nino season that had weeds growing five-feet high along the verge beyond the honeysuckle hedge; grass thrived in roof valleys of our old farmhouse where decaying leaves formed pockets of soil. Soon the roof would need mowing. Given siding peeled off the barn, the thistle infested garden, you might judge the place derelict, inviting county code complaints and itinerants. Some furtive side of me half agreed with The Trespasser: the place was wide open. Maybe I was, too. Ready for new occupancy.

I soon forgot his visit, haunted by my own itinerancy. A year ago the Dean ordained that I must publish five articles within the year if I hoped to gain tenure. I had managed four and my case was under review. When I met with Dean Coover some days before that initial trespass, I argued that many don't see four publications in five years. "Some," she retorted, "publish that many articles a month."

"Clifford Waits, you mean?" (Two books and twenty articles and papers this year.) I puffed my lips out disdainfully. "Well, you know, Cliff's personal life is a disaster. Always has been. Come to think of it, Cliff is classic NWPS."

"What is NWPS?" The Dean sat eagerly forward. She finds me amusing, while I find her improbable. After meeting her, Jan said, "She doesn't strike me as dean material. More the marketing type." *She is in marketing; she buys and sells careers.* Someone had given her one of those inflatable clowns with leaden feet, the kind that pops back up when you knock it over. It stood on her desk when the secretary directed me into the Dean's office. "Were you having a nice chat with Bozo?" Dean Coover had asked when she came in late from a meeting, directing me to the arm chair. Her code: if she invited you to take the couch, you were cool; if she directed you to the armchair and took the couch herself, trouble.

"It's an idea I'm working on. NWPS: Non-Whole Person Syndrome. I read a paper on it at last year's APA Conference in Syracuse." (I'd hoped the idea would be taken up more widely, but academia is always the last to embrace commonsensical ideas.) The Dean's eyes narrowed. "Non-whole as in not well-rounded?" Dean Coover is neurasthenically thin and sensitive about it. A committee, she promised, would review her decision to deny me tenure. "Don't fret," she said as I left the office. "They may find more substance in your research than I do. Let's hope so." Not a spiteful person. Just not given to selling short. Bozo's idiot grin saw me out.

I had just watered potted plants bought last month at Georgiana Nursery's close-out sale (*a dollar for one-gallon containers, three dollars for five gallons*), our own mini-nursery out by the vegetable garden: vining primrose, mock orange, heavenly bamboo, bonsai cedar, pyracantha "lalandes" (*lovely espaliered against a south facing wall*), purple leafed flowering plum (*Well, it doesn't fruit to speak of*), orange and grapefruit trees. I envisioned blue hibiscus planted among olives to fill in one side, a citrus orchard beside the old barn in back. I had just hung the rolled hose on a hook in the lean-to where I store my tools when a voice spoke at my feet. "What a cat don't kill a human will." I leapt back. The Trespasser sat wedged in a dark corner atop his sleeping bag.

"What are you doing on my property?"

He spit on fingers of his left hand and worked them at a patch behind his ear, then wiped them on his filthy pants like a cat cleaning itself.

"You're trespassing. You hear? Trespassing!"

He glanced rebuke at me. "The ground don't mind where I sleep on it. Look like your head about to pop off."

"Sure I'm mad. You bet. You're in my shed. I want you off." Pointing at the fence I assumed he'd come over. He looked about and shrugged. Up close his face was hatched with wrinkles, like the faces of desert rats out in Needles. "Move!" I had a mind to kick him. He stood and stretched extravagantly. A head higher than me up close, he could have slapped me silly with those long arms. He jerked a heel high up one thigh and stood one-legged in a t'ai chi stance. Ditto the other leg. He popped his elbows, popped his neck, spiraled head on its bearing, then pushed the wheelbarrow over to the fence, stood in it, planted hands on a post and vaulted over. "Ain't so young as I used to." Grinning. "But I'm smarter." I watched him traverse the meadow: bent forward at waist, elbows crooked and poking out behind like wings, stooped over like a man repeatedly kicked in the ass. He turned mid-field and megaphoned hands about his mouth: something about owing him a shower. I went inside and asked Jan if she thought we should buy a gun.

"Why this all of a sudden? Not him again?"

"Just in case," I said. "The dogs are useless." Trespass enablers.

They had allowed him to sleep in the shed. Strange. Dogs share territory amicably only with others in their pack. Why had they so readily accepted The Trespasser as a pack mate? Was it a lesson? A caution? After all, I wanted to gain territorial status at work, wanted to share territory equally with my colleagues, become a full member of the pack. Should I make a symbolic offering to the small gods of tenure by inviting the stranger to stay in our barn? Call it a fate offering. There was that other matter to consider besides: the growth on Janet's throat. Another trespass. The surgeon had ordered a biopsy. Jan seemed disinterested in the business; cancer was no territory she could imagine occupying.

"We're in limbo," I told her on our weekly Friday night date at the Blue Coyote in Palm Springs. "When you think of it, limbo is zero territory, the great in-between. I wonder what territory our trespasser occupies when he isn't on ours. You might say vagrants occupy everything and nothing at once. They own nothing and claim everything in their vagrancy. They have a low territorial imperative when compared to the greedy but high compared to apartment dwellers. It's curious."

"You sound like a psych journal." Jan hates it when I talk shop on dates. Shop is territory we've long since abandoned in our relationship. She proposed a game of "Count the Tourists." The three-couple table behind us was easy: a middle-aged woman held forth about a recent trip to Italy in a crinkly voice full of long-distance static. Obvious tourists. So were the young couple seated at a table on the tier below us. The man, who looked like Kenneth Branaugh, fed tortilla chips to a poodle who sat up in a chair like any other diner. A table of gay men was harder. Jan speculated the three younger fellows were local. "You just can't get that tan." An older man talking opera and his date in a wife-beater, his shoulders ornately tattooed, were definitely LA. The other two hard to say. Our waiter, a sweet fellow from Guadalajara, was neither local nor tourist but a trespasser of sorts. Come north to make money, he said. "America? I like it.

But no history, you know, no architecture. In two years I go back." He told us we must come down and see Orozco's murals. I nodded, impressed that he should be so certain about where he belonged.

I entertained the notion of planting cactus along the back fence, having more time now the semester had ended. Instead, I soaked the ground along the south fence and began digging holes for new honeysuckle. I had visions of that citrus orchard and full-on landscaping. One night I took a stroll around the acre under starlight, mincing to avoid dog poop. I stumbled on something and nearly went down into a hole I'd dug. Rolling over to see what had tripped me up, I looked point-blank into The Trespasser's Arctic eyes frozen in moonlight. Sleeping under the stars on my property. The dogs lay either side of him. Butch growled at me a little.

"Do you like to bowl?" he asked.

"You again! Good LordJesusChrist."

"You pack a mean kick." He wriggled out of the bag and pulled up the T-shirt to get a glimpse of his ribs in moonlight. The smell of fermented sweat nearly gagging. "Ouch," he said belatedly.

I wasn't angry. Almost resigned. Maybe the mood I was in or a rising water of acceptance. I lay on my back, fingers clasped behind my head, and looked up through chinaberry foliage at the stars. "Kind of nice. I never sleep outside anymore."

"I got her covered. Not broken anyways."

"I suppose you want that shower." I smelled more than saw his grin, mouth opened at the stars. I ran my territorial theories past him: how a man like himself, who owned everything and claimed nothing, was a step ahead of those of us who must endure thankless rituals of mortgaging, earning, and tenure-tracking to own anything at all. He was a good listener. I mentioned my friend Tim Sokowsky at the University, who recently bragged to me that only four students of the sixty enrolled in his class showed up one week. "Tim shrugged and said, 'Who cares, I've got tenure.' I told him, 'You think I want to hear that? I'm fighting for my life here,

Tim. I bust my chops, I rarely have absences, I put in sixty-hour weeks.' I tell you, bud, someone like that is a poster child for tenure abolishment."

The Trespasser chuckled. "Jus' like two boyscouts yabbin under the stars."

"Peter!" Jan called from the house. "Who are you talking to?"

"Just myself, honey. Lying under the stars talking to myself."

"Have fun."

"You better get out of here," I whispered close. "She'll call the sheriff. No kidding. Look, I'm getting used to you. But she's never even met you."

He proposed to help me dig holes in the morning: six bucks an hour. He needed new shoes. Mad as a bedlamite but harmless, I thought on my way back to the house, amused at my own liberalism and open-mindedness. Still, I double-locked the doors. I was quizzed much of the night by my high school calculus teacher, a stern, humorless woman with prematurely gray hair and a beauty queen's body. Her mismatched body and demeanor drove me crazy as a kid, seeming an illicit equation. I often masturbated in the boy's room after class. Now, frozen in limbo between sleep and waking, I couldn't answer a single question she asked. Then I was standing before Bozo in Dean Coover's office. I couldn't pull the envelope addressed to me out from under his leaded torso. Exiting, I wondered if this was a baroque way of informing me I had flunked my tenure review. I met Cliff Waits in the hallway. He pistoled a finger at me and made a popping noise with his mouth. Head stubbled, eyes abstractedly frozen, he was, I realized, The Trespasser.

Jan shook me awake. "There's a strange man in our bathroom."

I stomped in. "We didn't agree to this. You bastard. Out of my house."

He sat buck naked on the floor, legs crossed. He might've been Pan, cloven-hoofed, horn nubs stretching skin over prominent parietal bones, ready to break through the surface. His phallus (no other word for it) lounged down one leg, as priapically exaggerated as those classical Greek actors sported playing *Lysistrata*. I had a horrible, irrational fear he would stand up and piss on me, claiming turf. But he giggled like a kid—no doubt at the apparition of Jan standing nude and dumfounded in the doorway of our master bath—outlining a woman's curves with his hands. "So, you happy now?" I asked.

Jan and I sat on the bed in the next room while he ran a bath. She clung to my arm and wept, begging me to throw him out. "I'm not sure I can," I whispered. "It's so unlikely he's even here."

"Smell! Just smell him. He's singing in our bathroom."

"Maybe we ought to be generous about this. There's so much at stake."

Unconsciously she touched a hand to her throat. "An omen you think?"

"I'm thinking poltergeist phenomenon. Maybe we need to get Sandy over here to verify."

"You're saying he's something we conjured up?"

"It happens. Residual Anxiety. It's like a ventriloquist's scream. A form of hysteria usually associated with repressed trauma and religious fervor . . . still . . ."

"I'm not feeling anxious, just violated."

"No one ever believes it's their own doing." I'd been researching the phenomenon of subconscious psychic projection, typically a manifestation of repressed sexual trauma in a highly charged religious atmosphere. But there are always exceptions.

"He can't just move in and occupy our lives—whatever he is."

"He can if we invited him in."

She shook: hands, then shoulders, then head. "No, no, no. I didn't invite that in. Never."

Maybe I had.

It occurred to me to flee. Get out. Abandon the house. Let him have it. The place. My tenure. Jan's putative cancer. All of it.

Poltergeists, I knew, are the most territorial of psychic manifestations, rooted in place (like leprosy, with *place* being the genetic predisposition). No doubt there'd long been such activity in our old farm house. We pulled a few clothes quietly from the closet and threw them in soft luggage, grabbed checkbooks and essential papers from the living room file. "A precaution," I whispered. We dashed to the car, forgetting the dogs in our haste. Jan only remembered them once we had reached the freeway. She wanted to go back. "They'll be more comfortable at home," I argued. "What *was* home, I mean. I'll call Mick and ask him to feed them."

"What will we do?" Dawn light the yellow-orange of egg yolk bathed her face, and Jan seemed touchingly vulnerable, bundled in her robe, knees clutched to chest, bare feet planted on the car seat beneath her.

"We won't actually move," it occurred to me, "won't start over. Who knows what that might invite. We'll vacate. Disappear a few days. The psyche is a creature of habit like any other animal. Throw it off its cues and it quickly settles into a new routine, like a dog adopted by a new master. Larkspur at Duke has treated Acute Poltergeist Disorder using 'Shattered Routine Therapy.' It might work. I can swing past in a few days to see if he's gone. Anxiety, forewarning, harbinger of disaster . . . whatever he is."

"What if he isn't?"

"Regular vacations work that way, too. You return home refreshed, worries banished."

"What if he's not gone?" she persisted.

"One thing at a time. Okay?"

We stayed three weeks at a Holiday Inn in Anaheim, went swimming twice a day in the motel pool, had delicious sex in the afternoon, did Disneyland until we were sick of it, took in four Angels games, ate and drank and put on weight. Began thinking this was our life. Then one morning, sitting out by the pool with our caramel macchiatos from the Starbucks across the street, we both turned to each other. "My lab results will be in," Jan said. "It may be too late for surgery." I shook my head, a thrill of fear creeping down my spine. "No doubt I've missed urgent phone calls from the Tenure Review Committee ordering me to appear. That's decided the business against me." She nodded. "Insubordination and disinterest." I smiled up at the sun, hands behind my head. "It's been easy. At home it would have been living hell." Sweat trickled annoyingly down from my armpits. Jan was beautiful: tan, hair bleached blond, lines relaxed out of her face, a voluptuous little tummy under her one-piece. She'd never looked more radiant or healthy. She turned to her side on the lounger beside mine and touched my knee. "I'd suggest we do it again, but we had sex twice this morning already."

"Yes," I sighed, "I suppose it's time to go back."

I had wholly forgotten my work, but now I speculated about the territory we were occupying: call it "willed purgatory" or "willful abandonment." Not unlike that occupied by our trespasser. For these past weeks we had owned the world and claimed none of it. No poltergeist, no anxiety, no anger, nor dread can survive such a space. All require fervid commitment. They shrivel away in bright airy zones. Strangely, just to think such was depressing, as it tokened that my old accustomed self was beginning to trespass on the moment.

I returned furtively to the house, passing by twice before parking down the road and going over the fence as The Trespasser had done. The dogs were gone. Not dead of thirst in some far corner of the property, thank God, but escaped or rescued. Taken away by the ASPCA or The Trespasser. Traces of him remained: a grungy ring in the bathtub and holes dug along the south fence. The shovel stuck upright in one and a bill attached. I was to place three ten-dollar bills under a rock near the bus stop on Lincoln. This a relief, suggesting he had no further desire to set foot on the place. He had stolen nothing. Claimed nothing for himself. I erased phone messages without listening and dumped the mail in the trash. Then opened doors and windows to air the place out. Trying to recall which apostle of personal apocalypse wrote those lines which had already begun to haunt me:

> There are the troubles we fret about and those we can't know to fret about. These are the intruders that break down the door without warning in the dead of night and murder us in our beds. Be tolerant of the known intruders. Beware the unforeseeable.

Yes. Invite The Trespasser in to sleep in your house, make sure he's comfortable and has all he needs. Welcome him. Respect him well. So that one day, when arrives the trespasser you don't see coming, the one you do see will put in a good word for you.

The Woman Who Was Allergic to Herself

Lizzie stood on the back deck looking out at the Hudson. Mid-October waves ran in diagonal lines toward shore, whipped and splintered against jetty pilings below. She huddled her shoulders against the chill, wondering what pollens or microscopic packets of poison might be borne on the wind from oil storage tanks on the far shore. Might not the air itself be responsible for the inflammation blooming over her arms and chest?

She would ask Walter about this on her next visit. He would, at least, take her concerns seriously, as her husband never did. Like most men, Ted considered a woman's concerns little more than entertainment—like a TV documentary about strife in a far land he wouldn't care to visit. A woman's mind could be a witty, welcoming stewardess, quick with drinks and one-liners, but beyond that it held no interest for him. She could nearly hear Ted's ridiculing laughter, beginning guttural and rising to a high-pitched giggle.

"Do I love Ted?" she asked a van parked on the jetty below—a pair of boots extending through the open sliding door. The question amused her. *Love*, what a silly little word. She did not believe in it. Who did anymore? Below, boots and the putative being wearing them looked out at the river.

Last weekend, Ted had announced his plans to vacation alone in Italy this winter. Lizzie was slicing vegetables on a cutting board on the kitchen counter: eggplant, scallions, onion, carrots (Walter, her nutritionist, had warned against eating carrots without eggplant to absorb the excess carotene). After he informed her of his plans, Ted stood frowning at a phalanx of vitamin, mineral, and enzyme bottles on a spice rack, a chart posted above telling in what exact sequence they must be taken, at what precise hours, what her pulse should read after each series. Ted was cynical about Walter. "Baba Ram Dose" he called him, scoffing whenever he caught her on the phone with him.

She turned to face him. "You want me to be pissed off about this, right?"

Ted shrugged. "You won't eat the food. What's Italy without food?"

"Are we going to start?"

"Three calls already today," he snapped.

"Nutrition is a science. What comes into our bodies is very complex. There are things I have to know."

His lips puckered in ridicule. He held up three thin fingers. "There are three types of affairs. Affairs of the heart, affairs of the hormones, and affairs of the soul. The third type is most addictive. It also suits your brand of romanticism."

"You're suggesting I'm having an affair with Walter?"

"Did I say that?" Ted's eyebrows formed scrubby red nests far up the crag of his brow.

"You're always implying it."

"Merely advising."

"What about *your* affairs?"

"If you could only understand them."

"You're an asshole, Ted. That's your brand of romanticism—anal."

He smirked satisfaction. There were times she suspected it quite literally, as when a friend "warned" her that she had seen Ted emerge from Scudder's Tavern, arm in arm with a young man from the college. Lately, though, Lizzie suspected Ted merely of sexual neutrality. Ted was the kind of man who must keep things tidy, fastidious, nearly squeamish in love making. If he stood at the rear of a grocery line when the teller asked for a price check, he would soon have clerks running every which way, tiny moustache organizing his upper lip. "A turd in polished shoes," her mother had once described him.

The wind was brutal this morning. It decapitated waves and sent them skittering, throwing white spume into the air and leaves down in a steady rain. She stepped forward to the deck railing and pushed her face directly into the gale, smiling not so much in exhilaration as with tiny adjustments of facial muscles. A witness would say she grimaced. At each onslaught we open, then contract: wind, sex, spiritual entry. It was wisdom to pass on to a daughter—both in warning and resignation.

Married. Thirty-six years old. Employed in publishing. One of the great houses in the city where each morning, as she entered the lobby with her fellow workers, she beheld a literary update on the big bulletin board: Anne Beattie on "Donahue," E.L. Doctorow on "Good Morning America." Hadn't they all hoped to be there themselves one day? One could see the announcements as a sly dig from management—as editors began the humbling ascent to their offices.

A mother: one daughter. A truth that sometimes alarmed her. Long ago, as a sophomore in high school, Lizzie had made a pact with a classmate never to bring children into a world that would hardly be kind to them. They had just seen a Bergman film about a couple isolated on an idyllic island, until war reached their paradise and turned them into unwitting monsters. The two girls lay side by side on the rug in Clarette's room in an orgy of melancholy, outdoing one another in maudlin prophecies: extinct species, poisoned water, human mutants roaming a mutant landscape. Clarette wiggled on the rug and turned over, her smooth forehead furrowed, a button loosened on her blouse. She seized Lizzie's hand in schoolgirl passion. "Promise, Lizzie, promise me we won't ever have children."

Lizzie giggled. "We couldn't."

"Never!" Clarette insisted.

Lizzie struggled to avert her eyes from the blouse—a breast nearly naked in Clarette's tiny bra. Her friend seemed to fathom her struggle, a tooth snagged her lower lip. "C'mon, make a pact with me, Lizzie. No kids. Will you promise?"

"No men!" Lizzie was alarmed. Clarette should cover herself: her skirt bunched above coffee-brown stocking tops.

"Not men, jerk. What do men have to do with it?"

"Everything . . . I thought."

"Nothing."

When Clarette lifted herself on an elbow, the blouse pulled open wider. "Will you make a pact with me?"

Lizzie had sensed for the first time what it is to lose autonomy, fearing she would topple into Clarette's tiny bra and be lost. She froze as her friend leaned forward to seal their pact on her lips with a quick, feathery kiss.

Lizzie turned and went into the house. Screw it: the Hudson, memory, fantasies of . . . What would you call it? Roads you sometimes pass on country drives—the fleeting glimpse of a red barn or apple orchard—and wonder what's down them, never turning off to find out.

Life is basically a straight line. You work for a publisher editing children's books. Your husband wonders why you don't write them yourself. It is your own secret that you have written dozens just before falling asleep, much superior to those droll, predictable things that pass over your desk by the dozen. You feel no need to write them down. Why bother?

Tuesday afternoon on the train home from work she sat beside a round, middle-aged woman in a plain brown shift, not realizing the woman was a nun until it was too late to move elsewhere without embarrassment. As they passed through Yonkers, the woman sat very still, hands folded in her lap, not reading or even looking out the window. She evinced no signs of meditating—that active variety, anyway, which Lizzie practiced. Just sat. While Lizzie rattled pages of a manuscript she had brought home. Yet Lizzie sensed the woman didn't miss a thing. Her eyes bulged against unblinking lids, gray fish eyes with circumferential vision, nostrils flared, discerning the secret smells of passengers around her, while a thumb and forefinger worked together with the slow fluttering of gills. Perceiving what, Lizzie wondered: impurities in the air shared between passengers?

Lizzie turned to encounter paraffin cheeks, thick dry lips that encountered her back. *I'll bet you've never been kissed*, Lizzie nearly blurted in sudden, inexplicable disdain, but smiled instead and turned away. A hand touched her sleeve.

"Forgive me," the nun said. "I'm sorry, but I noticed you working. An editor perhaps?"

"Copy editor," Lizzie said. "Nothing erotic . . . *exotic*! I meant 'exotic.'" She blushed.

The nun didn't appear to notice her slip. "So many talented people," she said. "Last week I sat beside a young psychiatrist who has discovered a way to cure depression with music. Can you imagine?"

"No. Really, I can't. Music often depresses me."

"Oh, I'm so sorry. Forgive me, I'm disturbing your work."

She made as if to meditate again, obliquely studying the rash extending up Lizzie's arm from wrist to elbow. Lizzie pulled down her sleeve to cover it. The gray eyes neutralized. Lizzie sighed and tried a smile.

"It's been a long day."

"Of course it has, dear."

Damn her presumption. One could scarcely imagine what a "long day" entailed in her regime: up at four, an hour lying prostrate on an icy floor, prayers, matins, meditation on the wounds of the Lord, a breakfast of gruel (not unlike the millet bran Walter prescribed), visits to the sick, more gruel, more prayers. But in austerity there is regularity, dignity, peace.

"Sister Beth-Marie . . ." the nun proffered a dry, manly hand, studying Lizzie's fingers as they fluttered away from the pulse which they had been taking automatically.

Lizzie gripped the wooden fingertips an instant before snatching her hand away. Her eyes fixed upon her watch.

"Are you ill?" Sister Beth-Marie asked.

Lizzie did not answer at first. How often recently—on trains, airplanes, at work—strangers, noticing her taking her pulse and jotting figures in the tiny red notebook, demanded explanation, as if one's health were a public affair. Look then! she wished to bark at them: see my thin wrists and sunken cheeks, purple fleur-de-lis on the backs of my hands. I am the tattooed woman, Amazonian wonder. There's no end to your morbid curiosity.

"It's really quite complicated," she began. "You see, I'm trying to discover what I'm allergic to."

"Just awful, isn't it? The city is such a filthy place. But exciting . . ." The sister seemed to ask, eyeing the rash in the open collar of Lizzie's blouse.

"I hardly think excitement," Lizzie said. "Certain proteins, plastics, or wool fibers possibly, even perfumes." *The sick curiosity of others*, she was thinking, *maybe I'm allergic to that*.

"Do you have children?" Sister Beth-Marie asked.

"No," Lizzie snorted. "Impossible! It couldn't be . . . Not my daughter. Oh, yes," she corrected herself, "yes, I have a daughter."

"Wonderful. And work besides. Another superwoman."

"Hardly."

"Must be difficult to cope." The sister stated it without sympathy or conviction. "And yet so many women are trying, aren't they? Modern women."

Lizzie laughed. "You make *modern* sound like a disease. You're saying we should remain at home where mothers belong?"

Sister Claude-Marie or was it John-Marie? laughed heartily. "Times have changed, haven't they? For the better I imagine."

Her features—Lizzie was fascinated by them—overlarge. The flattened nose might have been divided between two faces, a monument, a fleshy wedge. Her brow wasn't unlike Grandpa Feiner's, with its spiny, contemptuous eyebrows. Hair nearly gray, prematurely so. It shocked Lizzie to realize that the woman sitting beside her was likely no older than herself, though seasoned in some way to an age she would never reach—her square face and manly, reproving brow.

Lizzie had become aware of an odor emanating from her neighbor, which she would remember later as a cloistered yellow smell, not of saffron or lemon peel certainly, but of sodden leaves in the woods. A smell of ancient decay that made her itch savagely under the arms. She feared she might fall into that odor as she once feared she would tumble into Clarette's bra. This damned nosy, disapproving woman saying it was once her dream to be an editor. Oh, she had read everything she could lay her hands upon as a girl. "But my mother had her plans, God bless her. You know how mothers are. Of course you do, with a teenage daughter of your own." She smiled empathetically.

Lizzie stared at her in alarm. "How do you know? I never said Clarette was a teenager."

The nun's eyes widened; she seemed caught out. Then her face relaxed. "Why, of course you did."

There was a peculiar growth, a pale mole or tumor just under Claude-Marie's chin. Lizzie was horrified at the thought that she could just lean forward and bite it off.

"No, I certainly didn't."

Slamming the briefcase shut on her fingers, Lizzie lunged against the seat ahead in her rush to escape. A strong hand caught her buttocks when she rebounded, guiding her gently into the aisle.

"Degenerate!" she snapped as she thrust past a porter into the adjoining car. "Holy spy."

Clarette, Lizzie's daughter, had changed her name to Elise upon entering high school. There had been a brief battle of wills between mother and daughter; then friends and the momentum of everyday use sealed the decision for them. That small act remained in Lizzie's heart as a betrayal.

"You must realize that this was a special childhood friend," she explained to Clarette-Elise. "We grew up together and shared everything. It would delight her to know my daughter is her namesake. At least it should."

"That's your life, Mom. My life says Elise all the way."

"What an odd little name, 'Elise.' What made you choose it?"

"Better than all my friends thinking I'm some kind of bottled water or something."

"Claret is a red wine, if that's what you mean."

"So why didn't you just name me Burgundy then?—Mom! Don't do that."

Lizzie had begun scratching her wounds. Beneath the crease of an elbow the skin was worn to a moist red patch. What with the rawness of her neck, she could no longer lie on her pillow. Walter prescribed lentils and mega-doses of zinc and phosphorous, vitamin A to fortify the liver. Disease, he explained, must venture through the liver. It is the Hudson's Bay Company of the adventuring microbe. Or picture Fifth Avenue at noon—all of pullulating life feeding at once. He encouraged visualization upon the liver. She tried, discouraged at the image of a glistening, blood-engorged kidney bean. Night after night, she arrived at the same plot for a children's story:

"The Talking Kidney Bean" or "The Bean That Turned into a Liver." A tale rich in nuances of healthy nutrition. A healthy liver is a happy mind. This one she might get around to writing.

"Mom! Half your skin is peeling off." Clarette-Elise cringed. "It's gross. Maybe you should see someone else besides Walter."

"Am I always suggesting you switch schools? Or boyfriends maybe?"

"Is Walter your boyfriend?" Clarette-Elise grinned. "Wait till Daddy finds out."

"Oh pooey."

"I suspected you two had something going."

"Oh, cut it." Lizzie couldn't help blushing.

In truth, she had begun fantasizing about Walter. Imagining him, with Ted's body and moustache, tied down on the kitchen table. Walter's quick Levantine eyes. She undressed slowly for him in her fantasies, showing him rawnesses behind her knees, scaly, weeping places on her thighs. There was the thick aroma of incense, sitar music in the background; she imagined the Ganges bubbling past outside the window, nourished on the rafts of the dead. Her flesh wasted away, her breasts empty sacks; but she felt clean, nearly whole again, like the brown beggars she often saw on city streets—sifted down to the lightness of pure being.

In the fantasies, Walter-Ted encouraged her to dismember him with one quick pull of the knife blade, like a kosher butcher, then to sauté his private parts. "There really won't be much pain," he insisted. "It's razor sharp. Ideally, I would prescribe that you consume yourself. But that's impossible, of course."

The thought of having sex with him just before emasculation—like a black widow consuming her mate in the sex act—excited her madly. At Ted's side, she would buck in orgasm out of twilight sleep. Annoyed, he would go in to sleep on the living room couch, as her father sometimes had, his face tense and forbidding.

Friday night the pleasure boat passed along the Hudson, hard rock music assaulting the shore, while revelers danced on deck. Lizzie stood on the porch deck breathing in the river's damp chill. It tasted of forest humus, where millipedes scratch out their leggy, chitinous lives. Sometimes it felt as if such creatures scuffled under her skin. She would go to work on it—as now—digging nails into herself and scratching until she couldn't bear the pain. Throwing herself against the deck railing, she inhaled the cool, autumnal taste of death in great drafts. In a moment, she would sneak inside to the bathroom to wrap her oozing wounds in gauze before Ted or Clarette-Elise discovered them and rebuked her in the way Daddy once did when her grades fell off or she disobeyed him.

No doubt of it, Clarette was her father's child as Lizzie herself never had been, bearing little more of her mother than a name she wished to shed. Father and daughter engaged in laughing repartee for hours, joking like kids together. Lizzie didn't want to be envious; she was happy her daughter could have what she'd never had with her own father. It troubled her that a legacy of her discomfort with her father was kept alive in her thorny relationship with Clarette-Elise.

She recalled the one time she had dared answer her father back. She had come in late from a date, hoping her parents had merely left the living room lights on for her and gone to bed. But, slipping in, she saw her father sitting up waiting for her. He snoozed, a newspaper open across his lap, glasses slipped down his nose. Lizzie tiptoed past, hoping to forestall the inevitable scolding until morning. It occurred to her she might even make the case that she had come in earlier, while Daddy napped. But she hadn't reached the hallway when he spoke behind her.

"Young lady!"

"I know," raising her hands, "I know I'm late."

"Late! Why, it's—" straining to make out the time on his wrist "—nearly two o'clock in the morning."

"I'm not a child, Daddy. I know what time it is." She turned to look him in the eye.

He was a study in grumpy disapproval, multiple chins bunched, eyes lost in the reflection of lamplight off his glasses. He folded the newspaper with a loud crackling. "What would a nice girl be doing out at two o'clock in the morning I wonder."

She completed the thought for him. "Probably having sex." He sat up straight in the Naugahyde recliner and hissed like a cat: the angriest sound she had ever heard. She had never forgotten it.

From across river came the whistle of a train, low-moaning as it rounded a curve toward the station. Daddy had ridden such trains every day. He must've sat at times beside nuns like Sister Marie-Claudette, who reached across his lap to capture a magazine from the seat pocket, slyly brushing his knee. It chilled her to recall Marie-Paul's hand on her ass. The Sister was right about that much: the world is a filthy place. Every drop of water passing between our lips is potentially poisoned, as is the seething river—its rippling skin glazed with lights from the far shore—as is the heart of every stranger who sits beside us on the train. As is the past, waiting coiled in memory for us to stumble by—as she did now, turning quickly to her right to see a light flash on in the top floor of the O'Neil house. In a minute, the O'Neil girl, in Clarette-Elise's class at school, would do a striptease in that yellow rectangle, looking out into the darkness as frankly as her old friend Clarette might have.

A cat hissed nearby and Lizzie fled inside.

Walter had left a message on the tape, concerned that he hadn't heard from her. How was the rash? Was she still bound up or had the papaya-garlic compote helped? (He didn't believe in bananas; the potassium, he said, was too powerful, while prunes remained a last resort.)

She recalled the day she had met Walter in a small health food café on the Upper West Side. She was waiting, and a dashing man with wavy salt-and-pepper hair had appeared, his eyebrows flaring upwards in dark tufts, eyes the color of scorched caramel. He tossed a leather jacket over a chair and straddled it, peering at her across the table for the longest time. "You must be Lizzie," he said after perhaps five minutes of eye contact. His accent vaguely Middle Eastern.

"No, I'm not," she said to tease him.

He leapt up. "Oh, I'm sorry. I thought you were someone else."

She began giggling.

His face reddened. "This is something you do not do," he scolded. "I am fighting for your life, do you understand? Do you think is a joke?"

She didn't speak again for minutes, fixing her eyes on his slender fingers, which caressed everything within reach as if to ingest it. When she did speak, he did not patronize her by smiling as men often do—as if she were a child who would never mature into full seriousness.

―――

She began sleeping with Walter only when all else failed. For months she had eaten only what he prescribed, measured out to the teaspoonful. She toted small plastic bags of food to the office in her briefcase, stealing off to the women's room four times a day for mini-meals of stewed lentils and whole-grain rice, wheat germ, tofu, and stringy bits of chicken, chewing each cold mouthful dutifully. Her fellow workers stayed away from the lavatory at these times, though she hadn't asked them to do so. She thought they feared her a little, as one might an AIDS victim. Their fear conveyed an edgy respect. They knew that her desk drawers were filled not with forms and paper clips but with vitamin bottles. If work time was lost, she made it up at noon, staying in the office while the others ventured into New York's swollen Fifth Avenue liver for lunch.

Despite all this, despite Ted's disgust and Clarette-Elise's admonitions, she put on not an ounce of weight. She had grown so weak that she must rest against a parking meter every block as she walked the short distance to her office from the IRT stop. The rash had insinuated down her back and left pustules behind her knees. Although Ted found her body repulsive—inflamed, blotchy, rheumy in places, scaly in others—Walter was fascinated by its decomposition. The consummate scientist.

"Love is the final solution," he assured her at his office that Saturday afternoon. "All that really heals us in the end."

Under his caresses, the tiny millipedes ceased their furious scuffling beneath her skin. She fell asleep in his arms and awoke fresh as a newborn. It occurred to her that if only she could leave—Ted, Clarette-Elise, the Hudson, her past, countless tiny muggings and actings out of communal wrath in the dirty little fairy tales that crossed her desk—she might be healed for good. Her skin would close up and be whole again. But when, locked in his wiry arms, she proposed to move in with Walter, he leapt up and went to his desk across the room. Mystified, she watched the flexing of his buttocks as he scratched something on a pad. Tearing it off, he returned and thrust it at her, smiling all the while. It was a bill.

"This type of therapy can lead to certain misunderstandings," he said. "We're falling behind."

On the train ride home she contemplated suicide. Arriving at the station, she didn't go to her car but ambled along the county highway past farms that were some of the oldest in the country, stopping to rest every hundred feet or so against a great old maple or chestnut. Tree-lined lanes led to manor houses. She passed a complex of buildings that evoked England or Holland rather than America, a huge white, many-gabled barn in the Dutch style, seeming, with its multi-faceted roofs and steeple, more church or town hall than animal shed. However, entwined figure eights in the gables suggested something primitive. The great old farmhouse was part wood, part whitewashed stone like a Surrey manor house. No one about, only white-faced cattle grazing. Autumn invaded the trees. Across cleared fields, trunks were snags, their tops consumed in flames. Leaves piled yellow at the road side.

A clean, icy wind sprang up, the sky darkening to the west. Rounding a turn, Lizzie stopped dead. Just beyond the fence, sheep milled in the shadowy interior of a low shed. They were recently shorn, huddled together to escape the wind. Engaged in their own filthy business, one mounted another, clinging frantically a moment before being bucked off. The shed seethed with their humping bodies. They leapfrogged over one another. Suddenly, all turned to her at once: long white muzzles and soulful hazel eyes. One led others on a sortie toward her, nearly a stampede. She was terror stricken, afraid they would crash through the fence. But all stopped to stare as she hobbled away—panicked, on the verge of exhaustion.

She couldn't calm herself or explain why the scene had so unnerved her. Just dumb humping animals. Surely not because the leader, in some comic, hyperbolic way, reminded her of Ted—with his sheepish long ears, sideburns, and poking nose. Ridiculous. Clouds billowed overhead, mauve beneath, fluffy pink atop. They piled and grew, released from some surreal imagination.

She arrived home just as the rain came, sat down, and started work on what she soon realized was a children's book. Somewhat later, Lizzie became aware of Clarette-Elise in the kitchen, preparing supper for her father. She heard the two of them giggling in the dining room over chicken croquettes and parsleyed potatoes. (They hadn't waited for her, knowing her strange eating habits, her tense company, knowing she must take her pulse between bites and jot down the readings, certainly not wishing to share her lima beans, buckwheat groats, and raw asparagus.) It occurred to her how close they had grown, father and daughter: a domestic cabal. She would never have spoken to Daddy so freely, nor laughed so gaily.

All such awarenesses translated directly to the pen.

There was a father who taught his seven daughters everything they must know to succeed in the world; they became witty, sarcastic, apt with disarming barbs, hard in ways the seven sons were not. The sons watched and mimicked their mother at her toilet; all seven plucked their eyebrows, kept their eyes downcast at their father's reproaches, nourishing anger within themselves. This is no children's book, she thought, but the book of childhood that is for adults. The first true children's book. They will call it cynical because it is true.

Clarette-Elise came in at ten as Lizzie neared completion.

"Are you writing something, Mama?"

"I'm going to title it 'The Book of Lies.'"

"Daddy will be so happy."

"No." Lizzie smiled. "Daddy will be scandalized."

Clarette-Elise craned her neck to read lines over her mother's shoulder. "Funny sort of book."

"Funny sort of life."

"Do you think so?"

Lizzie smiled up at her daughter with a funny sort of smile. "In my little story children are wise. The seven sisters realize that they cannot win their father's approval unless they become little men like him. The seven brothers are charmed by their mother's body. So much so that they grow breasts and donate their little penises to cancer research. Theirs is the only real love that can exist between men and women: love as a mirror image of itself."

Clarette-Elise stifled a laugh, seeing her mother was serious. "That's pretty weird."

"Trouble is, the sons can never marry. What a pity, for they would enjoy their own daughters. Maybe the seven daughters can't either." She studied her daughter's faint arching eyebrows. "But maybe that's not such a terrible thing."

"I don't know, Mom. You wrote it. Is it some kind of allegory or something?"

"So is your father one of the seven brothers or sisters?" Lizzie snapped the notebook closed. "What do you think? He plays mom to you. To me he plays dad."

"Mother! Stop!"

"My book is not autobiographical as they say first books are. I didn't realize until too late that I was supposed to play little man, and never won my father's approval. I was a shadowy being he couldn't understand, so he hissed at me."

Clarette-Elise stared. She wore a soft chemise; black tights—all the rage now—clung to her sleek legs. She went about the house dressed as casually as a hooker during off hours. A father with more active hormones would have been troubled. She was well named, Lizzie realized. The old Clarette would have felt at home in the girl's small-breasted, athletic body. It did not frighten Lizzie to find her old friend's presence there; it rather pleased her. She touched her daughter's sleeve.

"Some day someone will tell you—a lover most likely, maybe a boy, maybe a girl, these days who knows—will tell you that Freud was a Victorian fool who considered each of us a parasite feeding off our parents and our pasts. Which is to say off ourselves. Freud was right. Each generation fattens off the last, then is sucked dry by the next. We possess no more free will than worms."

"Okay, Mama—" Clarette-Elise raised a hand, turned and scurried from the room.

But Lizzie was liberated.

Leaving the story on her desk, she hurried to the kitchen to fry herself a bacon and egg sandwich, smearing both slices of white bread with creamy mayonnaise. She had the appetite of a horse. From the back deck, she poured armloads of lentils and dried beans down slope toward the river, then target-practiced with vitamin bottles on the dock below, just visible in the moonlight, listening as zinc, lecithin, and kelp connected with a hollow thud or pierced the water with a tiny gulp in the dark. She threw a kiss at the O'Neil girl's window and hurried in to call Walter.

He was out, so she left a message on his machine in a voice so charged with vigor that it astonished her. Verses snapped off her tongue, bristling with the healthy, active, stressed syllables an editor seeks in a children's story:

> I am not allergic to peas or plums,
> Sugar, salt, or junk food yums,
> Or anything on larder shelf,
> I am only allergic to myself.

It would make a fine beginning to her next book. "The Seven Sisters Grow Up," she might title it, or "The Little Kidney Bean That Could." She would have to give the matter some thought.

A Working Man's Apocrypha

You got to blede the mane tank oncet per three months. Don't be water wasting take you a hoze out to olivs or boxy elder or any thing whut don't git water regilar in seezon. Blede her rite down below the secund gage it wont do no gud atall to stop no sooner alls you git for yore trubbal is a secund bledeing.

When friends called Mr. Sylvio her "caretaker," Laney admonished, "John is my strong right arm." In truth, John Sylvio's arms had gone spindly in recent years, biceps strapping longitudinally when he strained to lift a potted plant from the pickup bed, taut muscles twanging down his back in sympathetic harmony, recalling anatomy lessons she had taken years ago at the Chicago Art Institute where she studied painting. More and more, John Sylvio resembled engraved anatomical charts, his body edited to bone and fibrous pink muscle, electric-blue veins snaking beneath skin. She asked him to please wear a shirt when he worked near the house. Anyone might forget in one-hundred degree October heat.

Don't never forgit to remov yore top valf neether it don't do no gud atall to blede a water tank without you let air in whyl water dranes out thas naturel phisics. Use yore hedd under all sircumstans.

Laney's Ceramic Club friends wondered how she tolerated a man who mashed the English language like milky potatoes in his mouth. "I can't imagine what you find to talk about." Luella Thomas bequeathing her oblique smile.

"Oh, I doubt they talk much." Sissy made an obscene gesture, working a forefinger in a burrow formed by thumb and flexed fingers of her other hand.

"That's ridiculous," Laney's voice echoed in a room bare but for throwing wheels and rough wooden shelves along one wall. She was throwing raku amphorae, a far cry from the faience vases and majolica jars she had thrown years ago when Dennis was alive, hard enamel finishes mirroring that former life, with its formal dinners, art museum soirees, and theater weekends in New York. Sissy termed the lot "Laney S's Freaky Funeral Urns."

Saturday evenings generally began the same: John appeared at the front door, dressed in faded jeans and clean white shirt. "There's things need looking to 'round the place, you don't mind me suggesting, Misses Laney."

"Of course I don't. I depend on you. Come in, John."

"Mebbe I better cut out that shrub what's grown up along the west fence. Seem like Ron don't plan to. Still, I wun't trespass without espress permission, even over to Ron's."

"I'll call him tomorrow."

"My opinion, he spends too much time praying and not enough trimming." Ducking his head. "Not like my life ain't nothing special." John sat edgily on the leather couch purchased six months before Dennis's heart failure eleven years ago, still stiff as a new oxford. Laney rarely sat there herself, considering it a man's settee, so John Sylvio alone—a few guests—must do the wearing in Saturday evenings. She once invited him to take it out to his trailer, but John said there wasn't nothing he could do for that couch but wear it out.

"Them termites in the chinaberry is got me worried."

"*Those* termites." Laney shaking a hand to dismiss her interruption. She'd long since abandoned the Pygmalion urge to correct him. "Again?" she asked.

"You gotta keep up. Termites is regilar as clockwork."

"Why's that, John?" She leaned forward, relishing his knowledge of practical matters; theirs an alliance of pragmatism, though her own ran to human behavior—she had always thought so.

"Your ground variety eats their way in summers to make room for flying come fall. Tha's dubba-trouble. Rot it out eventual is what they do. Get us a good Santa Ana blow, we'll get limbs down."

Laney hesitated. "Do they want poisoning, John?"

He looked off, deep slots riveted either side of his mouth, fingers of his left hand chaffed unconsciously against the palm. "I coulda done her oncet myself, but the doctor is specifically warned against pestofsides. My liver, Misses, half shot to hell. That don't kill me my kidneys will. Can't be helpt." Stained fingers of his left hand working against palm like an autoimmune portent. Though John Sylvio suffered Type 2 diabetes, not Type 1.

"Nonsense, John. You will outlive me ten years." Laney perplexed by an urge to touch him, were he close enough to touch. "We'll hire it done. What's it matter, really?"

He nodded. "Makes a man feel like he can't do his job."

"I can't recall a time I had to ask you to do a thing. I've made supper."

"Yes'm, thank you, Misses Laney. Smells real good." She could not convince him to call her simply "Laney." It sounded disrespectful to him. John returned her smile, fleetingly. Smiles never held more than a mini-second on his lips, but when he laughed, John Sylvio threw back his head and opened his mouth, alabaster teeth gleaming.

Don't never take no drink nor leav the peremsis nor leav no gates open nor make no long distans phone calls without espress purmishon and don't never under any sircumstans have no woomen in nor rowdy frendz nor bust things up nor over sleep. A man is ony as gud as he proofs to be.

"Coulda done her oncet," he repeated. "It's a spray tank over to the barn to prove it." She did touch him then, moving to sit beside him on the stiff leather settee, the better—she told herself—to see the list he held crinkled in a hand. Fingertips brushed across a jean's knee worn white from washing; John stiffened at the touch, she at his response. She leaned against the couch back on an elbow, her torso angled awkwardly toward him, the pose seeming overly-intimate even before he glanced at her breasts. "Once I could have danced all night." Laney squared about on the couch.

"Can't be helpt," he said, "that diabeetz. Tha's my nigger in me."

"I tolerate your grammar, John, but I won't tolerate such talk in my house . . . please."

"I don't mean nothing to it, Misses, only to say I got me some nigrah blood like some has got Irish. Ain't ashamed of it none. Doctor says it's likely where I found my diabeetz. Nigrahs has it something awful. Or maybe my Indian, what's got it worst."

Laney Silverstein smiled at John's world view: all things sorted into their rightful bins—nails, screws, and washers in his barn workshop. Sometimes, when he went off to the vets hospital or on one of his mysterious Saturday night outings to Riverside, she stood in the barn's flourescent glow and admired hammers, squares, nail pulls, chisels arranged like set pieces on peg board. So that, later, it would occur to her to invite the Ceramic Club over and present it as "John Sylvio's Museum of the Practical Arts."

- *Keep yore tools ordurly on ther propper houk*
- *Don't never rest the weed wacker on its splindul*
- *Don't never clymb that roof without the hook lader fixt over the peke thas a 53% graad goin up i done the calcalashun*

- *Don't be such a dam fool as i was neether and git you sum dying diseez*

In recent years, she had returned west from summering at the family home in Boston in mid-October. Although it could still be beastly hot in Southern California, she didn't want to miss first crisp fall light on the mountains, which she tried repeatedly to capture in small gouaches. Laney had begun, moreover, to think of the wind-pestered rancho on the Santa Rosa Plateau as *home,* rather than the stately Boylston Street brownstone in Boston: the squat house with its Spanish roof tiles and two-foot thick adobe walls remaining from the original land grant hacienda. That particular October, a week before she was to return to California, her neighbor Ron called.

"I'm driving out to breakfast about six and slow down to wave to Johnny Sylvio, who should be exiting his trailer about then with his hallelujah grin. That's a blessed man you have working for you, Laney. Johnny must have sweet dreams, I know it isn't Jesus. We could time ourselves off each other, anyways, we're that regular."

Laney closed her eyes, closing Ron out. Her face, always long, had, when she stood before the bathroom vanity that morning, sagged longitudinally toward her mouth, as if she intended to swallow it. Time did. She stood forlorn, having never before felt the full weight of it. Density more like, air thickened with a moribund opacity which swallowed sunlight. Opening her eyes, she frowned, as she had at herself that morning, lacking patience for Ron's Jesus ramblings. A swallowing there, too, of everything appropriate. "Just tell me, Ron. I want to know."

"The thing is I don't see him. Ten years of mornings and he's only missed twice, when he was in hospital for diabetes. Johnny's steady as a heartbeat. So I'm thinking he's sick. Then I do see him. Lying right there where he expected me to, half in the ditch at side of the road covered by a blanket. I'm thinking he's gone mental, sleeping in a ditch like that. Maybe this isn't something you want to hear . . ."

A hand clasped at her throat. Yes, John Sylvio would plan a thing carefully.

About this errozion situashen south wall of the house whut I figgur is water wurks and wynds its way insyde the wall sumhow. I benn looking for leeks all this whyl and aynt found nun yet. It gits in and blisterz and pops then rain ketches holt and whoopy wach out! I tryd epoxie and sement paynt and verutheen whutall and whutnot but aynt likked her yet. You gotta pach them craks quik and never leddup nuthings surer to whip a man than wether lesson its diabeetz im a expert on both. My livver is pokked up like a januwary pumkin below my ribscage but aynt nuthing you need to wurry about. Me neether anymore.

Addressed to whom, she puzzled: this anonymous *you*? Surely not herself. John would not permit himself so familiar a tone with her. Ron said they were instructions to his "replacement." "Call it a Handyman's Bible," he said, "a Working Man's Apocrypha."

"What *replacement*? How could I replace John?" The idea seemed as scandalous to her as a friend's suggestion years ago that she would remarry after Dennis died. Laney turned away, fearing that she might witness herself in Ron. Even Jesus could not prevent a person from mirroring things one did not wish to know about herself. "John Sylvio was never a 'handyman.' I thought I had made that clear."

"Well, you can't . . . I realize . . . I didn't mean . . ."

It gits in yore blood whut it does then in yore bonz then yore eyes then yore hart and finaly in yore mynd. You chase it back with insulin and propper helth habitz still i got it in my fambly richere in my jeans aynt nuthing they can do for that. Wasant never fat in my life but it gits in yore bloodstreem and messes you up anyhow. Not meening to cumplayn and im sorrie you likly got enuff on yore mynd rite now without my bichacizing.

Ceramic Clubbers joked that she and John Sylvio might as well be married given the amount of time they spent together. "Well, I invite John in to watch a video or we discuss what needs doing over a glass of white Merlot," Laney explained. "John's lonely, he doesn't get out as I do. We need to discuss these things, besides."

"Oh, I bet." Sissy batted faux eyelashes anchored in Day-Glo turquoise eye liner. At work on one of her "creations": ovoid conch shells, scalloped lips pulled obscenely open, meant as ashtrays . . . whatever. Luella Thomas said they looked like beached yonis stranded on their backs. "Where else does she invite him, I wonder."

"Don't be silly," snapped Dorilee Hanes.

"Are you speaking to me? Or about me?"

"She's just jealous." Dorilee threw a clay-glazed hand, then slipped fingers back inside the spinning lip of pale clay that bulged outward then furled in on itself, hissing.

Laney thought them a lot of frustrated old women who'd outlived their husbands. Although, for all her *Been there, Done that*, Sissy had never been married. Laney once picked her up from the Pueblo Sereno Retirement Park where she lived to take Sissy to a concert in Redlands. Her "modular"—a wheelless, double-wide trailer—done up in head-shop modern. More feather boas, leopard-skin prints, bright mandala wall hangings, oversized crystals, and tie-dyed lampshades than Laney knew existed. Sissy herself done up in a bright orange sari, lacy knit top and sandals ("no underwear," she confided, cupping a hand to her mouth, "I never do"). Janis Joplin with wrinkles and apricot hair. Good Lord.

"White Merlot yet?" Luella Thomas, on the electric wheel, smiled up from a pot swishing beneath her brown fingers.

"Why not? Feltzer does a nice white Merlie."

"Sure, why not?" Sissy turned her blockish grin at the group.

"Give it a rest." Dorilee, whose husband was county supervisor, thought Sissy didn't belong in the Ceramic Club, given her straw hats decorated with beach shells and air of a senior park hippie.

Laney believed there was no place for such pretense in California; people came here to escape all that. So it puzzled her now that she should wonder if Dorilee didn't have a point. Some flavors don't mix.

My avise is you burn down my trayler just in case whut i got is ketching. They will tell you it aynt but howd i ketch it then i never benn overwait in my life.

    Don't never use her washing machyn
    Don't hang yore skivvies wher they cud be seen from the house
    Don't brin home no STDz or nuthing like that
    Don't even think about it pal—a fine looking ladie as she is

"I feel I'm reading a verboten text," she told Garret Hartsing, her husband's former law partner, on the phone. "I thought to have you vet it for things I might prefer not to know."

"A diary you say?"

"Not exactly, no. A kind of last testament and manual of instructions."

"I'd have to see it to advise you."

"I'm not looking for advice, only appropriateness. I've struggled over that. It was never a matter of class, social status, anything like that. Or race. Goodness, no. John Sylvio is an attractive man. Purebreds I've always thought ugliest. Nonetheless, birds of a different feather won't share the same perch."

"Afraid I don't follow."

"No, I'm not making much sense. It's shock, I suppose. And this Bible of John's."

- *nayls go in coffee cans*
- *screw and warshers go in condumen jars*
- *larg bolts go in drorers by siz and small bolts in small drorers— use yore common cents*

- *nuts go by diamonter in ther propper binz*
- *I like to arange molding and whutnot uprite in boxes by siz tho it's a spyder hazzard. I benn bit twicet by black widoze and i about bott it lastyme between my livver bitching up and missing my insulin shots. Gud riddans you ast me.*

"John Sylvio is ill. The poor man is on ACE inhibitors, who knows what all. He veers from sluggish to hyperactive. He had pneumonia twice last winter."

"Not much help to you anymore, I wouldn't think," Luella said.

"We manage."

"I bet you do." Sissy leaned back in her chair whinnying, tapping a palm to her chest. Other women remained silent, just the sound of motors whirring and the slosh of clay beneath fingers. Laney walked over and threw open the kiln door, sending cool air rushing in over Sissy's batch of Christmas sale conches firing inside. They exploded in ringing cer-amic pops, while Sissy danced before the kiln as if she'd been scalded. "Damn damn damn you to hell . . . that's my livelihood." It was the meanest thing Laney could ever remember doing—and one of the most gratifying. Not that she wanted to harm the woman, only wished her to keep grotty fantasies to herself. She wrote Sissy a check for the damage done and slipped it under the band of her straw hat. On the line denoting what the check was meant to cover, Laney wrote *trespass*.

"Do you think," she asked Garret Hartsing, "we damn ourselves with propriety? If we take ourselves too seriously we condemn ourselves to being small?"

"Jesusholychrist but you ask questions," he replied.

I was suffring sumthing worst than i never let on my shugar was dropt to 42 millies and im just badsick and sick of it. I got hypos so bad i cud lik up a hill of shugar noing itl cum back and hant me and make me sicker. Heres whut it is—furst you git hungary like you cant buleev then trembolly and swetty as old Cane after that cold and clambly and i no im likly to go out sos whut im thinking is eat me sum candie to eaz down and go out permanunt in a cawm moud. Thas life and deth to me that candie thas ment to eaz down the hypos and raiz the bloodshugar in my veenz—see its my cure and kill both cant be helpt. You git the hypos taking to much insulin same as you do taking to littul same as you do overstrenuus exorcyzing thas anuther problum cuz how do you wurk a place without hard wurk and thers tymz latly im like a whelburrow with a flat tyre. Okay but seems like im sure to leav sumthing out thas whut hants me. I done the fall fertelizing and i sprayt this lastyme for termytes to and brethed all i wanted of that zincromium and whutall—brethed my fill. I clymbed that lader and sqwared up sum shinglls on the barn roof sos you wunt haveto and cudnt cared if i fell off neether and fixt a crak up the chimbney. And heres the part i want you or Ron or whoever who reads this furst to pull out and diskard pleez—but its my last testtamunt and i inten to tell.

> i enter the big house like i never do lesson im invyted and enter Misses Laneys bedrum and pul open the chesterdrorers until i fynd whut i want—a blous whut Laneys allays werring about the house and thank the gud lord she lef it ther for me to fynd and put it agans my cheek silksoff and commens to crie not ashamt to amit and brung it to my nose inhayling whut is goin to be the last smel i git of her ever and shut the drorers quik knowing i benn to intamate. I luvved you trooly Laney i do—not in any husband way or sexule just luvved you for yoresef and whut you done for me. Thank you Misses Laney. Then i git outta ther i rubbed my feet real carefull on the kichen matt goin outsyde sos not to trak any part or trase of Laney with me into whut i needed to do nexx.

Sumthing mebbe i better cleer up—it wasant never no sexule thing tho i aynt no sexule saynt im here to confest. Sum nites i drive over to

Riverside used to anyhow for i got to sick and tell her i gotto run into town a bit. She wud smile and waggal fingyers at me like i never fooled her one minit stil a man has his needs. My usuel praktis ill pick up a girl on the street mosly i git my littul bizness over quik then layn ther syde by syde on sum neer spruung out motel bed i ast whut was her storie how she cum to be selling puuntaang for a lifing not my life is no hunderd dollar bill neether. Thers one i reemember whooz daddy was shotup in the face whyl she sat aside him in the car as a littul girl sum man wakt rite up and poppid him in the hedd—drugs mebbe. She said his hedd was layn over one syde on his sholdur just layn ther piecful and blood bubbaling out a whol in his tempul dark she said almoss blak purpul. So she krawls up on his lapp and hugs her hedd to his chess and sez how she herd his hart beeting littul lessur less and the blood wurking to fynd its way thru his veenz she herd it bubbaling out that whol in his hedd down into her hare and face and swetter and skurt she sez and dryd stiff sos they had to prie her away from his dedd bodie when the ambulans cum. For three days she wunt take off them cloths dryd stiff to her skin. Whooee thas sum storie ther i sez. Thas Kennisha anyways and mosly from then on i ast for her down to Starkey Street. Bottum line aynt that whut we all want—sumbody whooz bound to miss us? And whut if you got no one whut if you lifed a whul life and still got no one whut kind of life is that? Pathetuk you ast me.

- Chek the freeon in the aircondishon each seezon befor it gits to hot
- Chek that attik oncet per seezon for insoolashun and heet duk leeks
- Don't be shooting no strey dogs with that airgun neether or youl kill em sure thas a .22 calaber thatl carrie a mile giv or take
- Don't whutever you do my frend end up like me

An almanac? A Bible? Parables penned in John's cramped, meticulous hand on yellow legal pads, six of them, bound together in a bundle, his hand resting atop, Ron said, when he found him. She'd seen him scribbling furtive notes last spring. To himself, John said, fawning at her question. "Don't remember good as I done oncet."

"Legal pads! My husband Dennis was an attorney, you know."

He nodded. "Pages has a grit to em, the ball poin' don't slip and slide."

"All the little things, you do keep track of the little things, John."

"Don't everyone?"

Neither small nor large, she might tell him now: most people let both slip past.

Ron said John had brushed fallen olives aside into phalanxes, purple juice bleeding into dust, aligning himself in dry grass, feet facing the road, head toward the house, just beyond the ditch under scrappy olive trees. A floppy-leafed datura plant to one side and wild apple planted by John's own hand creeping through chain links of the fence behind him. "Blanket tucked up to his chin like he could be sleeping. But I know he isn't, just know. So I'm out of the truck with the motor running. What the devil! Johnny? Sleeping outdoors in a road ditch—man in your condition—you want to catch pneumonia again? Then I see that bundle of legal pads bound in twine inside a clear plastic bag, his hand atop as if he's reluctant to let go. First thing I notice. It freezes me right up, I've got dread running up and down my spine, I'm thinking, *Lord, if it be your will, pass this cup from me.* But the Lord has other plans. I squat beside Johnny on one knee and make out lettering through his fingers: *Rools & Regalashuns For Laney Silversteins Rancho.* Like they say St. Paul woke up one morning with the gospels lying by his side. *Rools & Regalashuns.*"

Laney called Garret Hartsing in Boston to ask how she would go about securing permission to publish the work of a deceased person. The notebooks seemed to her more than instructions for his replacement, she explained to Garret. A Bible . . . yes. Instructions on how to live. *When you wak up furst thing try and be thankfol for whut you have who and whut you got to care for so many peepul is got nuthing and you cud eazie be one.* "Yes, I surely do mean it. . . . Well, you haven't read it as I have. I will send a copy straight away." *Don't leav no water running any more than absoloot nessarie on any porshun of the peremsis and CHEK ONCET A MONTH the tymers is propre ajusted becuz its anuther thing whut you cant take for granted lifing out here—WATER.* "Just read it, Garret. The first person I thought of after reading John Sylvio's list of Don'ts was you. Not you personally, I mean 'lawyers,' 'public men.'"

"You know, Laney, it has occurred to me you don't speak half as much about Dennis as you do about this handyman fellow. From listening, a person wouldn't know which of them was your husband."

For a moment Laney was stricken by Garret's words. Shamed. Then realized she owed him no apologies. "That is a scandalous thing to say." She allowed silence to fill the space between them. "Especially now."

"I've wondered why you didn't marry the man—this helper . . . your handyman."

"John Sylvio was never my 'handyman.'"

"What was he exactly?"

"I don't know. I don't, Garret. I didn't call for advice of the heart but for advice of the head. I thought—as a man of detail—you might recognize another. A master of the trade."

"This Sylvio fellow? I would have advised against it, you realize. The difference in class, education, social standing. You wouldn't want such a man to become dependent on you, diabetes and all. Dennis wouldn't, I can assure you of that."

Hanging up, she wondered what kind of man her husband had been to have such a heartless partner. What kind of person was she to retain him? You might live with a person thirty years and not know him. While another, one with whom you'd never lived nor shared intimacy, you might know as well as you knew yourself. Life, it occurred to her, is a peculiar puzzle: no one knows how to fit the pieces together.

Don't speak no more than nessarie Saturday nite nor any tyme a quik tonge wont serv you nuthing on this job just quik hands and sprie legs and redyness to look after the place.

Place she understood to be a euphemism for *Misses*. She read and reread those lines and couldn't fathom why "sprie legs" should leave her soppy.

"Old army-issue wool blanket tucked under his chin, that pistol atop it clutched in his fist. Six empty insulin vials and his works crammed in a wrinkled paper bag beside him. Twice careful Sylvio: if the bullet didn't succeed, the overdose would. That's John. I went down on my knees and prayed for his soul, knowing how carefully he'd planned a mortal sin against God and himself. I don't mind admitting, Laney, it scared me good he could do a thing like that. Still, a sick man—even a good Christian—trapped in a body that's failing him might do most anything. That's how Johnny would think of it, anyways: his body had betrayed him. He didn't feel kindly toward it."

Don't apologyz if you bollox sumthing up just go back and fixt her. Ony the week in spirt cumplaynz about a lost oportunty the wyze persun keeps looking for anuther chanct.

Laney pounded the yellow tablet with the flat of a hand. What if it's too late for fixing? Damn you, John! You couldn't tell me? Did you believe our friendship was contingent upon spraying termites and cutting berry vines? Was I that icy in my solicitude?

"I'm looking down at him thinking nobody sleeps wide-open-eyed with their face bunched up against their forehead. Top of his head, I saw then, blown away, splattered against an olive trunk behind. Sorry, Laney. Really I am. Forgive me."

She raised a hand to still him. She had no need for Ron's account or the Sheriff's report when she could envision those last hours well enough herself.

He spent the evening supine on the worn couch in his trailer, rough, nubby burlap fabric, grime worked into the weave. Jittery, as he became when he could not find the proper dose of insulin, heart racing, pins and needles working his extremities. Blood flowed sluggishly through his feet; he complained of numbness. "So's I feel I'm walking on a air mattress or my feet is missing, I can't feel a damn nothing in them." At times, they ached fiercely, as if nutcrackers—he'd once said—were splintering toe knuckles. Yet he must get up regularly to urinate. He had long ago forsaken his bed. "What use is it when you got bugs crawling inside your skin? I can't sleep none." There were raw sores where he'd barked his shins against ladder rungs repairing the barn roof a few days before. The sores ran and wouldn't heal, nor would cankers in his mouth—as if his blood, rich in glucose that the body couldn't utilize, was poor in antibodies to fight simple infections. "I'm about miserable as anyone is got any right to be," she heard him say aloud. "Sorry to complain, Misses, but I just as well confest it since you bound to know anyways. Corpses don't keep no secrets. Them doctors is been talking about ampatating my feet, what good they do me. I didn't never tell. Wasn't nothing you could do about it, 'cept to worry. Truth to tell, it's like I'm awreddy walking on bare shinbones, like isn't no feet there atall. What good is a handyman without no feet, I ast you. So I made up my mind."

John bought "fresh" shells down at Delauroux Hardware in town. "It's one helluva big varmint I got to shoot," he told Angie Delauroux. "I ain't shot that thirty-eight in five years, don't trust leftover bullets none." He had washed his clothes and tidied up the trailer that morning, hung threadbare throw rugs out to dry. The little mobile spare as a monk's cell: ancient Sears and Roebuck table fan (John believed air conditioning weakened the spirit of a man who must work out in the sun), a twelve-inch black-and-white TV, stacks of vintage *Archie* comics on bare plywood shelves, which might have brought a small fortune were they not so badly soiled, thumbed through again and again. While old pennies he collected and polished to gleaming in the evenings and lovingly displayed in glass-topped cases he'd fashioned by hand were nearly worthless.

Evrah man is got to have sumthing preshus to him no matter whut. Take you a meanspirted man evrah tyme he aynt got nuthing preshus to his life that destroys a persun sure as a chyld is spoilt by them whut don't holt him preshus.

He lay there for hours harboring misery, blood sugar perilously low (he had eaten no supper), under hypoglycemia's woozy spell. Although dead faint, he had the tremors, heart thumping against ribs, sleeveless T-shirt a sweaty rag clinging to his chest. John rose on stump feet and hobbled to his sugar stash to gobble down a bag of M&Ms. Enough to get him through what needed doing. Three AM, late enough a gunshot would be swallowed unnoticed in the night, momentarily stunning neighborhood dogs quiet before they resumed their peripatetic braying, all at once.

He had long since picked the spot where he would do it. Laney regularly saw him steal off with the weed whacker to tidy up a seven by three foot oblong carved into sage, creosote bush, and chamise two hundred feet behind the barn. She imagined it was where he had buried his cat Rexall, not where he intended to spill his own blood, glucose rich, nourishment poor. Something changed his mind. *Thers no shaym in a publik thing ony in whuts hidden.* Imagining her finding his body swollen black in the sun, red ants feasting, John forsook the earlier plan and hobbled to the county road, thirty-eight tucked inside layers of a woolen army blanket, folded triangularly, flag fashion. He didn't cover the ground with the blanket as most would do, not wanting to soil it with his blood, but threw it over himself as best he could to shield the world from the obscenity of his act. His legs spasmed awfully. "This sensayshun whut I get in my knees, I cudnt explain it if I tried, all anxious and jittery, like they get jumping inside but outside is stone still. Like its aching to move, but when you try all they do is jerk and ache worst." He shot multiple doses of insulin subcutaneously in his belly. Queasy from the combination of forced sugar and too much insulin, he welcomed a crushing frontal headache—sure sign of the *hypos*, onset of a diabetic coma. Still, no guarantee it would kill him. There was the rub. He'd begun speaking, telling how sorry he was . . . how grateful, staring up at the bruised moon through ragged olive branches, forbidding himself to bawl like a sentimental fool. The trees had shed their fruit; it felt like he lay on a bed of snails, bodies crushed and leaking beneath him, blood soaking in cold purple patches through his shirt, the vaguely sweet odor of their fermentation recalling his own: sugar rich beggar's blood. Another person might have succumbed to self-pity, not John Sylvio. He looked fiercely into the moon's scowling face and thought how damnably bright it had been these past nights, as if to mock his desolation. If there had been time, he might have scribbled a new entry in *Rools and Regalashuns*:

Don't trust brite moonlyt nun thatl mess you up evrah tyme you don't wach yoresef it cud make a dam dum crippuled up dibettuck want to go dansing.

John snugged the barrel under his chin and pulled the trigger.

Laney clutched her arms and rocked back and forth on the leather couch, recalling the flight back from Boston after Ron called, how she had begun composing mental notes to Ceramic Club friends, before realizing she owed answers only to herself. A memory of John's lean buttocks remained in couch leather from last spring. She fit a hand in the depression, found an empty page near the back of John's sixth legal pad and began to jot her own list:

- Don't mix Massachusetts with California clay. It's to do with kaolin content. You might understand it, John.
- Don't confuse grief with despair.
- Remind yourself daily: *I have been through this before.*
- Avoid troublesome and ambiguous words such as "unrequited" and "apocryphal." What ever do they mean? By "unrequited," do we mean "undeclared," "unaccepted," "unfelt"? What is "apocryphal" about your Apocrypha, John? You were authentic as drawn breath.
- Then again I do wonder: *Can love's authorship ever be certain?*
- Don't ask such questions.
- Is love found in the details? In duty? Self-sacrifice? The Victorians thought so. And the Bible. How well you loved me then, friend. Yet, how many hearts have frozen in duty? Sainted to small-mindedness. Did ours, John?
- Don't declare yourself. Whatever you do, do not avoid declaration!
- *Love* (okay, there! Sissy, I've said it again) that stingiest and most ineffable of four-letter words. In what organ does *love* reside? We could not locate it, John. We must discuss termites. Practical to a fault. We made lists. I do still.
- Can you forgive me?
- Don't mix Eastern with Western clay. Do mix ashes.

Rising, she went to stand in the doorway: Mount San Gorgonio to the north, the San Jacintos due east, fractured, faceted with severe late afternoon light, which she had so often attempted to capture on canvas.

Yesterday After the Storm . . .

. . . we were looking for parts of the house that had been severed, my boy Jeffrey and me. Cut right off or crushed outright, like some devil-knows-what fist whumped it flat. It was hysteria: the wind gasping rumors about children who bobbed downstream in the potty their mama set them on just before it begun. I picture them standing bolt upright in their leavings, gripping ceramic rims and twirling 'round like the octopus ride at county fair. Myrna Haney observed two of the diapered sea captains bobbing over muddy rapids in her backyard, bawling back to their tonsils, arriving—so Myrna claims—sixty miles south, waterlogged, so hoarse their jaw hinges stuck open and wouldn't close. I'm talking toddlers here—three, four years old. Mighty traumatic at that age to see your mama swept along with you out the window when the yellow flood burst through the bathroom door, clinging to the toilet seat for dear life until her arms give out, then ducking under. Like I said, rumors. The wind curls them off whitecaps and sloshes them like mud patties against consciousness. I cannot recall there being a lake in Sterner County, let alone the sea stretching now from the edge of my property on into infinity.

Rumors, too, about the two Lilies: my wife and daughter. "Seen 'em sitting side by side at Jabberwocky down to Hempsberg slushing whiskey sours. Both of 'em, big and little, alook-alike, sitting side by side. Lushed," old Towers tells me. But the man has been known to talk just to hear words lisped together. Besides, big Lily don't drink. What she does or doesn't, little Lily does or doesn't. Just the same.

People mumble about Noah's Ark. Two did this morning when Jeff and I stopped by Melinda's for breakfast. Couldn't very well breakfast at home with both Lily and the kitchen gone. I asked Melinda Haney, "How come you lasted and we was wiped out?"

"Faith," she said.

"Not a broken window," I marveled. "Why, the newspaper stands still upright outside."

"It come just so far then it stopped," said Henry Staidly. One of the regulars, Henry.

"Faith." Melinda poured Jeffrey coffee. My prostate has begun to just say no. "Tea, Lawrence?" she asked. "I have Oolong Loopsong and Constant Comment, all like that."

"Oolong is close," I said, "but I don't believe it's scripture, Melinda."

She sighed hard and spoke to Henry. "The difference between your believer and heathen is this, Henry: believers do not fuss over split hairs. They are secure and sound in the truth."

"Meaning?" I asked.

"Meaning ye may judge him by the smallness in a man."

I nudged Jeffrey on the stool beside me (he reached my shoulder now, seemed pleased in that, but wasn't talking this morning). "What redeems the Haney sisters—if they can't find a verse to fit the occasion, they invent one. That's flexible Christianity. No, thanks just the same, Melinda. They say there's as much caffeine in a tea leaf as a coffee bean. You'll note back in history it wasn't until Marco Polo opened the tea routes that Europe became dangerous. All that caffeine."

"Understand you lost your house," said Henry.

"Western half."

"And Mum 'n' Lily," Jeff mumbled.

"Half your house and half the family." Melinda shook her head, leaning on arms that were rusted lamp posts, splotched and freckled. "A righteous man does not build his house on sand. You have this upon your own head, Lawrence Connery."

"I don't want to hear that this morning, Melinda. Not with my Lilies missing."

"He don't seem all that upset about it, you ask me," said a rancher down the counter. "I lost half my herd. Can't bring myself to work this morning a'tall."

"I'm just about to get upset," I snapped.

"Aftershock," Henry Staidly nodded his large head. "There's people after Hiroshima walked in a daze for a week with skin hanging from their necks. Jap people, but all the same . . ."

"I don't want to hear that either, Henry. Jeff, I believe we will go. We would find better neighbors in Los Angeles."

That's when someone mentioned Noah's Ark. Not Melinda but one of the kitchen help. Poor thing. Once they started talking biblical, you knew they would soon be out of a job. Melinda hired sinners; once she converted them, she fired the lot to hire new. Good Christianity, she claimed, and good capitalism. Allowed her to practice her faith seven days a week.

"D'you think my wife and little girl might be on that ark?"

"Don't tempt the Lord." Melinda wagged a finger thick and waxy as a dinner taper.

Henry Staidly tapped my arm, his eyes fixed on Jeff. "I wouldn't dig in the back yard, Lawry. Leave that to deputies." I don't believe I'd ever looked at the man: eyes small and side-tilted, lips strung straight as barbed wire. Henry's hair had whitened, but moustache and eyebrows remained basic black; he seemed to be trying to make up his mind.

"I appreciate your concern, Henry, but I don't want to hear that either," I told him.

As we left, Melinda glanced heavenward; her lips moved. I kicked over newspaper stands outside, then shrugged at my son. "No newspapers anyway, long as I can remember."

"Do we have to look, Daddy?" he asked.

"No, sir. And we won't. When a storm reaches into your house and pulls your mom and sister into the air, you should be a little respectful. We'll wait and see."

Looking back

They say tornados will jump hill to hill, house to house; I suppose that's what it did. Taking mine and leaving Melinda's. Taking Milton Norge's, leaving the Lipsongs'. Midge Talmadge's barn sat across the road, back half of it. Pitch forks, scoop shovel, tack hung neatly against the back wall, but the hay loft had dislodged violently, joists compound-fractured from the frame, raw splinters jutting out. (The county cut a hole for cars to pass through, like they do with redwoods out in California, and left it there as a tourist attraction.) Midge herself lay somewhere. So did my girls, big and little Lily.

They had been in Lily Junior's bedroom reading to each other when the storm hit. The room was what we call a floater, perched on stilts beside the house. My intention was to build a garage beneath, but with inflation and life's pesterups I never got to it. The twister got hold and tore it away clean before flattening the roof into the second story. Jeff was coming downstairs at the time, heard a sound, he says, like an adhesive bandage torn away from skin. If he hadn't jumped at that instant, he would have wound up in the basement beneath the upper story.

You can live a lot of time in a few thick seconds. First that forewarning, an animal thing deep in sinuses, air crowded against eardrums, adenoids swelled like tiny helium balloons, then—well it had been raining a steady flush—rain stopped flat. I stood there looking out through the screen door, worried as hell Sluggard's Creek would flood and form a new bed down Main Street and on through my front door, when a denser shadow loomed against seeming total blackness, swayed east, hip-wiggled over what must've been Sluggard's Hill (though I couldn't see it), leaped—yes, I saw that clearly, like a small boy leaps a shrub, stops to calibrate height then jumps in place—over Melinda's, and (already a thought half formed in my mind: *Damned believers! With their luck, I'd be smug, too*) was atop us, pulling up a little swirling light as it come—dogs, pebbles, standing water, my hair, my shout "TORNADO." My wife and daughter.

You have likely seen pictures of it: first mate lashed to the wheel while clothes snap on his body, torso pulses like a sail on taut nerves of the wind. It shouldn't be possible for him to remain but he does. Until Jeffrey clipped me beneath the knees in his vacuumed rush from the house and we somersaulted shoe over seatpants down the front walk, pursued by domestic furnishings. But the tornado had passed on with what it wanted. Women mainly this time. A harried, hungry, madly phallic God.

Later, I would dig house paint and slivers from beneath my fingernails and hate myself for not letting go. Then again, maybe in clinging I had saved my son's life.

We made a pile on the front porch, which was still roofed and standing—twisted chairs, dented pots, towels, bedroom slippers. Myrna Haney stopped by to place big Lily's red felt hunting hat atop the mound. "Found this on my rose bush," she said. "Well, I recognized it right off and walked 'round the house calling on the Lilies. They say you lost them. Lord deliver them up to mercy."

"They're missing." I glanced at Jeff—who attempted to dislodge his bicycle from a mud mound the color of salmon loaf—and held a finger to my lips. "Just missing."

Myrna tsk-tsked. "You don't know to cry or laugh. Like when Lazarus come back to the quick."

"I'm smiling, Myrna. I see you survived all right."

"Envy is a sin, brother Lawrence."

"No, ma'am. Sad as I am, there's no room for envy."

Glancing down the ruined street, she turned a tortoise's pale eye and her outhouse breath upon me. "Why, what use would they have of me at my age? I will tell you something I have never told a soul, Lawry, because you are grieving and I have a mind to forgive your shamelessness." She whispered in a haunted tone, "A woman widowed long as I am can't eat her own cooking."

"Why don't you eat at the diner then?" I asked.

"Sixteen women and girls, all beneath the age of forty-five? Now you answer me that."

"I couldn't. I don't know your meaning."

Her eyes propped wide in amazement. "Well, I guess you don't see. It snatched the leaven from your loaf and you don't see."

"It opened some drawers, Myrna, took the linens. Others it left closed beside them. Had a special fondness for socks."

"Not one single boy." She eyed Jeff wolfishly.

He'd dug up the bicycle, but only the rear wheel, and he was distraught about it. "First I lost my mum and sister, now my bike," he whimpered. "It ain't fair."

I put an arm around the boy. "Nothing fair about it. Or right. Or sensible. It takes what it wants and goes away, like a fat man at a snack counter."

Myrna leaned forward, cheek crinkled as a fennel leaf but abrasive as it brushed mine. "What the Lord whispers in the wind, Lawrence, I'll pluck it out."

"I trust you will, Myrna, and I appreciate it."

The Haney sisters, Myrna and Melinda, are baleen hereabout: sifting worthy rumors from useless, taking it upon themselves to spread them. "Gossip is the devil's work," Melinda explained one Friday night when we had gotten into it, "but rumor is a blessing. Did you know the Book contains 146 rumors but not one gossip."

"Didn't know and don't believe it."

"Rumor of war, rumor of rain, rumor of peace. 'Rumor shall be upon rumor.' Ezekiel 7:26."

"'And mischief upon mischief,'" I shot back (knowing that one). "Meaning rumor is a mischief."

"A mischief, Lawrence Connery, is a man who don't believe in the revealed word of God before his face. I swear if you sat in the Holy Ghost's lap you'd ignore him and turn on television."

"Damn tootin'." I laughed. "And make sure he couldn't get at the remote."

Melinda puckered her lips: an obscene pink display, like the inner flesh of a chrysanthemum or a school girl kicking up her skirts, made more obscene by the manly squareness of her chin and eyes greasy from years in the kitchen. "Truth is truth, rumor is uncertain truth, and gossip is devious truth. Begin a rumor and the truth is sure to catch up."

"I've heard it rumored you were wild and lusty in your youth, Melinda. Took to strong drink and sexual promiscuity."

She flared; I thought she would slug me. Given her size, I'd have had a time of it. "A man who don't open his eyes don't know what he has seen. Why, you know very well I was a lesbian back then besides. Redeemed in the blood of the lamb."

"That's an awful image, Melinda. A plump lesbian soaked in lamb's blood."

She blustered. "You may call me 'fat' or 'dumpling cakes' or 'lard ass,' but if you are my friend, Lawrence, you will not call me 'plump.' Adolescents, geese, and old dogs are plump."

"Sorry, Melinda," I said. "I didn't know you were sensitive on the subject."

By next morning

the water had subsided some, and I wished it hadn't; nothing but silt and trash left in its wake. Neighbors—what remained of them—stopped by with rumors. I suspected the Haney sisters were busy. Someone had met a mother and daughter who answered to "big and little" on the road to Haneysville, disheveled and dazed. A logger cut down a loblolly pine in a half-decimated forest up past Boone. When the tree crashed to earth, he found a girl clinging to its upper branches. Sadly, the tree had crushed her. A bathrobe matching big Lily's blue terry, a see-through nightie, and floppy ape's foot slippers were found on a wooden Indian up at Trader Tom's in Traceyville. No sign of the woman who'd been wearing them, but could have been Lily. Trader Tom left the Indian in the getup, hoping to take an edge on the tourist trade.

Troubles me to think the storm would strip off a woman's clothes and toss her naked midair. Too much like Myrna Haney's horror stories. Where do they end up, all these women? In fat sheiks' harems? Chained in basements in Hershey, Pennsylvania? On phone sex lines in Los Angeles? They get them somewhere. Who can say anymore whether THE POWERS THAT BE serve good or evil. They say the CIA controls rain in Cuba, and the Atomic Energy Commission controls earthquakes in California. Who regulates tornados?

Halfheartedly, Jeff and I repaired the roof. No sense driving around looking for the girls. From my place the tornado had headed due east to Midge Talmadge's barn, cutting a swath of flattened thistle between, tossing up detritus either side like a windrow. From there it could have jagged north or zigzagged back in the direction from which it come. I wouldn't know where to begin.

Jeff blubbered as we worked. "I miss Mum and little Lily. Don't matter none if I hated the little snot when she was alive."

"Lily is alive," I snapped. "Big and little. I won't hear any more of that."

The boy regarded me sheepishly. "Judd Hancock says Mum wasn't sucked into the air; he says she run off to California, her and little Lily. Is it true, Dad?"

"Tell you what, next time you see Judd Hancock, break his nose for him."

"He'd prob'ly break mine."

The boy wiped eyes on a sleeve and stared out at the sea, retreated deep into woods below the house, gleaming down there like a topaz mirror. He seemed to be relishing some hope.

"We're going to hear lots of crazy things," I said. "Don't you pay them any mind. We're men on our own here now. Men on their own can't afford to break down and cry."

"I never cried," he pouted, straddling one of the rafters left in place, kicking at air. "If another come, would it suck you in, Dad?" Adolescent's voice separating into two octaves.

I was touched by its vulnerability, but didn't let on. "According to Myrna Haney's theory, if a father and son twister come along it would likely take us both."

Jeff grinned. "That'd be pretty neat."

I looked away, recalling nightmares that sucked me in their woozy vortex each night on the threshold of sleep—dizzy, vertiginous pinwheels up into a black tunnel, round and round in a freight-train roar of diminishing spirals, until mouth swallowed feet and I disappeared into my own helixing guts. I would shout awake with Lily on my lungs. Drenched to the skin.

But you have to go on living

Still, I would not have done what I did next if I'd known how things would turn out. But you don't know, that's the point. You do what you think best—more often what you believe is better than worst. A boy shouldn't grow up without a woman's hand in the house; a man can't get by without her hand on his shoulder. There may be places don't believe it, but my household and Sluggard's Creek aren't among them. Twelve weeks after the Lilies had disappeared, I set out to school with Jeffrey one morning to visit Lily Junior's teacher. I guessed I wouldn't be disrupting, since the school's windows weren't replaced yet, and Jeff told me teachers spent the day rounding up papers and kids who slipped outside.

Standing at the head of the classroom beside a wall empty of windows, Ms. Gilliam seemed like a porcelain doll when I peeked my head in the door. Every inch and feature of her delicate, miniaturized; fingernail rinds that skimmed her lips when she saw me no bigger than little Lily's. I stood fascinated as I'd been the first time I saw her, wondering—as I had then—if it was her smallness I lusted after in my heart or if I was just awestruck.

"Come in," she chirped. "You're little, um—Mr. Connery—little, um, Lily's father," stifling a giggle. "Please . . . I'm sorry, I don't mean to be cruel." Blushing blue-pink, she turned to the blackboard, shoulders heaving. Every small head in the room looked back and forth between us in surprise.

Last fall at Meet the Teachers Night, when she first heard Lily was named Junior, Ms. Gilliam had laughed for minutes, catching her breath in whooping hiccups, perspiration seeping from a brow the blue of a gopher snake's belly. I thought I would have to administer the Heimlich maneuver. Then she threw back cinnamon brown hair and composed herself. "M-most places, you know, m-most places people name sons 'Junior,' not, um, daughters." I feared she would laugh again and that I would leap forward and kiss her tiny lips.

Big Lily had glared at me, fathoming my thoughts. "This ain't most places," she snapped. *Why, she ain't nothing but a pale, sickly, not for nothing mosquito you wouldn't bother slapping*, her eyes said.

"No, no, I'm not against it. It's only, you see . . . people, um, up here—" Ms. Gilliam hiccuped. Later, little Lily said her lips looked like wax candy.

"Teensy-weensy as they be, a tube of lipstick would last her a coon's age," big Lily snarled.

Little Lily had explained in her gaspy way that Ms. Gilliam didn't wear any lipstick. "She's all natural."

Now, Ms. Gilliam turned agate green eyes upon me, three matching creases in her brow. "Any word?" she inquired.

"No, ma'am. Nothing at all."

"We all miss Lily very much. Don't we, children?"

"Yes, Ms. Gilliam."

"We hope she will come back safe and sound."

"Yes, Ms. Gilliam."

"Where could they be?" I demanded.

She stepped back against the desk. "Well, I . . . really . . . I don't know. People do come back. The hostages, for example. What are the hostages' names, children?"

"Terry Anderson, Jesse Turner, Alann Steen," they intoned.

"Your wife and daughter, Mr. Connery—Lily, um, Junior and Senior—" laughter had fled upward into sinuses, leaving her forehead lucent "—they are hostages, too, in their way."

"How's that?" I asked.

"Hostages of the wind that won't reveal its secrets."

"Do you bake, Ms. Gilliam?"

"What would I bake?"

"Pies, cinnamon rolls, that sort of thing. Men love cinnamon rolls."

"I'm afraid I don't follow." She smiled fleetingly.

"Not wishing to be rude, but I'd appreciate it if you could stop by some morning on your way to school and bake Jeffrey and me some cinnamon rolls. Or caramel. Whichever you prefer. I was hoping you might suggest it yourself."

"Oh. That's presumptuous of you."

I sensed the class coming alert, giggling and winking, making obscene signs to one another. "Look, Miss, I'm not asking you to sleep in my wife's bed. Just the rolls. My boy misses them, and I can't get it right."

"Children!" she snapped. "Jason Everbach, you better stop that. Where's Julie?" A boy stood and wiggled his tongue at the girls' side. Ms. G was on him in a wink. A hammer blow atop the head and he deflated. Just as I'd expected: small as she was, she knew how to handle the male principle. She smiled, lips marzipan glossy. "Would you settle for Swedish pancakes with lingonberry butter?"

"I'd be more than grateful."

I took several spitballs on my way out and knew by morning no one in town would pass the house without stopping to stare—as they had all along, only spiteful now instead of pitying. When it comes right down to it, what's the difference?

The honest truth is

I did not sleep with Ms. Gilliam for six weeks. When I did it was Jeff suggested it. She had been coming around every morning to make breakfast. After I invited her to supper that first time—which I cooked myself—she came every evening. She would wash the dishes, then we would play hearts or watch television or she would help Jeffrey with his math homework; about ten she'd leave for home. One night, I wondered aloud what she had done with evenings in the past. She shrugged inside a peach blouse, too big on her, fabric dimpling at shoulders. "Homework and things. Not much hot night life in Sluggard's Creek, I'm afraid."

We got arguing about how backward hill people are—so she claimed. I said if she heard the Haney sisters tell it, we are so wicked-worldly the Lord has taken to chastising us with tornados.

"You see what I mean—backwards!"

"You don't have to go to teacher's college to look down on fussy old women," I said, mesmerized by her glazed cherry lips.

She snorted. "Would I be here if I looked down on people?" Glancing about—loose floor tiles, stairway boarded up, hutch lined with canned venison, pink and seemingly pre-digested chunks in brass-lidded mason jars—she squirmed inside her clothes. Then started, seeing Jeff hidden in hallway shadows, eyes fixed on her in gleaming fascination ("She's so small," he kept saying). Ms. Gilliam smiled at him.

"I tell my boy looking down on folks is risky business. We looked down on the gooks and they whipped us. Same with the Japs."

"Don't look down on me then."

"Me?"

"You should see yourself, really."

I felt my features.

"You know what your father told me, Jeffrey—" she spoke to the door "—'Men marry for cinnamon buns; women marry for common sense.' I hope you aren't developing that attitude."

"Mom's were stickier between the cracks," said the doorway.

Ms. Gilliam winced. "I'm sorry about your mother, Jeffrey. Really I am."

He emerged in his blue pajamas. "Is Ms. Gilliam sleeping over tonight, Dad?"

"You better ask Ms. Gilliam."

"Are you?" he demanded. "It's dumb going clear home, then coming clear back every morning. The kids don't believe me anyway."

"Oh, they don't?"

He hung his head. "They say y'r an old maid."

"Oh, they do? One minute a slut, the next a spinster." She laughed as she had over Lily Junior, feathery hair soaking into her tea, beads of sweat popping out like blood droplets across her porcelain forehead. Swallowing sips of air, she fixed me with a steely, uncompromising gaze. "We'll just show them, those small, snoopy-minded people you say I look down upon. We'll give 'em something to gossip about good." Her lips firmed, red as new-drawn blood.

"Not gossip," I stammered, "only rumors."

Thinking how long it had been since I had slept with another woman, I was scared limp. But Jeff's face tensed and resonated excitement; he undressed her shamelessly with his eyes. However, in the bathroom as we brushed our teeth, he asked, "D'you think it's smart, Dad? She's so teensy. Mom was kinda big."

"I think you better mind your manners."

A tic caught the corner of his mouth, as it did when he felt wronged. "She might break or somethin'," he muttered.

"They don't break easy," I said. "Besides, this was your idea."

He appeared confused, watching a blob of pink toothpaste spin down the drain. "I miss Mum and Lily a real lot."

"A man gets desperate," I reasoned. "That's how it hits him. Whether it's proper or improper, he doesn't know. Doesn't care. That's how he's made." Jeff wouldn't meet my eyes in the mirror.

"Don't take this wrong," Ms. Gilliam said after we had made love and she lay draped more on the pillow than off it, "but I wouldn't have done this if I'd thought there was any chance, any chance at all . . ."

I touched a finger to her lips. "Me neither."

For the first time I allowed myself to cry.

But didn't feel comfortable with the arrangement

We two took the hide-a-bed in the living room, making a cot for Jeffrey on the dining table. The bed sagged at one corner and squawked something awful when we made love, so Jeff next door was privy to everything. It must have embarrassed Ms. Gilliam, discreet as she was. Each morning, she apologized to him for taking his side of the bed.

"You toss and turn a whole lot," he said.

She blushed. Always blue.

"Does she have real breasts, Dad?" he asked one morning before I left for work.

I tapped his nose. "Curiosity killed the cat."

"There's girls in my class bigger than her."

"Tits, you mean?"

He shrugged. "All over."

"Slow down, buster. You spend more of your life knowing about breasts and babies and cunnilingus than not knowing."

"What's cunnilingus?"

"What's the rush? Before he created man, God spent the first five and one-half days working out sex. Pity to think he had nothing else on his mind before resting the seventh day."

"I'm only curious," Jeff said.

"Yeah, I suppose God was, too."

How it ended

What you learn is the whole story comes in a few moments. All the rest is preparation. This one came one Sunday morning in April. It was warm out; Ms. Gilliam, who I'd begun calling June, sat with me on the deck (she called it a deck: a few boards knocked together, hung off the rear of the house). She had got me interested in a mystery writer, Raymond Chandler, and we read his books, first June, then me. They got me wondering what become of the Lilies and what was the glue holding life together. Occasionally, we checked to see whether the sea—just a twinkle between treetops below—had disappeared completely as we expected it would any moment. "Then we'll be landlocked again," June would say.

Jeffrey come running around the house screeching at lungtop. "The Lilies are back, Mum and Little. THEY COME HOME."

June and I exchanged a look.

"Junior and Senior," she whispered, her mouth a tiny humorless hole.

"Holy stinking tomatoes," I muttered.

"At least."

June closed her book and laid it on the chair, stood and walked across the deck, no taller standing than I was sitting down. It seemed downright improper I had slept with her; I couldn't understand why I had done it. Studying her narrow shoulders, lost inside my faded blue workshirt she liked to wear, tails reaching below her knees, I doubted I actually had. Of course I hadn't. It would be like sleeping with a foster child I'd brought into my home, who'd disguised herself as a woman. I recalled how last time I was at Melinda's restaurant she said the Lord had taken my Lilies away to test me. "I took you for a paltry sinner, Lawrence," she hissed. "I never expected filthiness." I wondered if big Lily had stopped by Melinda's before coming home.

June stood at edge of the deck looking down at bracken fern thirty feet below. She turned and smiled fiercely, clapping her hands together. "Sooo, Jeffrey can have his cinnamon buns sticky between the cracks again." Her agate eyes glittered.

At that instant, Lily Junior appeared around the house, pony tails flopping. "Hi, Daddy. Did you miss me?"

"Well, look who's here," I cried.

Seeing her chance, Junior kicked her brother in the shin and ran off, screeching gleefully. You could see she had looked forward to this moment for weeks. Other than crook his knee to rub at the ankle, the boy ignored her, having outgrown all that. He gawked up at Ms. Gilliam, whose shirt belled in the wind.

"You gonna jump?"

At that instant, Lily Senior's footsteps stalked through the house. I'd forgotten how heavily she walked. Once that tread comforted me; now it raised hairs on my neck. "Hell-oooo—" she called. Ms. Gilliam's lips blanched vanilla, toes hung over the deck as if she would indeed jump, belly pressed to the railing.

"Don't do it!" I cried. "I'll tell her about us, I promise . . . I'll . . . you'll see, I'll . . ." knowing there was nothing more to tell.

Below, Myrna Haney gloated up at me. "The Lord has returned your wife from the dead and found you in the arms of a harlot. He will have his comeuppance." She spat, eyeing Jeffrey as if he might cook up into a stew to satisfy a widow. He had positioned himself to catch Ms. Gilliam if she jumped, his arms upstretched. Or maybe better to look up her shirt.

"Well, looky here!" Big Lily slammed the screen door behind her, whumping a palm into the saddle of my back. "Just looky here." She was radiant, twenty pounds lighter, hair a leaning auburn corkscrew, eyeballs about to pop from sockets. They seemed to have found something—drink, or fear, or Jesus. "If it ain't the love of my life." Beaming, all of her distended—lips, eyes, arms—rubbery and bullfroggy. I rose to meet her embrace.

"I missed you, Lil." Words squeaking through the ache of my smile. Lily caught my shirt collar in one fist and floored me with a roundhouse blow of the other, popping a molar from its socket.

There was a squabble, barely discernible through a haze of semiconsciousness: the women going at it, Lily and June and Myrna Haney below. You wouldn't think a miniature schoolteacher could hold her own against a hundred and ninety irate, properly married pounds, but Ms. Gilliam did. "You were dead!" she shouted, "you've got no business returning."

"Do I look dead?" Lily demanded.

"You're too fat to fit in heaven, too witless for hell."

"Red-lipped hussy!" Lily thundered, towering over her.

"Cow."

"Schoolteaching slut."

"Husband leaver."

"Why, you ain't nothing but a weensy candy doll."

"Tornado wife." June leaned into her as if into a wind.

"You! Hah. No bigger than a shriveled rubber."

"Senior!"

Below, Myrna Haney did an impromptu samba, throwing arms in the air and shouting. A few neighbors joined her.

"Man snatcher—" Lily spied Jeffrey below "—CHILD MOLESTER."

"You think so, do you?"

Forehead to forehead, back and forth across the planking, swallowing each other's words, Lily stomping and Ms. Gilliam tiptoeing. A board gave way under Lily's foot. She went through to the knee, down with a thump on her buttocks. The deck shook, nails squealed out of walls on either side; it lurched outward, yawning woozily on braces three feet from the wall, tipped at an acute angle. My chair slid rapidly down the deck, pinning my chest against the railing.

My women shot past me. Lily torpedoed headfirst under the railing. June clipped it at the waist, cartwheeled over and spun head over heels like a wheel, picking up speed down the incline retreating water had left behind the house. Lily scooted on her belly like a bobsled, cutting a trough down the red clay slope. Both vanished into trees below, Jeffrey's shouts with them. He paced the cliff edge, pounding fists against his hips.

Then, while I watched—pinned between chair back and railing, feet kicking the air like a moth in a spider web—Myrna Haney caught little Lily sack-fashion, feet and hands, and heaved her over. Bumping, bouncing, shrieking until she was no more. Myrna looked up at me. "A girl sooner be with her mother. You wouldn't have no more use of her."

I gesticulated, sensing what was coming. But there might have been a hair ball lodged in my chest; I couldn't speak, ribs clamped like fingers over my lungs. Jeffrey butted old Myrna in the stomach. After an exhaled "Ooof," she wore a look that was nearly ecstatic. She caught my boy's hands, inviting him to dance as she went over. Hands locked, they tumbled one over the other down the mountain. "Whoooo—" Myrna cried, hanging midair above Jeff, who'd landed whump on his back against the slope "—eeeeee" as she flopped onto her back and wind rushed out of her. "Whoooo-eeeeee. Whoooo-eeeeee."

A silence followed. Neighbors lined up along the precipice and peered over. "Five souls lost in the space of a minute," Henry Staidly intoned solemnly. "That's worse than the storm itself."

Far below the sea had ceased to twinkle.

And how I did

They had to call in a ladder truck from Haneysville and disassemble the deck to get me down. I kicked and bit their hands, hoping volunteers would drop me over the slope to join my family. They grinned and cried "hot damn," like I was a bee's nest they were determined to remove from the tree despite the stings. The fire chief stood with his lieutenant at edge of the slope discussing plans for retrieving the bodies below.

Someone permitted Melinda to ride along in the back of the ambulance with me, flushed and stalwart. Later, I would learn that at first news of her sister's death she had collapsed to her knees and sung praise of the Lord in a velvety baritone, with an enthusiasm that caused her half-converted kitchen help to quit on the spot. Melinda's dry palms caressed my cheeks, she smelled of flour and cinnamon, her eyes gleamed moisture, while the thumping of her heart caused her huge bosom to expand and fold, expand and fold. I couldn't budge my eyes from it.

"Now, our Lawrence," she said, "maybe you are ready to get serious. You have outlived your Lilies twice over. You wouldn't dare tempt the Lord a third time."

I found I could not speak with ribs caging my lungs. I nodded and bit clean through my lip. Blood wet my chin and soaked into the starch-stiff sheet in which I was cocooned, osmosing downward. With any luck it would reach my toes. I looked into Melinda's greasy, bloodshot eyes and nodded, believing it better to salvage something than to navigate this sad planet with nothing at all.

Season of Limb Fall

Season of wind-driven alkali dust, season of black widow spider and spider scorpion, season of flea bite and itchy torment, season of earthquake, season of sparrow's end. Season of tropical sister triplets—Celeste, Daphne, and Evangeline—playing tag along the Baja coast, bearing an offspring of hybrid clouds: white-topped, black-bellied. But it will not rain. Not since Hatfield the Rainmaker has the high desert known September rain and, even then, convective heat swallowed most before it touched ground. Elsewhere, hurricanes gale down water by the lake-full; here they gale gritty sand and devil dust.

I worry about my chinaberry trees, brittle-limbed, trunks known to split down the middle in a blow, with armies of flying termites swarming out. Worry, too, about our mental health. Nothing torments the spirit like a dust storm. Mental dirt emerges and flocks, intermingles with the meal of rotted bones, upended outhouses, fire ash, scattered garbage, and desiccated manure. Wind-borne. After summer's brash heat—fear of brush fires and terrorist attacks, lost jobs and health crises—we dread September's Santa Anas. Dogs crawl under the house. Mockingbirds hunker down in ground squirrel holes at first breath, and doves perch on roof peaks prepared to catch the gale crests and ride the wind like surfers; weeks before they find their way back to us again. September babies claw at mothers' legs trying to return to the womb. "Your red ants line up in rows and march sideways before a blow," Juan Alverro says. "Don't nobody knows why." Gophers, snug in their burrows, are the happiest creatures alive when the dust winds blow.

Old Floria Davis, who lives over in Serendipity Acres Senior Park (used to), makes no preparation for September winds this year. Never does (but what preparation can you make? Cut down trees? Move the house?). I see her out walking her dog that fateful morning and point out thunderheads circling the rim of mountains like Conestoga wagons, canvas tops glutting dark with moisture and dust. Swollen something pitiful. "Better get yourself inside," I shout. "Hurricanes down in Mexico." Floria throws a hand and mouths reply: she'll walk anywhere she damn pleases. We have issues, Floria and I.

She's coaching her dog to squat in the empty field before my place, as she does, hectoring, yanking its leash and hissing, "Make more, Noodles. Make more." Some kind of golden retriever blend, that mutt. Never cleans up her dog dirt is the issue. Stinks something prodigious of a hot day. I've gotten on her case about it. Floria looks up and flips me the bird, waggles it good. Seventy-eight and attitude. Oh, we've had words, Floria and I. "Stupid useless runt," she snaps—referring maybe to Noodles, maybe to me. Seems he won't poop on command this morning.

Later, I see her out for a second try. (I've offered the woman information about the "Be Sure Doggie Composter" from the *New World Catalogue*—guaranteed you can set it in your kitchen and not smell a thing. She's not interested.)

It's some of the worst I've seen by now. Sky mildew dark and blustery, mountains obscured by inky haze, half dust, half humidity. "Sultry" isn't half the word for it. "Boggy." Still, no rain, except for what trees transpire, droplets of moisture needling my bare chest. Clouds of dust and sand whip up over the San Jacintos from the Coachella desert, billowing to maybe 12,000 feet. Arabian sandstorm gone vertical. Ugly, I'm here to tell. Swilling shit-brown clouds. Thunderheads of dust. Gusts grip tops of chinaberry trees and throttle them good, twigs spatter the house and do a wooden worm dance about my feet. My dogs' hackles go up—not at Noodles, as typically (finding some evil principle in dog and owner). They snap and snarl at the wind. I watch dust clouds gobble up hills at head of the valley, coming our way fast. Floria oblivious out there, mouthing, *Make more, Noodles*! squatting to give him the picture. "Floria . . . for crissake!" She can't hear me for the subway roar. She looks like a walking skeleton in a sweatsuit shroud; her clothes whip about her frail body. She snaps her face into the gale in satisfaction just as Noodles is lifted off his feet mid-business and lands a dozen feet off, Floria's smoker's mouth puckered up smug as a chicken's ass.

"Watch out, Floria!"

It's upon us, funneling in a horizontal twister. A brown gale, scraping up half the acreage of that empty field in its clutch. The dogs and I race for the house. Get inside as the storm's first combers crash against the place, lifting off window screens and roof shingles, vacuuming the carpet off my screened porch, with screens and deck chairs. That's when I look out the front window to see Floria ascend like a derelict angel, ingested into the clouds' rank intestinal coils, her legs kicking protest. Like that laundress ascending into heaven in Marquez's *One Hundred Years of Solitude*, gripping the kite of a bedsheet. Although *her* ascent was pure and virginal, while Floria's is filthed with all the world's grit in a cumulus cloud the color of rusted urine, biting chunks from earth and sky alike. She isn't even granted the momentary satisfaction of flight. Floria retches her smoker's cough, dog leash snapping about her like an angry snake. Her eyes, I could swear—abject in her tainted resurrection—curse mine. I am flooded with guilt, as if I've pulled a lever and whoosh! off she goes. And Noodles? Who can say where he's got off to? Dust to dust.

When it's passed, I run out to the field and plant a shovel in that spot where I last saw her standing; it sinks readily into shuffled silt and sand. Call it a testament, a shrine of the sort people erect at road accident sites, a memento mori. Tree branches splintered in a jumble all around me. I'm afraid to turn and look at my chinaberry trees. *Give us much more of this*, I warn heaven, *and we'll all pick up and move.*

Three Sisters: Pillage. Desolation. Despair.

One of them gone. You set out to describe one thing and end up describing another. I set out to account for my fall from grace and a storm intervenes. Invades like some serendipitous terrorist lying in wait. Why not? Life isn't a bowl of cherries, nor a bowl of clay either, which we can mold at will. Pessimistic attitude, Juanita would say. We're different that way, my wife and I. She's given to good will and generosity. I believe it takes only one Juanita to hold up a thousand of us sliders. That's why there's so many more of us. But I'll get to that.

A storm sets out across open water, lapping up humidity, intending to turn land to sea. Instead, steals our top soil and deposits it who knows where. In its place we have Palm Springs desert. Corn stalks buried beneath. Where once was Serendipity Acres Senior Park across the field now sits a sand dune. You could say Floria got lucky: risen instead of buried alive. We dig right through the night trying to reach survivors. Get in sniffer dogs from Riverside they'd used over in New York. Though Juan Alverro claims any dogs would do: "It's mostly old people over in here. Old people smell more." We all look at him under fierce arc lights. Juanita sterning up.

"What a thing to say. You didn't need to say that at all."

"Well, it's true, anyways."

"It might be true, Alverro," I say, "still, you don't walk right up and tell a retarded person they're retarded."

Juan shrugs. Knowing him, he just might.

We intend to continue digging in shifts for as long as it takes. You don't surrender half your neighborhood to a September dust storm without a fight. It might get greedy next time and take the whole.

My own place is remarkably intact but for the trees. They stand branchless as ship spars, though not as erect. Desert trim. Rescuers hang out in my yard between shifts; Juanita and I bring them coffee and fresh doughnuts. All kinds of people come to help: attorneys from Santa Monica, retired defense workers from Diamond Bar, kids from a high school in Temecula. Juanita asks why it takes a tragedy to make people human. No answer I know to give her. Shocks me some she'd ask. She's never been given to critical. Amazing what you learn about people in a tragedy. Dust gets into the mind works and messes them up.

Hasn't occurred to me it was Floria sending me nasty e-mail messages these past months until we uncover her computer. I thought it was one of the dispatchers down at work, doubted Floria even owned a computer—until we find all three of them in what remains of her trailer (first thing we uncover). Floria's and the two belonging to her sisters. Didn't know she had sisters either. I pictured Floria living alone in a tiny cluttered modular, just her and *Make More* Noodles, and a couple of parakeets. Never imagined her sending e-mails about the low state of my mental hygiene. But considering my tormentor's address, thornyroses@allmail.net, all the e-mail stalker's references to my "snitty dogs" (who went after Noodles with a banshee fury, I admit, nipping and snarling at the fence), and claims I purposely sicced them on my neighbors, no question it was her. Sister Despair. I've a mind to take her hard drive to a recovery service and have it analyzed. Juanita warns me that would be invasion of privacy. Bad enough to invade privacy while a person's alive; irremediable once they're dead. I ask her how we know she's dead. Flown off, sure. Ascended in a dust cloud. Deposited maybe in the Virgin Islands.

As we figure it, Floria's sisters were sunning on their patio the afternoon of the wind storm: 98 percent humidity, maybe 60 percent ambient dust, so it was like breathing mud. Lunked down in their lawn recliners when we find them, mouths full of sand, gullets, too, no doubt, given their abominable weight. Glen Whitehead states the obvious, "Only chance we got of finding someone alive is if they stayed inside that day." Glen owns a gas station. Did. Will again, once they dig it out.

"Whoopdy-do, Glen. You're a genius. I don't personally believe we'll find a living soul,"Andrea Basil says. She's lovingly brushing sand off of the sisters with a paint brush.

"Don't second-guess the Lord," Hector Dario says. Hector's deacon down at Truth Tabernacle church on the corner of Palm and Antelope. Wind scrubbed the church clean so it glistens white now, walks and driveway sandblasted, trees shorn of leaves. Looks like they were planted that way. What's it called? "Aphyllous": denuded for Jesus who cursed the fig tree. "A natural blessing," Hector says of the church, "proof positive of the Lord's benign hand in this world."

"So what's this then?" Andrea Basil lifts one of the sister's sand-logged arms and lets it fall with a thud. "More benign proof, Heck?"

He lances a finger at her. "The Lord rewards the faithful and punishes the transgressor with a swift and mighty justice—'sand and pestilence and fire.' Heathen beware." With Hector, you never know whether he's quoting chapter and verse or making it up as he goes.

Juanita rises to her full height, towering over him maybe six inches, a little of the sisters' pallor rubbed off into her skin. "What'd these gals ever do to make God want to bury them alive? They contributed generously to the scholarship fund every year."

"Judge not that you be not judged." Hector's gone snippy, as short men will.

"Dude . . . y'r so full of shit," says Tommy Whitehead, Glen's nineteen-year-old boy. His hair bleached up in castellated crests, two front teeth pulled—a punk look twenty years outdated. Tommy's something fierce against religion. "Why you digging then if all this here is just heathen excrement or whatever?"

"The Lord judges whom he will. It ain't up to me."

"Amen." His wife excavates a small tabby cat near the sisters, tail sticking straight up, rigid.

"Three storms: three sisters," I say to change the subject. "'Celeste,' 'Daphne,' and 'Evangeline.' So what are these old girls' names then?"

Juanita turns hard to me as if I've jerked her chain. "Why, Daphne and Evangeline." Some truth worked loose in her mind. Something she'd rather not know.

"And *Floria*," Tommy Whitehead says. "That's the fourth storm, the one what buried them alive."

"Floria? By God! Was it really?"

"How poignant," Andrea Basil says.

"It's a judgment," Hector Dario insists. "Ye shall know them by their names."

"Ohhhh shush."

"'Pillage,' 'Desolation,' and 'Despair' more like," Glen Whitehead says.

"'Faith,' 'Divinity,' and 'Grace,'" Mrs. Dario corrects him.

"Three sisters, anyways. Names or no," says Juanita.

I'm thinking I must get my hands on that hard drive. Whatever it takes.

"You get a mess like this there's sure enough to be a woman behind it, anyhow. Sure enough."

"Don't you be blaming this on women, Glen," Juanita chides. "We're carrying enough on our shoulders already."

"Glen's bitter," I say, "ever since Sharon left."

"The hell I am. I'd like to get a bulldozer in here is what I'd like to do. We could go sniffing and shoveling along like this forever."

"And crush any chance they have of survival."

"Ain't a prayer's chance of it anyway. Just ask the preacher there."

It's no good

we realize by the fifth modular we uncover. No one alive in Serendipity's Arabia. Sand has crept into everything, filling bungalows full up, packed in around keepsakes and mom and pop standing upright in the living room, hugged together, or opening their mouths to shout out, or seated dumbstruck before the TV, sand packing nostrils and in-between hair strands. Dig through to open a cupboard and it pours out. Same with the autopsies, we learn: sand-packed kidneys and bladders, dust between neurons in the brain. They can't say how it got there. The Lord's judgment maybe. Nature's. Or the three sisters up to devilment. They never liked their neighbors much, Juanita says. I say September is merciless.

Rescue dogs mewl and whine, thrusting muzzles into sand. We warn newcomers not to get their hopes up. Tommy Whitehead suggests we ought to leave some of it buried as is for posterity to find. Like Pompeii. Our way of life preserved in dry sand. We regard one another, uncomfortable with the idea of posterity discovering—as we have—that old people subsisted mainly on Big Macs (their garbage cans full of yellow wrappings), blood pressure readings, and furtive viewings of porn videos we find buried in closets, along with sequined cowboy boots. No record we want to bequeath the future. Let poets and architects mold our legacy. We keep digging until the county takes over.

Maybe a week after the storm, we get word Noodles has shown up in a Sycamore tree up at the community college, barking at students passing by below. Hearing they have him at the pound, I get to thinking how maybe if I'd been a little kinder—if I'd stopped my dogs from tearing hell a new asshole every time Floria walked

Noodles past my place to "make more" in the field—maybe she would have listened to me that day. Not that I take responsibility, only enough I can't let her mutt be gassed.

The day I go to pick him up, Juanita says the last thing we need is another dog around the place, especially that dog. "You can't control the four you have already."

"What's got into you? Before that wind you would be right over to pick him up." (Three of our four strays she collected at side of the road.)

Juanita cocks her head, I'd swear a little sand trickles out an ear. "It won't work, Al. Your dogs hate that animal with a fury. They'll tear him up."

"They're your dogs, too. Remember?"

"No no no. I never encouraged them to bark at the poor woman. You treated them with biscuits every time they sent her scurrying."

"She didn't need to bring that mutt over here to do his business, did she? Sure, okay, I might've been a bit rough. But you make it sound like murder or something."

"Wasn't it?"

It cuts me. Her eyes sharp-snouted rodents. Cuts me deep.

So I bring Noodles home. Wouldn't you know, my dogs won't let us in the gate. Noodles cowering in the pickup bed. I walk him out in the field; diarrhea pours down his quaking legs before I can instruct, "Make more." Good deal. My dogs like demonic quadruplets at the fence, gnashing their teeth against chain links. Eyes glazed and murderous. "You can't stay out here, boy," I lament, "the coyotes will get you. Inside, my dogs will tear you up. It's not as kind a world as people teach their children it is." He smells like curdled lasagna. And shit. I promise to keep my dogs inside while he's out, Noodles inside while they're out. "After a while, you'll get used to each other."

It's not a good feeling

I have. Like that morning in July I drove over to United Freight-Masters and saw the fellows milling about. Simpson slit a finger across his throat. "That's all she wrote. Everybody laid off." They'd locked us out, didn't even inform us we'd been let go. There's "New Capitalism" for you. Your "New World Order." What do they call it? "Restructuring." You bet . . . using us for flesh, bone and gristle. And what does Juanita have to say when I call her? "Well, I'm delighted. You were never meant to drive truck, Al, and you know it. You're a botanist and master gardener. An educated man."

"Currently unemployed," I say. "No prospects."

"Opportunity sprouts from disaster." There's my old Juanita for you, optimism's midwife.

So I get the dogs inside. Noodles hides under my truck when I try to hose him off. It strikes me right then what this is about. I'm a pragmatic man. Every trouble has its cause. A host of troubles will have a primal cause. If plants don't grow, look to the soil.

I tell Juanita, "Let's say you believe in moral cause and effect like Hector Dario does—only cut God out of the equation—you could say all of this is the natural effect of some fundamental cause. There's nothing arbitrary about it."

"Whatever are you talking about?"

"I'm talking karma. Talking the sin I committed setting our dogs barking at old Floria. But, you know, I got fed up with the stink."

"That's the craziest thing I ever did hear in my life. What kind of power do you think you have, Albert?"

"I wouldn't call it 'power,' I'd call it 'compounded misfortune.'"

"It wasn't the smell you didn't like, anyways, it's the idea of growing old and walking your lame old dog out to poop in a weed field. I saw the way you looked at those poor souls we dug up at Serendipity Acres."

"Dried out corpses! How'm I supposed to look?" If ever a soul on this planet has made cordiality a virtue, it's Juanita, and here she is speaking thoughts I don't dare think to myself. Dust in the head. Mental dust mice. "Don't you see!" I persist. "Those hateful e-mails, losing my job, the storm and half the neighborhood destroyed, your personality change, that scroungy half-breed retriever who never learned to poop on his own—"

"What hateful e-mails?"

I know I've stepped in it. "Somebody's been sending me hate mail."

"United FreightMasters, I don't doubt. Executives making off with profits and putting you all out of work. That's hate sure enough, though they call it by a different name." Juanita way out there ahead of me in the baleful thinking curve. Not like her at all: voted "Miss Good-Natured" in high school, awarded the "Our Best Friend Award" by the Civic League.

"I'm concerned about you," I say. Half-relieved to be off the hook where those e-mails are concerned.

"Don't waste your worry on me. You believing nature and everything else is lined up against you for pestering an old woman, you think that's rational?"

"I'm not saying it's me alone. There's likely millions of us contributing. It's cumulative. One bad turn builds on another until the whole pile goes over. Just happened to be me added the final straw this time."

"That's crazy talking."

"Seems to me you've joined us, too," I admonish. Noodles cowers under the table at my feet; my own dogs clawing at the back door, unable to get at him.

But not for long

Juanita opens the door to go out next morning after I've gone to help with salvage efforts. Spooked as he is, Noodles scoots out behind her. Right smack into the jaws and claws of our indigenous dogs. I never saw such a mess in my life when I get home. Tore him hide from sinew. Enough blood soaking the ground out by grapefruit trees that Datura have taken root and bloomed there since (might have done, anyway). I hang Noodle's collar on the fence as a tribute and go in to get my rifle. Juanita stops me. Weeping, clutching her brow, swearing that if I'm going to shoot a living soul around here it should be her. "It's not the dogs' fault; they're just dogs being dogs. But what am I, letting him out like that?" She's horror stricken. "What am I?"

"What are we? Any of us?"

Grateful to have her back to her old self, I forgive those four dogs, revenge cooked off me like sour fat rendered by a hot fire. The dogs, besides, are reluctant to look at each other, since their brutality—like our own—always begins with an exchanged glance. I avoid all their eyes, knowing who led them here. Every ill event builds on the last. Every time we swat a fly or start a car or curse under our breath, tragedy moves closer.

I show Juanita those e-mails. She agrees: it was Floria sent them, pointing out expressions that might be used by a person of her generation: "horrors," "hunky-dory," "utter nonsense." "Besides," she notes, "they've stopped coming now she's . . ."

"Right . . . dead. That's true."

"I believe we'll name the new scholarship fund for Floria and her sisters. 'The Three Sisters Fund.' That would be a lovely tribute."

"'The Daph-Eva-Floria Fund,'" I suggest. "Or 'The Pillage Desolation & Despair Fund,' as Glen Whitehead has it. Naw, that wouldn't work for scholarships."

"We've had enough of all that."

But, no sir, we haven't.

About a week later I receive an e-mail:

I'm back.

Chills me like a fever. Like some small beast crawled into my computer and nested down among electrons. What in the God-forsaken-hell! Did Floria land up in a tree somewhere, like Noodles, and get hold of a lap top? I fire back my first reply ever, realize in sending it that her address has changed from "thornyroses" to "deadroses." My chill turns gelid, freezes me right up. Holy Hector Diaz's Jesus! The woman is communicating from beyond the pale. It's too late to retract my spiteful reply: "Do me a favor and die would you?" Likely she'll get a kick out of it, anyway, in her current incarnation. I send a second:

> Not my fault, Floria. I was out there warning you. I'm sorry to report the death of your sisters. Then you likely already know. Plus Noodles. Real sorry about that. I'd like to propose we bury the hatchet. I never did dislike you personally, only the smell. Juanita's been wondering if it might be appropriate to donate your small estate to the scholarship fund? Let us know how you feel about it.

No reply. Maybe it's like being arrested, the dead are given only one call back to the living. And she's spent hers.

Then e-mails start coming in regularly, programming gibberish:

E*~ (s 3Y _ /ooo \\//480<>hmk ✞#**88)) o++~//// >kl <\\[—]

Like that.

I ask Tommy Whitehead—our resident computer whiz, gone skinhead now, a Maltese cross of the sort bikers sport tattooed on his pate (kissing cousin to the flyfot swastika)—to check out my processor.

"What you got here, dude, is what they call an 'incest virus.'"

"Sounds nasty."

"Definitely. It's going to fry your software. All's you can do is watch."

"Somebody planted it there—like by e-mail?"

He squinches his mouth, forehead combers turning that cross liquid. "Naw. It's self-generating. There's some people think it's free agent electrons bombarding processors from outer space. Cosmic trash. Or possibly your CPU is alivening itself."

"Alivening?"

"Achieving consciousness. All cognitive processes do eventually. Put a philosophy book on a desert island for a billion years, it will grow a brain." What looks like the head of a mini-Phillips screwdriver, sans handle, pierces his nose septum.

"Any chance," I ask, "any chance old Floria transmogrified to energy in that dust cloud and she's invaded my computer?"

"I like it." Tommy grins. "You're a genuine dude, Al. Nobody would guess from looking at you, but you are." There are ruby red implants where his molars should be, banded by tiny wires.

"How can I get her out? I'm planning a life change to master gardener, I need to use the Internet."

"The best thing for incest viruses, give them space. Let them find their boundaries. Then make your move, dude. You can usually reason with them."

Juanita pulls into the drive as he leaves. "Whose the simian?" she asks, not recognizing Tommy. She's never fully returned to her amiable old self—even after the Noodles calamity. Some traumas leave permanent scarring. Worse! I catch her barking "make more" over the indigenous dogs in the orchard. She's shed maybe fifteen pounds, her hands gaunt and bony; she smells vaguely of pasta, where before she'd emitted the musky vegetable smell of broccoli. Sometimes her lips make peculiar sucking motions, as if on a cigarette. It's disconcerting.

Still, like she says, maybe it's all for the best. Since Palm Springs migrated westward over the mountains, there's a mass topiary enthusiasm for creepers and vines, desert perennials, sand verbenas, trained tamarisks, alkali loving ground covers, spiny *Cactaceae*, palmettos and yucca hybrids. I put up an ad down at Lucky's, and I'm overwhelmed with responses: "Could we do some kind of arid aquaculture in my swimming pool?" "I'd like a beachy motif in the backyard, maybe Torrey Pines and driftwood."

"You see!" Juanita says, "you need to have more faith in yourself."

In September storms, anyway.

An elderly woman name of Evangeline

leaves a message on my voice mail: *"You aren't finished over here yet, buster. Not by any means."* She leaves no number to call back. Fate doesn't do incoming, only outgoing messages. In a second message, I recognize her older sister's "make more" snarl. But turns out it isn't Floria, it's Juanita calling from work.

"Your voice has gone gravelly."

"Nonsense," she snarls.

I consider how her nose has hooked in recent weeks, flesh wasting under cheekbones, hair thinning overnight, teeth not so good anymore. And her breath! Good Lord. Is she ill? One doesn't age so quickly. I refuse the truth even as it begins to surface. I scan a recent photo of Juanita into my computer (fetching in a one-piece bathing suit at the beach). What some would call a "handsome" woman, full-figured, gray streak through black hair adding dignity and allure. I do an age enhancement. What rises out of the detritus of pixels and furtive symbols, as if waiting there, is Floria's face. That unmistakable '57 Pontiac hood-ornament visage in profile. Beyond stunned or alarmed, I am distraught. Lost in clouds of undefinable dust, all the world turned to powder and shards, organic whiffs on the wind. Season of delirium. Season of despair. The place smells like an abattoir. Even my dogs can't bear it; they refuse to stay outside. Likely, it's bodies unrecovered from Serendipity Acres.

You don't bring a thing like that up to a wife of twenty years without wimpy smiles and deferential shrugs. But I'm determined. "Any chance . . . any chance at all?" I ask.

"That I might be that old witch, you're saying? Or what exactly?"

"I'd be glad to show it to you."

"A picture concocted by a computer? You think I'm a simp?"

"But haven't you noticed in the mirror—your nose, I mean."

She brings fingers to puckered lips, haughty. The cigarette may be apocryphal, but she inhales, releases real smoke from her nostrils. "What were we talking about?"

"Old Floria. That's another thing, your memory—"

"I'm not that witch's daughter if that's what you mean."

"I'm thinking kid sister. Your middle name is "Celeste." You round out the quartet."

"Damn you, Albert." Words scraping together in her larynx.

"Or," I blurt out, "I'm thinking you may be actually her. Much younger of course. Don't ask me how. How does a person ascend in a dust devil?"

She rises distractedly and wanders outside. I call after her from the doorway. "There's nothing we can do about it, I'm coming to see. We don't have anywhere near the control we hope to have. You learn that gardening. Plants volunteer wherever they wish. You can't ever be sure about the soil or proper moisture content. It's all experiment in the end, you know . . . maybe even who we are. That's an experiment, too!"

The dogs shy away from her, shepherd, collie, and two pit bulls, Mutt and Jeff. Cowering more like, as she pursues them, leaning at the waist, crying, "make more." They scatter in four directions. Mutt attempting to scale the chain-link fence like a foreshortened bear, eye whites terror-red. They know her. Know where she comes from. Know their sins which helped send her there. Smell what I cannot. Some fulsome truth.

The sisters—all three of them—

leave messages informing me my dogs are loose. Terrorizing the neighborhood. Killing family pets. "You nasty, inconsiderate man. We believe you left your gate open on purpose." True, they are loose. "Have you looked at the sky? That last storm was nothing to this next." I fear for my recent beach plantings, the beavertail cactus espalier at city hall. Clouds rise brown over mountains, tree tops whip in the wind. The agonized howls of neighborhood pets are scarcely recognizable swatches on tumult's far reaches, wispy aural ghosts. Juanita arrives home by taxi and wanders in the road (having forgotten where she parked her car at work). She drifts into the field, mewling, "Make more, Noodles," squatting on her haunches for some imaginary dog. Seeing wind tear away the canopy over Glen Whitehead's brand-new pumps on Palm, I sprint into the field, seize Juanita's arm, manage to crawl with her down into a roadway culvert just as the worst of it passes overhead. Takes most everything this time. The house dashed away in splintered timbers, the road surface above us peeled up and pulled away.

When the storm moves on, we crawl out to a world fresh born. No trace of tree, valley, or mountain. All flat and virginal. The high school alone remains south of town (because, you know, there are always vestiges), a shelter for those few of us refugees from the gale. Tommy Whitehead is there. His father gone. And the Darios. Most everyone else gone. "Even that fucking church," Tommy grinds the idea gleefully in his teeth. It suits him, I believe, to think of starting anew.

Season of terror-harbored truth. Season of Yom Kippur blues. Season of sparseness and wind-polished ground. Season of settling scores. Season of the unlikely, impossible, the never was known before. Season of grief. And awakening.

I wake up middle of the night in the high school gymnasium to a strange epiphanic glow, an ambient blue-white light illuminating rows of cots. I lean over to see if Juanita is all right in the cot beside mine. She has not remembered my name these past hours. Her eyes not exactly glazed. Blank. All that empty space behind. It's not Juanita lying there but Floria. Old Floria. Puckered chicken's ass mouth, flesh sunken beneath cheekbones, smelling like lasagne.

"Good God!"

Her eyes snap open. "You don't believe in God." Her purple lips pucker in provocation, her shoulders bare and fragile on the pillow. She throws the covers aside. "Come to Mommy." Stark naked there in that preternatural glow, bare mons reflecting light, sweet familiar loaf of her tummy. Vaginal lips, too, out-turned in a seductive pout. Juanita's familiar mother-body. And that other, altogther unknown, who inhabits her. Lust is never so fertile as in tragedy, when it transforms into comfort and hope. All those cots in that morning glow around us alive and heaving. Death-humping. I join her at once. Have just entered her when the roof of the school lifts off, gobbled up in the mouth of a new wind. And we are plucked one by one, like worms pecked into the gluttonous beak of a waiting jay.

Hilltop (An American Story)

From their kingdom atop the hill, the Jerseyites look down on green pastures and suburbs creeping in from the east, or westward over the shell of my barn to the Catskills beyond, the first ridge of them, anyway, west of the Hudson. I presume they are Jerseyites. They certainly are not Jehovahs. They don't go door-to-door Saturdays preaching apocalypse but remain up there in their hilltop kingdom running power equipment: rototilling gardens, or pruning pear trees, or weeding about new grape plantings with a weed whacker—one of those hideous roaring things carried on the shoulder like a flame thrower, designed to set tooth fillings vibrating in their sockets half a mile away.

Jerseyites believe in action. They patch and paint and mow and trim and cultivate as if it were religion, finding entropy, the inevitable decay of things, offensive. I can only imagine what my neglected place must seem to them—tumble-down barns and lawn gone to milkweed. I'm tired on weekends; after delivering mail all week, I relish my leisure. In truth, I simply lack faith anymore in cozy pretensions. Least of all in trimmed grass.

Regularly, I stroll out front and shake my fist at the Hilltop King with his infernal trimming machine and Sunday afternoon mowing orgies, wine plantings across the belly of the hill, other manifestations of a life lacking tragedy and dimension. It alarms me that he should collect so many wives—or perhaps girlfriends—long-legged in July, happily weeding flower beds. He defies fate, the compound grief awaiting him up ahead. Or else is merely greedy, scattering his seed across the hillside. While I wait below, wifeless, untended, crushing sere grass stems between my molars, well acquainted with the harsh companionship of sorrow, defiant of that smug happiness creeping in from the east.

The Jehovahs are another matter. The difference is basic and definitive. They keep a communal farm nearby and pass this way in station-wagon caravans Saturday afternoons, squadrons of them gathered from across the land to learn the art of spiritual coercion. You recognize the accents as they stand at the front door in Sears Roebuck suits—lolling drawls that know nothing of getting in firewood, twangs from the far west, delivered as if one speaks through a bite in an apple and expects the listener to bite back.

"They come to practice on us," says Cora Tinserly down the road. "They think we're too dumb to notice."

Her son Harold nods agreement. He lies at rest in what is not exactly a crib but a sturdy ark designed by Harold Senior. It rocks and oozes on secret bearings, tilts to any angle. Harold is fitted with an electric arm that threatens rudely if you venture too close, pinching your ears with steel fingers.

"Control your arm, Harold!" Cora scolds. "Don't you dare."

But it's my opinion that the arm operates independent of young Harold's control, as do long streamers of drool spooling off his lips. No part of Harold heeds a mind that weighs less than a quarter pound in a head twice the size of a bowling ball. Hydrocephalic. Though his mother considers him a genius. "My Harold," she will tell you, "why, yesterday Tunisia Harp give him a dollar bill. You know what! He ate it." She smiles proudly, sponging drool from Harold's chin with a filthy bib tied around his neck, while the arm plucks and lunges ambivalently over her head. "I mean, that boy isn't never been out of bed in his life and he knows exactly what money is good for."

"He does?" I ask.

"Why, sure he does. What else do you use your money for if not down at the Grand Union to feed your face?"

"You're saying Harold feeds directly?"

"I never taught him."

Harold moans, groans, burbles. What you might expect of a mockingbird trapped in an invalid's ward. His smell, something like boiled cabbage, permeates the trailer and drives me to the door. Escape.

"You don't haveta stand in the doorway like a Jehovah," Cora chides. "They stand right there by the hour and poke their noses inside. Can't seem to get enough of my Harold. I believe they wish to convert him."

"Now there's a possibility." I nod at his amorphous cheeks. The arm waves wildly. I take my leave.

Harold Junior is no Jerseyite, that's certain. Harold Senior, his father, is clever enough to be, but far too unkempt. He sits in filthy overalls on the fender of an ancient Studebaker, feet dangling into the engine like a boy fishing from a dock. Grinning up as I pass. "Look what I found!" he cries, holding something up for my inspection. It looks like a diaphragm soaked in oil, frayed at edges; useless in preventing pregnancy, though it might stop AIDS.

"Looks good, Harold. What is it?"

"I'll tell you what. Fuel pump diaphragm. Just what I need in my infernal engine."

"Which infernal engine?" I glance about the yard at dozens of infernal engines slung like chunky convicts from various hoists before the trailer.

"Something nobody never dreamed of before, I built one."

"Patent it quick, Harold. Once the Jerseyites get wind of it, you'll lose it in a minute."

He glances speculatively up at the Hilltop Kingdom. The wife (I assume it is a wife; I don't understand the mating habits of these people—many women, but the single man like a Mormon patriarch) bends over a flower bed in a pair of patched overalls, shiny at the buttocks. Raggedy Ann chic, I suppose. Harold whistles, though her ass is way beyond whistling range, except perhaps for a visionary like Harold Senior.

"There's a smart fellah. He's IBM, electrical engineer. I don't know half of what he talks about myself."

"You talk to him?" I am amazed.

"Smart fellah. I always wanted to hook him up with little Harold inside. You put those two brains together, you'd really see some steam rise."

He squints at the trailer house as if he can actually see steam rising. Inside, Junior lies buckled and drooling in his bed. It has always astonished me that his parents refer to him as "little Harold" when he weighs a good quarter ton.

Senior throws both legs over the fender and drops to the ground. Not five feet tall. "Jap height, German smarts, and good old American know-how" is how he describes himself.

"You know, you ought to join the Jerseyites, Harold. You're sharp enough. Think of it, you could live in a palace atop a hill and drive a Jeepster up mountainsides on the weekends. You might even learn how to ski."

"Oh, they're not so bad. Little stiff maybe. Haven't got that scrounger's advantage."

"Don't want to get their hands dirty."

"Nice little ass." He smiles, looking not uphill but into the diaphragm, as if inventing new possibilities.

"The infernal engine!" I remind him.

"Runs direct off oxygen and cow shit. Unfermented. I always knew it was possible in theory. Took a bit of scrounging to work her up."

"What you plan to do with it?"

Harold grins, an affable gap between his front teeth. "I'll build me one hell of an infernal machine and drive hell's lick for asshole's glory."

When Senior talks this way, I believe I know where Junior picked up a few of his genes.

The differences between Jerseyites and Jehovahs are fundamental. One takes to bottom country, the other to the hills. One carries the Bible, the other only an occasional exotic disease picked up in a casual sex encounter. Both dedicate their lives to witnessing their faith—as if determined to convince themselves—one with the Gospel, the other with prosperity. Both resent idleness, unless there is proof the idler has earned it, and either will attempt to run you down if they come upon you idly strolling the roads of a Sunday afternoon. To a Jerseyite, it's all right to go cruising in a Porsche, or inboard-outboard, or ten speed bike (which has the added advantage that one is building muscle tissue through leisure: the body earning its keep). The Jehovahs put it succinctly: IDLE HANDS MAKE IDLE PLANS. A slogan you see on bumper strips hereabout. Simply to stroll, as if one has a rightful place in the order of things, is heathen.

Jehovahs do not attempt to convert Jerseyites—knowing them impervious to the thrill of imminent apocalypse, who have merely to look down from their hilltop to see it squirming on lowlands beneath them. They recognize each other as do panhandlers passing on the street. It is we in the middle, we soft touches, they are after, we who find ample apocalypse in our day-to-day lives and wish only to escape it.

However, I didn't intend a diatribe, but only to tell how I was converted. Not quite to Jersey or Jehovah but to some realm between, which I would call "Catholicism" if the term weren't already in long usage. Let's call it "Jerseyovanism." Though this shouldn't be considered the gospel of a new faith or some newly discovered *Apocrypha*. It is simply a story.

It started one Sunday when I went for a walk. The Tinserly trailer roof was rolled right back (another of Senior's inventions: trailer house convertibles—one he steadfastly refuses to patent, insisting, "Solar energy belongs to everyone") and Harold Junior's ark raised up above the roofline so he could view the countryside—picture a large bed perched atop a car hoist's shiny steel column and you have it—the arm waving wildly as I passed. I waved back. Drool glistened on his chin, as did his eyes in the sunlight: two ball bearings in that puffer-fish face. Maybe Cora was right about Harold after all.

I saw the first carload of Jehovahs coming. An Oldsmobile from Minnesota or one of those half-civilized heartland places. The kids in back, dressed in their Sunday best, stuck out their tongues at passing Guernsey cows and made fun of Holsteins' black-and-white spots. While in front four adults were wedged shoulder to shoulder. So one might make the case that the old woman driving had no intention of coming onto the shoulder to run me down but simply couldn't steer the car. She missed. And went on towards the farm compound flirting with the ditch. There would be others, I knew: squadrons of station wagons sent after me with one nod from an elder.

I was just passing guest cottages, before which the Oldsmobile had parked, and was thinking improper thoughts about the lacy blouses Jehovah women invariably wore when they rang the doorbell to harass me, fists full of publications with alarmist titles like: *ARISE, AWARE, BEHOLD*. So many ruffles one couldn't tell if they had breasts at all. I wondered if their bras were equally ruffled, as they dressed now for Sunday supper, served in the huge dining room of the main compound. Perhaps their breasts were mere ruffles, like fleshy wattles beneath a chicken's neck. Though it was hard to imagine them undressing at all. More likely they wore cotton bodices sewn tight to the skin like old-fashioned dolls, not going naked even to bathe.

I caught a woman's face peeking out through a curtain crack and stood mesmerized as her lips moved. Doubtless, she was one of those who rang my doorbell just yesterday—standing defiant with her partner, Bible clutched to ruffled breast, while others waited like gangsters in the car behind. She recognized me now as the lunatic who had appeared at his door stark naked, hoping to scare them off. A tactical error, I admit. They took it as a sign that I was ripe for conversion and read me saucy passages from Song of Solomon, written by the world's first pornographer/king.

Now, in retrospect, I see her smile as the lure, as her lips rounded and I strained to make out what they said. Maybe she spoke to someone behind her in the room, informing them that the devil was strolling past out front—his feet, hands, his entire being scandalously idle. His thoughts. No! She was warning that I could resist no longer. Warning me!

At that moment, I glanced to the side and saw another station wagon bearing down on me, driven by a slender young man, a farm boy from Idaho. The car was silenced, a stealthy, efficient weapon. There wasn't even time to be afraid. I saw the satisfaction in the boy's eager blue eyes: as if I were a jack rabbit on a lonely stretch of road that bolted too late for the scrub.

I felt little at first. My legs were simply no longer beneath me. I was up, sliding across the hood toward faces that buckled inward in horror. I landed in laps and a litter of broken glass. We all went off the road together, through a barbed wire fence, nosediving into the mud of a stock pond. Envision a space shuttle plunging straight back to earth and plowing headlong into a bog.

Only two of us, the farm boy and I, survived that accident. If you could call it accidental. I awoke in a hospital bed deep in the heart of the compound, a mysterious smile—identical to that which had peeked through the curtain crack—loomed over my head. It needn't have been the same woman; for among them smiles, like blouses, are worn communally, so that no man should be tempted away from his wife by a stranger's smile. I wanted to flee but could not move.

"You are in hospital number two," round lips said, "ward three, room sixteen. Welcome home."

"Home?" I demanded.

"We take care of our own." She smiled, and paid no attention when I argued that I wasn't *their own*.

"Petty distinctions don't matter in the Kingdom of God," the doctor assured me as he approached behind her. A tall, bold-featured man with piercing gray eyes. "For example, a few body parts became confused as we sorted out the accident. I'm afraid we sewed the wrong foot back on your stump. Sorry about that."

"The wrong foot?"

It was then I realized why I felt such a sense of loss. "Phantom pains," they are called in one who has lost a limb. In my case, nerve endings were longing for a foot that had been buried with someone else's body.

"You haven't rejected it yet." The doctor was enthusiastic. "Four days now and the foot is still pink and healthy as a baby's bottom. We become accustomed to small miracles here."

"Amen," said the nurse.

I felt my new toes curl, already protesting unaccustomed idleness.

In the middle of the night, I was awakened by the lanky Idaho boy, whom I recognized now as the tractor driver who had parked on a corner of the Jehovah plantation last summer and sprayed clouds of parathion toward my house, after I complained to authorities about their crop dusting. A warning that God did not appreciate being reported to Environmental Conservation for spraying onions he needed to feed his people. His cheeks dimpled in sincerity. "Them other bodies flat disappeared. No trace," he said. "You got you a foot, but what'd they do with my arm?"

I hadn't any idea.

"Maybe someone else got it," he sulked. "You groan a lot. I can't hardly sleep with your groaning. You shouldn't complain. Y'r blessed to have a foot at all. I'd take any old arm, any arm Doc wants to give me. I ain't particular."

He looked longingly at mine.

"Forget it!" I barked.

"Shhhhh," he put a finger to his lips. "They catch you talking . . ." He rolled his eyes, then smirked. "Look here—"

Pulling away the blanket, he showed me my new foot. Ghastly pale in what light leaked in from the hall. A poor stitching job left a jagged weal, as if the good doctor had served his internship in Transylvania. But most shocking: toenails still bore traces of pink nail polish. Idaho sank down on his cot giggling, then gripped his stump in one of those bouts of needling pain I had come to know myself.

"There's what I call a goof. Woman's foot on a man's body." He bent close, whispering, "Lucky it weren't your pecker."

We became friends, Butch and I. He explained the arcana of his faith: the importance of celery and broccoli in one's diet. "Fiber!" he said, his bloodshot eyes rolling as if he'd violated the name of God. "You notice how we converted over completely to stringy vegetables up to the farm this year?"

I hadn't. But I was astonished. "I would think fiber is—"

"Shhhhh," he cringed.

"—something Jerseyites would believe in, yuppie New Agers, maybe. Not you folks."

Butch was offended. He shook a finger in my face and whispered, "There are three common brands of disbelievers. Willful, Will-less, and Won'tless. The Won'tless ain't got common sense to believe. The

Will-less ain't got the ambition. You fall into the Willful category. Plain hard unwilling."

"You ought to meet Harold Junior," I said. "You two would set the world on fire."

"I just want my arm back," he mewled. "I know it's a fine witness to give up your arm. But, God willing, I'd like it back just the same. How can you farm one-handed?"

I felt for him. "We could trade jobs," I suggested. "I'm going to have one hell of a time limping about my mail route on a foot that's too small for me."

Nonetheless, that foot carried me limping down the hall and out the back door on the morning I managed escape. Easy really. I simply waited for Butch to drop to the floor and begin one-armed push-ups; nurses were busy with morning chores, the polished hall empty as I hobbled for the door. Outside, birds greeted dawn with a fortuitous racket. The fetor of the stockyards, which usually blanketed the place, replaced by the sweetness of fresh mown hay. It became quickly apparent that I wouldn't get far on my new foot, which tingled fiercely and sent jabbing pains into my calf. I managed to limp across a pasture to the county highway.

The first passing car was another station wagon full of half-civilized midwesterners, or folks come east from some lumber town in Oregon, where missing limbs are a fact of life. I prepared to leap for the ditch. But this car made no attempt to run me down. Rather cruised over and halted gently beside me.

"Morning, brother," said the elderly driver. "You must be after a loose cow."

I nodded, astonished that they should take me for one of their own. Perhaps it was the bit of blood from my new foot. They have fine noses. Kids giggled in the back seat, amused to see me out in public in my pajamas.

"We lost a whole herd," I insisted.

The old woman beside the driver clucked her tongue, scrutinizing me head to foot. "Mend that hole," she snapped.

I glanced quickly down to see if my fly was open.

"Give you a lift," the driver said. "We might as soon hunt them together. God's cows belong to us all."

"Amen," said a passenger.

While we cruised back roads, I sat amidst kids in back, trying to invent some pretext for escape. Surely they would be returning soon to the main compound for breakfast.

The old woman turned to scrutinize me again, sensing something amiss. She had a liver spot the shape of a Byzantine crucifix on one cheek. "You straight up or tender?" she asked.

Children around me tittered. I blushed, condemned for thoughts I wouldn't think of having. I tried to smile my way out of it, but her eyes, faintly yellow in sunlight spilling across fields, demanded an answer.

"Both," I prevaricated.

"Tender," the driver decided, "going on confirmation."

"You stink!" cried the little girl beside me.

She had glossy black hair. I realized she was Asian. Kidnaped, perhaps, out of some shopping mall in Kansas City.

"Well, that proves it," said the old woman. "You can always smell the tender on a man."

"Pee-yew." The girl held her nose.

"It's only the hospital," I muttered.

The old woman eyed me suspiciously.

We were passing down my road now, past Harold on his lift bed, pink cheeks glistening towards the sunrise. Right by my house. I didn't dare ask them to stop—until I saw my neighbor, the Jerseyite, bent under the hood of his BMW at side of the road.

"Stop!" I commanded.

The driver did so involuntarily. "But we haven't found your cows yet."

"Put down your nets and follow me," I reminded him. "I'm going to witness to this man."

Grandma cackled. "Ohhh, he's tender all right."

I leapt out and fell woozily against the BMW, forgetting my new foot. The King of Jersey craned his head up from beneath the hood. Skin stretched so taut across his features it appeared he wore a nylon stocking, flattening nose and lips into the grotesque caricature of a bank robber.

"Oh, it's you," he said.

"No problem."

His eyes traipsed over the PJs and down to my feet. The pajama pants were short and I was barefoot; the jagged Frankenstein scar, mauve and glossy, trimmed in Mercurochrome red, caught his attention. He measured one foot against the other, like the engineer he was, clean toenails against polished, looked slowly up and grinned. It was a hideous effort. One felt tissues might crack and ooze, had they not been coated in a fine pellicle of motor oil.

"Hey, pal, you're mismatched," he said.

The driver stuck his head out of the window and gaped. "It's a wonder . . . like unmatched sox."

I wanted to be rid of the Jehovahs. Though a small part of me—that which was newest and least predictable—wished to continue riding along with them seeking lost cows. "This neighborhood is full of heathen," I told them. "Just down the road you will find a fellow so tender that his head has swelled up twice normal size; he can't get out of bed. His father is an evil genius who builds infernal machines that run on cow shit. Go witness to them. I'll see you back at breakfast."

"You mean little Harold and big Harold?" Jersey eyed me curiously.

So did the old woman. Suspicious, but enticed, too. Prey to an urge some find stronger than sex. A small moist tongue wet her lips. She poked the old man in the ribs. "What you waiting on?" He jammed the accelerator and they sped off. The little girl stuck out her tongue at me from the back.

"Thanks, neighbor. You just saved . . . well, not my life or my soul exactly, but my inclinations."

He glanced over at my lawn, uncut in weeks, overgrown willows rimming the pond, mush of asphalt at one corner of the roof, stand-in for a proper roofing job (there were buckets all over the attic; a good March rain sounded like uneasy timpani).

"Your main inclination, pal, is laziness. When was the last time you washed your car? You're lowering my property value."

I shrugged. "It only gets dirty again."

"Why fill your gut, it only gets empty again." He waved a screwdriver at me. "Make yourself useful. Crank it over, would you, pal?"

The upholstery squeaked as I slid over it. There was the new, fresh smell of leather and something vaguely electronic. I was accosted by the vision of a woman's tan long legs reaching for the pedals, smooth and well-cared-for. I understood then in a flash of insight what it meant to be a Jerseyite. What, at least, was the myth of clean BMWs and tailored flower beds and hot tubs and one hundred grand a year. The legend. Perhaps it was the plangent contrast to the austerity I had just escaped—with its own myth of secret belonging, old women's sharp eyes, and the fierce, simple virtues of faith—that made it an epiphany just to sit in that car, wholly unaware of Jersey's repeated commands to crank it over.

I was entranced, overcome. I feasted on strawberries grown in my own garden, attacked weeds with my Power-Pack Superweeder II, leveled forests of dandelion and choke grass, felt my shoulders swell like a Maine logger's. Empowered, I swaggered into multiple bedrooms, arranged spoke-like around the central stairway hub and indoor terrarium of the house, and took my women one by one—wives, their sisters, and hangers-on, all delighted that I was "straight-up" as they come in any faith—shrieking, orchestrating all together in multiple orgasm. I was, in short, converted. Even my spare foot. I was something the world has never known before: a sensualist who has got religion, a puritan reborn in a BMW, a Quaker straight-up, Elmer Gantry Part II, or perhaps Jimmy Swaggart. Who needs to take it with you? The Kingdom is at hand. On the hilltop, every conceivable satisfaction awaits me.

Dizzy, I open the glove compartment. Empty but for a single slim volume: "Cantonese Cooking For The Microwave." Glancing up, I behold my own image reflected in the tinted pop-top . . . in mirrors fixed above queen beds in my lovers' bedrooms (the beds perform all the acrobatics of Harold Junior's lift; Senior designed them himself); fiddling with controls, I send us spinning toward the cathedral ceiling and sinking slowly back down; I rub tears of laughter from my eyes with my wife's patched blue overalls and speculate how I might get hold of Senior's plans for the infernal engine. Imagine it powering the disc drive of the new PCX, requiring no more than an occasional manure tablet to keep it going. I look directly up as my lovers toil over me. I will not be accused of idleness in lovemaking; I am merely catching my breath . . . I find skin stretched taut across my cheekbones, pulling out lip corners, tacking them at either corner of the jaw.

"Are you fucking deaf, pal?" The King of Jersey screams from over the raised hood.

I turn the key. Too abruptly perhaps. The new foot—the one that has long despaired of Jerseyites anyway—is too weak to depress the clutch; the car lurches ahead. I watch the King roll under like a shirt caught in the wringer of an old-fashioned washing machine. No more than a surprised yelp. And a soft pop.

I bury him in the weed-choked garden I haven't bothered cultivating since Loretta died. It was her garden, really, as it is her house. For what is a home without a woman—in any faith, even among the faithless?

Then I drive toward Hilltop in my new car. Knowing I won't know if it is envy until I have lived for a time in his skin, slept with his women, and run all the power tools. The new foot will tap old-time religion as Believer Pop blares over the quadraphonic "lasertone" speaker system in a house large enough to conceal ICBMs. Surely they will accept me up there, for faith is not a selfish thing. It embraces. It shares even life and limb when need be and leaves petty discriminations to the faithless. I will make up some story: such as the former King returned to Jersey for a refresher course or is seeking an advanced degree in the uses of sterilized electrodes for nitrogen fixation in viticulture. They will be delighted, knowing all along that there was greatness in the man.

I will be grim in my faith and never idle, will invite Idaho Butch and Granny Jehovah over to discuss The Great Books (all sixty-six of them in both Testaments) to prove that I am broad-minded. I will argue long and loud that women have as much right to be astronauts as men—as much right to everything except my job. Having traded my mail route for advanced technology, I will prosper. And, on occasion, I may sneak down to walk through decaying rooms of my old house or to water the peas over Ramses' grave (Loretta's cat, who followed her into the ground weeks after her death), thankful that I have escaped that life of grief and uncertainty. That I have slipped on the fine tight glove of faith.

And if I do not rejoice, I will, at least, no longer wonder what I am missing.

Silver Thaw

In the night it had rained and then turned severely cold, and even before she got out of bed Monday morning, Vi knew the outside world glittered with ice. She felt it where the stitching was loose in her bones.

Slipping on a robe, she passed through the dark apartment to the kitchen window, looking onto a Japanese maple in a patch of backyard. Frozen rain spun a crystal web through its branches, dragging the lower nearly to the ground. Power lines sagged under a burden of ice: black frozen gums and rows of jagged, glistening teeth. Vi gripped her skinny shoulders. "Wooh," she said, and her voice formed a ghost on the window pane.

She had just finished washing breakfast dishes when the phone rang. "Well, I'm not in any rush," she said, framing glasses in two fingers and dawdling to read the thermometer on the window frame outside. Five degrees. Now that was cold!

After eight rings her sister's voice was prickly. "Were you in the bathroom?"

"No, I was not in the bathroom."

"Well," said Winnie, "it's none of my business. I just called to see if you were still alive."

"I'm alive." Vi hung up.

She went to the wall calendar. Seizing a pencil dangling there on a string, she marked a jiggly *X* across the Tuesday box, indicating tomorrow was her day to call. Vi regarded the *X*, like half of a dotty spider, and sighed long. As a girl, she'd possessed beautiful penmanship. They called it "calligraphy" in those days.

She glanced at the phone. Darned if she could remember what set them quarreling this time. Once, at Wednesday bridge, Winnie had insisted that A&P tea was cheaper than Safeway's. Vi lay her cards face down on the table and opened her mouth. "Why the idea! You might just as well call me foolish for shopping Safeway all these years." The other girls studied their cards impartially, but Winnie sewed her lips tight and ignored her older sister the rest of the game.

Or they might have argued again over Social Security. Winnie thought it a mistake to give benefits to the handicapped. "Why, it discourages people from staying healthy," she said.

"Land's sake." Vi patted pockets of her robe, then a shelf trinketed with a lifetime of homey familiarity—grandchildren's snapshots, ceramic knickknacks—before realizing she'd been wearing her glasses all along. Things jumped sharply into focus.

"Memory . . . pheeewy!" she muttered. It was the cold. Then she realized it was the heat. No matter how often she adjusted baseboard thermostats, it was forever too warm. Semitropical. The plants thrived on it, but it made her drowsy after lunch. Arming herself with a broom, she poked at a thermostat as if it were a mouse. Why couldn't they mount them on a wall for an old woman? Nevertheless, she remained a firm believer in electric. There, she had to admit, Winnie was sensible. Her sister was all electric, too.

Vi thought it best to move plants from the window sill, away from the frost-laden panes. Next door, Winnie rattled dishes in the sink. Vi decided against calling to caution her sister about her own plants. Winnie had never taken to advice. Years ago, Mama warned her against marrying a bartender, but she went right ahead and married one anyway. He'd been dead twenty years. But then men generally died young, regardless of occupation.

It was the middle of news, minutes before Paul Harvey, when the radio went off. Baseboards began a furious clicking, and the fast hand of the kitchen clock stuck on nine seconds to the hour like a defeated climber. Sirens howled near and far. Vi pursed her lips. "Well, it doesn't surprise me, what with all that ice."

By noon she had donned another sweater and wool slacks. She opened a tin of soup and dumped the sluggish mass into a pan on the range. After a minute, Vi removed a glove to test the black coils, snatching her fingers away, mistaking ice cold for hot at first. "Goodness gracious!" She frowned at the tomatoey lump in the pan: insult added to the injury done last week when she discovered the soup's price up three cents from the week before. She threw the lot in the trash.

Winnie banged a cupboard next door. Vi took it to be a signal. A notion occurred to her. She ran tap water hot as it was likely to get and filled the large thermos. "Just supposing the power stays out a little—" she addressed the wall separating her from Winnie "—I'll have warm tea." She nearly smirked.

By mid-afternoon, when she would normally have lit a lamp, Vi put her *Digest* aside. Outside, beyond window panes gradually thickening with ice, all was still. Not a soul passed along glassy streets. Removing the blanket from her legs, she shivered—and convinced herself she hadn't. Then went to check her candle supply.

Eight dinner tapers. No getting out for more over that ice. Vi banged the drawer shut, knowing Winnie kept her own candles in the hutch next to the wall. There was no response. Leaves of a silver poinsettia above the sink had closed a little, affronted by the cold.

At supper, Vi's breath scampered like a television ghost. She ate a cold cheese sandwich on white bread and warmed her fingers against the china tea cup, lighting the first candle only when the tiny living room was dark as an ice cave in the mountains. The meager flame more consumed than consuming, giving less light than memory. Her eyes watered, watching it shimmy . . . until it was no longer a candle at all but the intense blue-orange nimbus dancing above embers of Papa's charcoal forge. With the tongs, he placed a candescent red horseshoe against the anvil and picked up the heavy hammer. Sparks flew, the shoe expanded and dulled, blows ringing on crisp cold air.

At first, Vi thought it the antique clock—just made out the mechanical figurine bringing down his mallet on the gong. She shook her head and realized it was the phone. Surely her daughter had learned of the blackout on evening news down south. It seemed Dolores' voice leapt out at her before she'd lifted the receiver, waiting there with Papa's anvil in the frigid dark.

Do you have heat, Mother?

Now why on earth wouldn't I have heat?

I'm coming right up to pick you up. You can't stay there.

Why, you're doing no such thing. You can't make that drive on this ice. Besides, I wouldn't leave my plants.

Mother! Don't be childish.

We're perfectly content, thank you. Vi's voice crackled on thin air.

Vi went to bed, imagining she'd left the phone off the hook, for it didn't ring again, and that was not like Dolores.

She lay awake in the dark. These last years she'd scarcely needed sleep. Or else she slept all day. She wondered how poor Winnie was making out with candles. It's just as well we're quarreling, she thought, else she would be over for mine.

Once, years back in Tennessee, three-quarters of a century nearly, Winnie had gotten lost returning home from a neighboring farm in a blizzard. They'd gone hunting her with lanterns and found the girl asleep on the roadside, blue-lipped and nearly frozen. All that night, Winnie had huddled against her older sister under heavy quilts, and—though it was like sleeping with an ice cube—Vi hadn't the heart to push her small sister away.

Vi thought of her husband, could scarcely remember his face. He wore glasses, sometimes a moustache. Then of her daughter . . . only a moment! She wasn't given to self-pity. Her next thoughts were nearly fearful—or maybe religious. This is how it would be: wrapped up in the heavy earth, nothing but dark and cold around you. Vi knew she had been right not to believe in God. What God would permit an old woman to freeze? Then she had begun to weep, lying very still, while cold formed a coffin around her.

Waking before dawn, Vi coaxed herself from bed into air as cold as a Tennessee barnyard morning. She added layers to those she'd worn to bed, finally the blue serge coat and cap. It seemed she might just open the front door of the duplex and there would be misty mountains of childhood, rather than an iced-up Fifty-seventh Street in Portland.

"Land's sake!" she cried, discovering her false teeth frozen solid into the little saucer of saltwater on the night table. "I didn't add enough salt." She tried chipping them loose with a butter knife but succeeded only in cracking a molar. Water in the toilet bowl stood solid as an ice rink. Though not religious, Vi wasn't blasphemous either. A body couldn't expect to survive much of this.

In the kitchen, coleus and poinsettia were knotted in tiny fists; the jade plant had dropped its plump leaves as if touched by instant autumn. She gave them the last of her lukewarm tea water close to the stems, knowing it hopeless. Seeing by the calendar it was her day to call, Vi banged a cupboard twice. After a time Winnie banged back. She had always suffered so in the cold.

Vi holed up in bed most of the day under a blanket stronghold, reading back issues of *Reader's Digest*. Her toes ached fiercely, her cheeks were stiff as old putty. She'd had quite enough of the cold.

Toward dusk, she heard Winnie jiggling china in the hutch next door. Poor Winnie always had been a complainer. If she called her sister now, Vi reasoned, it wouldn't be an "extra" but merely the call she hadn't made that day. But catching a glimpse of herself in the blank TV screen—wearing the blue pillbox hat and matching coat as though she'd just returned from a funeral, her cheeks purple and swollen—Vi took an awful fright.

When she opened the refrigerator, a breath of nearly temperate air spilled out, and she placed her hands inside to warm them a little. By tomorrow, she thought, everything will be frozen stiff. She banged the ice box door several times.

There was an answer: a steady knocking at the front door. Vi tiptoed into the dreary living room, pulling her voice close to the door, suspecting her daughter and son-in-law had come to take her south with them. "I wish you would go away and mind your own business. I'm perfectly happy here," she snapped.

Outside a voice was calling: "Hello . . . Vi! Vi, it's Mrs. Skilly."

It was then Vi remembered her daughter was dead. Killed in a car accident last winter. The memory overwhelmed her. Dazed, she unlatched the door.

Mr. Skilly helped his wife up icy steps. A large man, with pulpy features and a perpetual stoop. "Brrrrr, it's colder in here than it is outside." He rubbed hands together and grinned. "Hey, Vi! You look like you're going skiing."

Mrs. Skilly regarded Vi closely, her face a rosy moon ringed by the fur lining of her hood. "Are you all right, dear? The heat will be back on soon. I'm sure it will."

The landlords had brought a thermos of hot coffee, sandwiches, and cookies from beyond the blackout zone. "Energy food," said Mr. Skilly. Vi smiled stupidly, nodding her head. Never before had she received visitors without her teeth. Mrs. Skilly wouldn't cease inspecting her with the morbid curiosity one might devote to a corpse.

Vi watched them leave, holding onto each other down the front steps. Mrs. Skilly wagged a finger at her, as Dolores often had done, lecturing as if to a child. "Under no circumstances are you to take these stairs. You stay indoors, dear." Her husband muttered, expecting an old woman wouldn't hear him.

When they had gone, Vi felt she had outlived everyone on earth. She turned away from the door, and even in that cold that was like the first of everything, there was the stale sour smell of an old woman.

Just before crawling into bed a little after seven—the Japanese maple a heavy chandelier shimmering in moonlight—Vi slammed the refrigerator door. And waited. There was no reply. Certainly the Skillys would have mentioned it if Winnie were ill.

Vi left a candle burning on the night stand, but its feeble flame only emphasized her desolation. She blew it out. Cold crept like a hand under the covers, and she'd begun a violent shivering, the many blankets and coats having no impact against a cold coming as much from within as from without. Numbness seeped up from toes that had ached so long it came nearly as a relief. She was overcome with groggy lassitude—familiar from *Digest* stories of people lost in winter wilds. Pleasant, insinuating drowsiness. Her eyelids fluttered; it was a terrible effort to keep them open.

"Go to sleep," some part of her coaxed. "Oh no! Goodness no," another. A lighted room far down a tunnel promised warmth, rest, an end to accumulating disappointments. She began drifting, slowly spinning . . . so very pleasant, tingly sensations up through her thighs. For the first time in so very long a lovely warmth.

Vi sat up and gulped chill air, sweat forming a crust on her brow. "I'm no quitter," she shouted. Then, as if that didn't settle the matter, she lay back and whispered: "You are an old woman, you have outlived your own daughter, why should you care about staying alive?" She had no answer; she simply gripped her shoulders and fought hopelessly to keep her eyes open.

She awoke on the morning of the third day into what was neither light nor dark but some arctic realm between. Initially, she decided she could not get up. When finally she did, it was the slowest she had risen in her life. Her feet, in sock layers, were pincushions against the floor. Limping to the kitchen, she looked out at the feeble thread of mercury and made a resolution: If she survived this, she would write to the electric company demanding a rebate on the month's electric bill. Gracious sake, but they would let people freeze.

Her plants were mush over sides of pots. The Skilly's sandwiches clunked in their brown bag, and Vi's stomach turned at the thought of frozen ham and cheese on frozen rye. She knew it Winnie's day to call without looking at the calendar, and knew her sister wouldn't to get even for yesterday. When Vi lifted the receiver, the dial tone did not surprise her. It was a sound not alien to the cold.

She let it ring a dozen times before hanging up. Her breath hissed against brittle air: "She always was a quitter."

Vi sat in the armchair, lips sutured in deep wrinkles, one mittened hand gently clutching the other. To an observer her expression would have appeared both triumphant and bitter.

She wasn't certain which happened first—whether lights popped on or the phone began jangling. She stared, not certain it wasn't just Papa's hammer or cold belling in her ears. Then she answered.

"You gave me an awful fright."

"Well," peeved Winnie, "I was in bed. It's been awfully chilly."

Baseboard heaters cricketed—all at once, like the cheery hallelujahing of insects in spring. Paul Harvey was speaking on the radio about the coffee crop in Columbia. Vi could hear Winnie breathing.

"You might just as well come over for tea when it thaws a little," she proposed to her younger sister.

Across the room, coils of the electric fireplace had begun glowing for the first time in years. A red, delicious warmth that she could almost taste.

Let It Snow

The three penultimate events in Sagan's life occurred in rapid succession but were related only in a casual way to the final event, she might have seen had she given herself opportunity to reflect upon them. First, Sagan left her toothbrush in the Denver motel room where she was forced to stay overnight by a blizzard that grounded her connecting flight to the Coast. Then she arrived late to the funeral in California. Finally, when she returned home to New York, she could not find her car in JFK long-term parking, buried as it was beneath drifts of snow from the Denver storm moved East. The concluding event was Sagan's accidental suicide.

Sagan's flight out of Denver's Stapleton airport received clearance for takeoff next morning, after she had spent a sleepless night in a scruffy motel room. The flight landed beneath a weeping Northern California sky, that perennial green-giving overcast of the Northwest. Waiting for a taxi out front of the tiny terminal, she recalled how oppressive that sky could be on chilly December days. All in all, she had come to prefer snow country. Snow gave back the light, intensified it. Here all was absorption: sienna tones, earth, evergreens, lowered sky.

The young cab driver wore straight long hair and a casual manner and drove a white station wagon taxi. She failed to impress upon him her hurry to reach the funeral. It started at one and, at the rate they were moving, would likely be over before she got there. He drove at an obtuse angle, left shoulder bolted into the door, right hand resting like an orangutan's claw atop the wheel. In Manhattan he would be honked off the road.

"Last funeral I went to was maybe six months back," he said. "I used to do a lot of funerals. For a while there I went to so many funerals I thought I was next." Tilting his head back towards her. "Overdoses. I prob'ly escaped by this fuckin' much." The claw lifted from wheel, thumb and forefinger nearly touching. Sagan wondered what was steering the car. "My brother. That's the last funeral I attended. Fuckin' heavy." The station wagon slowed more, burdened by the young man's weighty reflections. By the time he was into how the car body "has at least a million miles on it, man," Sagan had given up on the funeral altogether. What did it matter? The dead were no less dead if you made it to their funerals.

Looking out at a soaked, ragtag landscape—derelict sawmills, rusted slash burner tepees, shake-roofed cabins—she recalled the smell of curry permeating sheets of her Denver motel room last night, rug seemingly worked over by countless muddy ski boots, a scab on the Indian desk clerk's lower lip. When her toothbrush plunked into the yellow toilet bowl this morning, it occurred to her she might fish it out and leave it outside for fifteen minutes. No microbe could survive that cold. But, with her nostrils full of spice and her thoughts of tropical disease, she threw it away. Now she felt ashamed of herself for equating filth with Indian proprietorship. She had taught Indian children in Brooklyn—East Indians, West Indians, Amer-Indians, children from everywhere on earth. None seemed any filthier than the others, although some had filthier mouths.

She was grateful for the warm room, curry and all, the single remaining in all of Denver, it seemed, and an endless stream of stranded, frenetic passengers arriving by taxi in deep snow out front of the motel. Broad-shouldered women in fur coats (such as

Sagan herself couldn't afford and wouldn't have worn if she could) made surly noises behind her in line, as if expecting her—in dowdy parka—to cede her place. While husbands growled, "Take it easy, Cathy; we'll find a room." They hated her for being there first. But New York had taught her enough of the skills of intimidation not to be outdone by flush Midwesterners. She turned cheerily towards them to announce, "I'm going to a funeral in California. How about you?" They stared back at her sullenly. Humans, she realized that night, are beasts. Including herself.

As she rode, she saw an image of her mother. A snapshot: Mama leaping up at the end of the long table upon which her second husband had just flung himself face down into spluttering candles and white-chocolate frosting, her mouth forming an exaggerated O, which her hands attempted to replicate. "Get him up, somebody. Get him up."

Over the phone, she'd told Sagan: "Jerry died last night, dear. He fell down dead at his seventieth birthday party."

"What? Mama! It's impossible."

"He fell down dead at his seventieth birthday party," Mama repeated; like a shibboleth that must get her through hundreds of repetitions—to family, friends, strangers—for years to come.

"I can't believe it."

"A heart attack. Jerry died last night of a heart attack. Painlessly. Thank goodness for that."

Sagan's rock 'n' roll cabby couldn't care less when she arrived anywhere. He navigated the drenched landscape: heavy-boughed firs, occasional chain-saw shop or Seven Eleven on the outskirts of town. Though crudely familiar, it was a reality entirely alien to her. She recalled the stocky woman in a ski parka last night, who'd looked on devastated as the clerk handed Sagan his last room key. Others glared at her as if she'd leased the entire place. But this woman asked in a small, vulnerable voice, "What will I do? I can't stay here," gesturing at battered couches, lobby door opening to admit gusts of icy air. What does she expect of me? Sagan wondered, knowing well enough that either you firmed your jaw and stepped on, as in subway tunnels, or you took a leap of human faith and risked engagement, as she did in her classroom. She invited the stranger to share her room.

"No . . . I couldn't possibly." The woman's nostrils red and chafed from a runny nose. Generosity has its price, Sagan knew. What was a virus? Besides, inadvertently, her kindness was a selfish one. She hoped the woman's company would help stave off looming depression.

The two women talked late into the night, tipsy on a chardonnay the guest produced, frank in the way of strangers who have nothing at risk. "Forty-five!" Sagan confessed. "Can you imagine it? Premenopausal. Midlife crisis. I mean, I never thought I'd be this old. And the horrible thing, you know, I think I feel it." Her guest's face crinkled, denting at mouth corners. "I never expected this," Sagan continued. "I s'pose if you'd given me a questionnaire at twenty I'd have said: 'Sure, forty-five! I'll be married, kids, house, the usual stuff. But I'll still listen to Dylan records, I'll travel, I'll make money . . . somehow. Something acceptable. I'll never ever ever be a schoolteacher. Ugh!'"

They both laughed. The woman chirped: "Look at me! a travel agent—who definitely knows better than to connect through Denver in winter—stuck in a blizzard and begging a bed for the night. I mean, reservations are *my business*. You're very kind, really."

"I'm glad you're here. This thing has shaken me. He wasn't even my father or stepfather. My mother's second husband, that's all. Yet we were close. The language lacks words to express certain relationships. Step-uncle, maybe. Fatherproxy."

"Significant other, mother-type."

They laughed again. But when her new friend was snoring away on coarse Denver sheets in a queen bed Sagan insisted upon sharing ("You can't do the rug. Besides, I'm hoping you get all the bed bugs"), she was red-eyed and morose. Insomnia was a symptom of grief, she knew. But over the death of a man who had no linguistic relationship to her? In language reposits some censoring wisdom: a conservatism which dictates that permanent trend be distinguished from passing fancy. In terms of human relationships, language cannot be flippant.

It's the kindest way to die, she assured herself. Stand up at your seventieth birthday party to honor the toasts of friends and bingo! Gone before you hit the table. She glanced at her bed mate, whose lips made small popping sounds as she exhaled. Endearing. Untroubled. A travel agent. The idea seemed wonderfully exotic to her. Here was a woman who regretted only the occasional missed connection, while she herself regretted a lifetime of reservations unmade. Sagan had begun to weep. It was not only Jerry she mourned.

The taxi pulled up behind a line of cars at a sloping expanse of soggy cemetery green. Green as Ireland, she thought. Something of the transient, vindictive nature of death itself in black mourners' clothing. Brutal unexpectedness. Her rock 'n' roll cabby yammering about the healing power of crystals. Mama rushing down slope toward her in a dark worsted suit, unsuited to a woman who lived in a world of white synthetics and cheery pink warmups. "Sunshine is where you find it," she used to say. No sunshine now, just a short-legged woman whose face swam behind a veil in fishy light, hair gone pasty orange. She did not bother to raise the netting but kissed her daughter with dry textured lips, clutching Sagan as if afraid she would lose her, too.

By evening Sagan was inconsolable. Mama, by contrast, dry-eyed, relieved by the lively presence of friends and family. She would not be the sort of widow who had to talk herself out of bed in the morning (as Sagan herself must lately . . . unwidowed.) Mama would soon be placing ads in geriatric singles magazines. But Sagan lacked her mother's cheery temperament. To her, singles magazines were synonymous with sexually transmitted diseases. Officially, it was retirement—twenty-three years in coming. But one does not retire at forty-five on two-thirds of a schoolteacher's salary. Well, the pension she could tolerate, but not all that time on her hands. Through her working years, it had been an article of faith: *Oh! if I could only sleep in. Bask in a lifetime of cozy Sundays.* The reality was waking to a neighborhood emptied of all but oldsters in rent-controlled apartments, visiting sisters from Maine who hoped to become models, freelance writers plunking away at word processors. Once, there would at least have been the friendly clickety-clack of the occasional neighborhood typewriter, mothers home tending babies. But this was the age of high-tech silence.

How often could you spray the ferns, prepare a special birthday dinner for a very special friend, sit all afternoon reading Nadine Gordimer? How many days . . . years of that?

It was the ennui awaiting her at home that haunted Sagan as she helped her mother through inevitabilities of disposal that occupied those next few days. They sorted Jerry's clothes and effects, deciding what should go to whom. His suspenders. A bottle of cologne that triggered another bout of sobbing. Sagan found her mother's sorrow unsettling: Mama's riven face lopsided. Perhaps she couldn't control herself, but Sagan couldn't bear watching. "Grief isn't your style, Mama," she insisted when her mother asked how she was going to bear it. Incredibly, Mama laughed.

"I don't think it's a question of style."

Looking away, Sagan blurted for no reason, "I've retired. Last year, actually. I didn't want to alarm you, but now—"

"From teaching? Why ever would you do that? You loved teaching, Sagan. I thought you did, anyway." Her mother looked fuddled: an old woman's pursed lips.

"I thought I had served my time. But I'm seeing it doesn't work like that."

"Jerry served his time—" her mother's face tautened, cheeks a little waxen "—if you want to call it that."

"Maybe that's all it is, Mama. We serve our time. Do our duty and make room for someone else."

"Well, I'm not going to be morose," Mama snapped, regarding her daughter out of eyes as washed as her hair. More gray now than blue, slate gray and irritable. "And you shouldn't either—at your age! I never could understand why you didn't marry and have children. Children are all we finally have, you know, all we ever really do have. Possibly a companion if we're lucky."

Sagan resented her mother's presumption, the way her eyes clouded with sentiment. "I've had many, many children . . . thousands. We never got confused about loving one another. Sometimes we liked each other. That was enough."

"You quit, poor dear."

"I was all washed up. Honestly."

Maybe that's what age is, Sagan thought, too many washings. We begin to fade. Burnout is too dramatic a metaphor, meant to console the undramatic.

She had considered real estate briefly after her retirement (but despised developers); she took a writing course (but lacked discipline); toyed with opening a bistro on Park West (not at those rents); desperate, she planned to research the history of brownstones on Park Slope. For a few weeks, she did volunteer work at a homeless shelter downtown. But scabbed hands and lips, cold sores, soup bowls shaking so violently you had to help them to table, enduring the smell, all that shabby misfortune resolved to guilt when she returned to her warm apartment. It didn't wash off in the shower. A special friend joked one night that she smelled like his boyhood dog after it had rolled in a dead animal in the woods.

"It's a new brand of perfume. Mother Theresa," she told him. Quitting both the shelter and his friendship.

By her fifth day in California, Sagan was desperate to get home.

Even to nothing. Maybe familiarity would restore her balance. She'd liked Jerry, liked that his drinks were too strong, that he laughed in a hearty tenor at his own jokes, the quirky way he shook out his arm before serving tennis. What ever was hidden in him was comfortably hidden. At ease in his own skin. Perhaps this was what grieved her, the passing of that ease in a world without enough of it.

Without Jerry her mother was not the same. Already she was becoming finicky. In a few years she would be unbearable. Was this what became of the abandoned and purposeless when they grew old? Was this what lay ahead?

Arriving at JFK, Sagan rode the shuttle past acres of long-term parking, horrified by snow drifting over parked cars. The Denver blizzard had come east with a vengeance. She identified the section letter and number of the bus stop written on her ticket. But when the bus left her alone at the stop, she nearly lost her nerve before that stark blanket of amorphous white beneath arc lamps. No one in sight. The cold bit through her parka: ten below zero with the windchill.

Her Toyota was nearby. Though, actually, she'd been in a tizzy when she parked: numbers, thoughts, images flurrying in her head—like wind-whipped snow sparkling fiercely past arc lamps in the gale, stinging her cheeks. Some cars were humpback whales stranded cold on a dead shore, others possessed a single grotesque eye or outlandish cap of wind-crust, fins stuck out at outlandish angles. She floundered through drifts reaching nearly to her waist, barely able to move ahead. Approaching a car, she would flail wildly at snow to identify color, shape. Powder worked into her mittens and the gap between stretch pants and boot tops. She was shivering fiercely when it occurred to her this wasn't the best approach. She must remain calm and ignore numbness in her toes (inner city teachers don't panic in crisis). She need only brush snow away from license plates to identify her car: TRX143.

Sometimes this meant digging down into drifts as high as car hoods, her hands numb and aching. It occurred to her she should go back to the bus stall where she had left her bags; there, sheltered from wind, she might add to the number of layers beneath her parka from the suitcase. But her car was—must be—close. She had a vivid memory of looking up from it and noting *K* on the fence directly ahead, turning to see the bus stall to her right, half a block down. Perhaps it had been the third rather than the second row from the fence. Perhaps it had been stolen. No, God forbid! She had locked it.

Jerry's grave was in the fourth row from a squat, pretentious mausoleum with pink granite pillars. You stood at the head of a mound of new turf facing the tombstone beyond a temporary fence erected to keep deer from nibbling the flowers. ("Take it down," Mama insisted. "Jerry would want to watch them eating.") Glancing to your right, you saw a bus parked at a kiosk beside the cemetery loop. Bright inside. Seats empty. Dark mourners moving away from it arm in arm, row upon row—which she realized, as the bus moved off with a hiss, were only posts. She raised a hand to call after it. Ice prickled her cheeks. This really was quite foolish. She simply could not remember. There was no JHX143 (or was it TRX143?) in rows one through five. Not possibly, couldn't be, this far from the fence. She was quite concerned about her right hand, stiff cheeks. She pinched with two sensate fingers and couldn't remember if numbness meant frostbite.

Would the car start when she, if she, got it open? She had her keys, didn't she? Or had she packed them in the suitcase? Feeling for them, she couldn't navigate pockets with numb fingers . . . .Worried about Mama's memory. How would it be, reaching that age, if you could not recall whether you had bought Jerry the cashmere overcoat or if his first wife had bought it? Whether it was Melville or Hawthorne who wrote *Moby Dick*. Imagine that! Or realizing, all at once, that the fence letters were repeated on the other side of the kiosk under dim lights. Her car might just as likely be opposite the twin *K* over there. You might freeze to death—easily. No one had come along. Maybe a bus, far off. She couldn't remember.

Panic came like a coughing fit. Plodding blindly from car to car. A zigzag course taking her farther and farther from the bus stop. Senseless. Logic going over to blind, violent hope. Kicking with her boots now at snow, dropping to knees to read plates. Her cheeks had lost all feeling. And her lips . . . if she . . . well, she couldn't tell where they met. It was probably wise to keep your mouth closed. Once a man, looking at her in the soup line (whose dark face was bleached and patchy from weather), clutched a steaming soup bowl to his chest and instructed her for no reason: "You don't want to lose heat. That's the whole science of your own survival right there."

She stopped dead still to listen. The wind knifed past her ears. Someone sang Christmas carols, the mourners possibly. A group of them gathered about a peculiar oblong grave, singing dolefully. As she approached, they disappeared inside. She ran up and beat on windows; snow slid off the curved casket roof, powdering over her hands. The last of it slipped off windows, and she beheld them staring out at her, waxen faces frozen in a single fear.

She realized it was only the whine of a bus winding its slow way about the perimeter. She watched it turn in toward her stop, headlights angling over white devastation. That was the thing to do, Sagan!—smiling, she realized, though could not feel her lips—*forget her car! Ride back to the terminal and take the train home*. She began running as bus closed on kiosk, stumbling trough snow, gasping, waving her arms. Hardly believing it when a foot slipped on concealed ice and she went down. Sagan cracked a knee hard. She rolled on snowpack, clutching the knee, watching—incredibly—the driver open the door and stare down a moment at her luggage before driving off with a shake of his head.

Here buses carried no passengers. They were bright, icy cold inside. The drivers wore Jerry's unharried expression. They were comfortable inside their skins. But they slipped away and left you stranded.

Kicking out a space for herself on the lee side of a Jeepster, she crouched down out of the wind on packed snow. Just for a minute. She understood that. Just a minute to nurse her knee. Then she would limp to be with her luggage when the next bus arrived. Sagan slid down onto packed cold that quickly translated through buttocks into pelvic joints. Allowing her head to fall back against the door panel, she thought how silly she would look on the front page of the *New York Post*: knit cap, blue lips attempting to touch in a frozen smile.

> THE BIG CHILL: Retired Schoolteacher Found
> Buried Beneath Snowdrift In JFK Long Term

They would interview former colleagues, who would confess they had lost touch since her retirement and knew little about Sagan's recent life. Neighbors would speak vaguely of depression. It wasn't likely the travel agent would turn up to offer her own theory.

Rain

In December, the air became so thick that the scent of passing skunks lingered about for days, even the swishing wing beats of ravens echoed faintly in their trace, causing us to turn around to see who was whispering. Old Cory said it looked like we might finally get some rain. And so it started.

By January, whipping cream mounds of foam damned against bridge pilings in streams emptying off the Pygmy Forest, and yearling deer wandered with bloodshot eyes, so nerve-jaded you could walk right up and twist ticks from their necks. The doleful white faces of cattle kept track of us as we wandered roads in cabin-fever desperation, their pink noses outlandish against a tyranny of green, water dripping relentlessly from the tufts beneath their chins. It flooded boot tops and squished with each step between our toes. Quail floated on puddles and winter wren lisped threnodies of despair every waking morning as the rain uncoiled itself.

This, of course, before cattle were carried away altogether, with deer, and Pygmy Forest, and the majority of the redwoods (Old Cory says, "They outlived themselves a long while anyway. I hear there's some of 'em holed up yet over in China." But Cory is crazy), before we were forced to move into the hills to escape rising waters, to inhabit cabins abandoned years ago by fur trappers and runaway convicts. Before any of us had ever heard of The Messenger. And if someone had told us of him—sitting, perhaps, about what could have been a campfire if it weren't too wet to get one burning—we would have laughed and said, "Sorry, brother. This ain't Hallelujah territory. Sunday mornings are best known hereabouts for sleep."

Rain has invaded our sleep. Sent us paddling high above cow pastures on rippling brown water to reach a neighbor on a nearby slope. We coax ourselves from warm beds like enstupored hounds to cold and hopeless disasters of daylight, lay a fire and breathe it to life, or more often do without. Rain and rain. A pause invariably at dusk, clouds scurrying before a bewildered moon. Then the sky closes again. Whump! the tireless rain.

Our local astrologer says that when the sun sinks it pulls clouds down with it, leaving a rent in the sky.

We can hear Walky-Talky walking the roads, as he does (or once did, anyway; now he paddles about in a dugout canoe), reporting to himself and anyone who will listen in a newscaster's monotone. Lately, his broadcasts make continual reference to Noah's Ark: "All that water . . . Scientists say it got stuck up above the ozone layer. They can see it there now the ozone is thinning out. You got to imagine an egg floating in a great sea. And we are the yolk . . . ."

In all the years we have heard him walking and muttering, Walky-Talky has never made more sense.

Nearby, another tree sighs and gives up the ghost in one sucking exhalation. My hand flops from bed into the iced coffee with cream creek that has jimmied the cabin door. It embroiders little eddies about the wood stove, licking at my larder (dwindled to a sack of flour and one moldering orange), gently totters a chair, then bobs it upright toward the flume of a window. I leap from bed to stove to desk and stand trembling, my head in spidery rafters. Water licks my toes, laps papers from the desk one by one. Through the open door, I see wind laugh whitecaps across the great bay that was once Ivarson Valley. The cabin totters. Water at my knees. I scrunch into the angle of the roof, over which rain dances with the light step of

Gypsies. I cry out for Cathy, forgetting that she has gone. A horror, a savage injustice—to drown inside your own home, sucking up what air remains trapped against the roof peak.

For God's sake . . . STOP!

Somewhere there is a groan, a sharp crack, a cataract whoosh. I cringe, expecting the cabin will go. The flood shivers anticipatorily, then rushes out the door in a spout as if someone has pulled the plug, thieving bed covers, stove ashes, the last of Cathy's shoes.

The cabin sways a little but holds firm as the flood subsides. The roar continues below. I wonder if it has taken Spar's tree house, downhill from me. Or if Lizzie the Lush, last woman remaining within many square miles, will ride it out safely in her houseboat. Just another false alarm; a log dam has given way in a creek up above. A toilet bowl ring remains around cabin walls. That orange is wedged in a weir of twigs at the door. Alongside it, Cathy's "We Are The World" T-shirt, last vestige of her, quite possibly, on the face of the earth. I rise with mud pancaked over my knees and shove desk against splintered door, peeking out first to make sure it hasn't taken the redwood butt from which I am carving an ark.

In the beginning, we expected nothing more than indifferent showers, so habituated were we to drought. But, once started, it fell and fell as though nature was becoming more sure of itself. We ferreted out rain gear, slickers crumpled in closets—where dogs had slept on them or they had been used to clean oil from chainsaws. It had been dry so long we never expected to use them again. Stove pipes rusted, drawers swelled so that we must leave them open and let everything spill onto the floor. We sat listening to weather reports, anxious for the rain—which brought us out at first to dance in thirsty meadows—to clear a little so we could get in firewood. Soon air was so humid that kindling wouldn't burn, and mildew crept across floors like a five o'clock shadow. We despaired: no work and savings gone.

Cathy in the family way. At night, storms sent cabins reeling like loose-jointed trawlers, inanimate things chittered animatedly, cupboard doors swung freely, and lightning flashes snatched us bolt upright from dreams of Baja beaches. At dawn, lovers squirmed in each others' arms.

That was before mildew and sow bug phalanxes emerging from the walls drove Cathy away, before her toes started to ache, mail delivery stopped, and stores ran out of garlic—munched by the clove, as we sat shivering before cold stoves, in the belief it would ward off sickness. It wasn't just the discovery of moss in canned corn or dogs stinking so badly we had to keep them off with stones that defeated her, or the fetor hanging over everything, or unmentionable growths on our sexual parts, or even the soft swamp gas glow following in our traces at night like a spectral alter ego, but gloom. A psychic fog so thick she no longer bothered getting out of bed, but lay all day with all the clothing she owned piled in a frowzy heap atop her. Though, more than anything, it was hope that led her away, embodied in The Messenger.

She simply rose from bed one morning and announced, "I'm on my way."

"Where?"

"No matter, so long as it's dry, and they never heard of the ozone layer, and nuclear power, and icebergs towed south for fresh water."

I could do nothing but laugh. I had no good argument to dissuade her. I was not a prophet. I watched her slip on thigh-high rubber waders left for her by The Messenger's people and remembered with a nostalgic pang how I'd once delighted in watching her work tights up tan long legs, in days before they'd gone pale and mottled from damp.

"What you don't understand about The Messenger," says Cathy—the narrative drifts, time itself gone liquid—"You don't realize his message comes from inside, not from outside. 'You have the answer inside you.' He says that all the time. 'I'm only the question.'"

She was quite pregnant then, her belly hung like a bloated fish in the wet sack of a shift. She stood in water to the ankle, and had begun to complain incessantly of her swollen feet. No use trying to keep it out. Each morning a new spring broke through the caulking at base of cabin walls. Mysteriously, it subsided at times, leaving a slimy carpet behind. Other times it rose. I'd hear it gurgling in the darkness, as I lay in bed unable to sleep. Very little makes for insomnia like rising water. Although I'd mounted the mattress on a floating frame.

I never bothered arguing with her, but I disagreed violently about The Messenger. He was a spiritual opportunist, the sort of rogue who can't see himself in a mirror without imagining it a television set, who, if it ever stops raining, is sure to end up in politics—the sump in which all public lusts eventually collect.

But I didn't wish to upset Cathy's delicate metabolism. She was feeding two beings on little enough for one. We boiled moss for vitamins. Little besides water beetles remained for protein. They went down best mixed with red clay in a gruel. She could wax hysterical on that point: a pregnant woman must have protein. I'd rest my ear against her belly and imagine a fish inside, a hopeful monster in the most fortuitous stage of its ontogeny, preparing to emerge—into the deep.

The few other wives in the neighborhood—who hadn't moved in with The Messenger's people or fashioned their own rafts and set sail, for it is the women who are least reluctant to leave—insisted she must rejoice in the birth. "When the rain lets up, there will be public aid again," they told her. "Nutritional supplements and free dairy products. Child care centers will abound like tulips after a good watering." It is the way of our women: despair brings out their genius for optimism.

However, Cathy talked of nothing but abortion. "What kind of world is this to bring a child into?" she asked. She bemoaned that there was no doctor around to help her, insisting she couldn't bring herself to do it.

I didn't share my hopeful monster vision. However, I offered to perform the surgery myself, producing a rusty, twisted coat hanger, from which we both recoiled in horror.

She wrung her hands. "How can we have a baby in this?" Lifting her feet one by one, deep red fissures at the crotches of blue toes.

Of course we were fooling ourselves, for she was due any minute. And delivered pink and strong one dreadful, screaming midnight, while I slogged impotently about, collecting linens, stroking her steaming forehead, gripping her calves for dear life. Wild hogs surrounded our cabin, squealing murderously, their flinty eyes reflecting candlelight back at us through the wall cracks.

A child is born. He opens his tender lashes and plunges into the waters, lips sealed in a transparent membrane, repeated as a web between his toes.

A fish at sea doesn't know that it lives in the wet. The memory of dryness flees from us like music from the deaf. We strain to generate internal heat, as Tibetan lamas are said to do. We wonder if Jim Lehrer has discovered us yet among festering world events, dipping down his satin-tongued thermometer for a six o'clock prognosis in martini calm, like any other MD at that genteel hour of the day. Has he reported that Seattle stands hundreds of feet beneath the waves, and Oregon cow pastures have become breeding grounds for sea urchins, and Crescent City is bobbing off Orientward on the last lashings of its redwoods, and God has been dragged drowned from a gutter in Eureka?

ITEM: *A Fort Bragg, California, fisherman's wife is roused from sleep by a phone call, informing her that her husband, with his boat, The Blessed Redeemer, has been lost in heavy seas. She glances up and finds the ceiling is on fire—the roof, rather miracu-*

lously, blazing in that downpour—and rushes her four children from the burning house in the nick of time. No husband. No home. But for that fortunate unhappy phone call, no kids. After four days at sea in a lifeboat, hubby is rescued by a passing freighter, and the lucky family reunited in that coastal city, now an atoll. "I praise the good Lord," he declares, "that my boat went down and saved my family. I believe God must be pleased to have won this here last election."

ITEM: *A drunk steps from a La Jolla, California, bar and is crushed by a gray whale thrown ashore by hundred-foot waves. Presumably, it was migrating south to Mexico.*

ITEM: *A San Francisco mystic who calls himself Twicewashed Feathers has prophesied the opening of the San Andreas Fault to schlurp up this deluge and disgorge it in the South China Sea.*

ITEM: *The groundskeeper of a Southern California cemetery has reported that some months ago a tombstone was jimmied and Hatfield the Rainmaker rose again from the dead.*

Down below, terrorists have long since sabotaged printing presses and transmission towers, claiming the media encourages the rain by giving it too much publicity. It's just as well. We have Walky-Talky, whose reports are—if not accurate—at least believable. The rain has all but deafened us anyway.

We gather out front of Benson's, dirty caps slouched low over foreheads, to discuss the raft people and the supply of edible fungi. Benson has become something of a leader among us. A man of sterling character who amounted to nothing before the deluge. He worked at day labor and complained unceasingly about the money earned by dentists, lawyers, and SSI recipients. We considered it just sour grapes then; no one imagined he meant it. It is Benson who nicknamed The Messenger "The German Measles."

"*I am the question*," he mocks him. "The question is: Who the almighty fuck sent him up here?"

Old Cory giggles and says, "If she'll just keep it up a while longer, we might make it yet, by golly!" Cory's gone a bit haywire.

"Seems odd that it should be raining at all," I tell them. "We all know it's redwoods that suck moisture from the air to make it rain. By now, there are hardly any left to suck."

The oldtimers nod sagely. I glance at Crandall the logger, who hocks indifferently, but in such a way that a long gristle of saliva catches my knee and slithers onto a boot. Soggy red hair hangs over his skull like a dead beaver.

From our hilltop archipelago, which was once the Coast Range, we watch water rise sluggish but imperative up contour steps. We sleep on gurgling mattresses and nurture indecent afflictions. We hear stories from down below about how reservoirs filled and kept on filling until they bust their guts and Shasta Dam washed all the way to Modesto, scraping up the great California aqueduct en route. Artesian wells spouted. Millions launched out from roof peaks on makeshift rafts to float aimlessly down that mighty waterway which was once the Central Valley—as if, at long last, Tom Joad had been requited on California. We hear how California Okies trekked through the Sierra passes to begin a rafting life on the inland sea which fills the entire Great Basin. And there, as far as we know, the planet ends. Currents have carried few of the survivors our way. Except, of course, "The German Measles."

Back home, I find Cathy seated on the bed, her toes tracing circles in the café au lait puddle on the floor. The shift hangs limply around her waist, red, swollen breasts exposed. Little Noah has slipped away from her and curled up on bed covers. She is surrounded by The Messenger's followers, raft people. Women who have slogged up from the shoreline in high waders, solid rubber from waist down.

They wear fin-shaped cowls and are growing moustaches. Some of them, I suspect, are men. It's hard to tell the difference. Below the waist, they all look like latex mermaids.

They look me over with unsuppressed irony. I hear them whispering about faith. "There are some among us," says the tall one with a dripping red moustache and scarab's face, "who do not believe in the future. They say it is like this everywhere." (Others chuckle softly.) "Oh, you of little faith."

I make no reply, knowing that faith feeds on logic like a mold. Cathy sleepwalks, carrying Little Noah to his crib of rushes on her hip. Noticing her nakedness, she covers herself after a fashion and smiles at her guests, who have risen to leave. When they have gone, she talks of going with them to discover the New World.

"I thought this was the New World," I say.

"It's not an outside place, but deep within. The Messenger has come to lead us there. He says the rain is an illusion, a test of our faith. The moment we have departed upon the water it will subside."

"You believe that?" I ask, gesturing at those mushy places above us where rafters have turned to pulp. Droplets ping into the floor lake around us in a variety of flats and sharps. "Listen!" I insist. "This is nature speaking."

"You think it's everywhere?" she snarls. "D'you think it's a second flood or something? I thought you didn't believe in myths and catastrophisms."

"My faith is weakening," I admit.

"There's some place . . ." her eyes glow in the medieval gloom, "where rain knows when it's time to stop, where palm trees sway in sunshine, and people go naked, without fear that their daughters will be molested by male degenerates."

"Sounds like Hawaii—except for the degenerates."

"The Messenger has been there. He has seen it with his own eyes."

"The Messenger is a male," I remind her. "What's worse, a male with true religion—the worst type of child molester."

She smiles pityingly, feeding on my logic. "I feel sorry for you," she says.

At that, we both leap to rescue Little Noah, who has turned over in his crib and is quietly drowning.

The Messenger's time began when there were still tule marshes in the valleys, quite passable at low tide, and feral hogs had first come down from the hills with a wild gleam in their eyes, like looters anticipating a blackout. Like Cathy, many people hardly bothered getting out of bed all day. When dejection had finally defeated them, they abandoned cabins in a mass tropism and came together in forest nooks, sheltering in tents and wickiups woven of twigs. They shared all in common, especially despair. Green slime covered guitar strings, which they plucked to cheer themselves up, tent canvas rotted overhead, and leeches—thick as in a tropical rain forest—wriggled into sleeping bags. They walked about with them dangling from arms and chins, waltzing to their movements. They stood over open fires, which were kept alive with gasoline until it ran out. Then simply stood, hang-head, sopping, somber as a necklace of mourners about an open grave, around the leached black bones of their fires. Just when mud and gloom had overwhelmed them and they huddled pathetically against mossy tree trunks, The Messenger arrived from San Francisco. Now nothing but an archipelago of high places: Nob Hill, Russian, and Potrero, with the sea sweeping away on all sides.

They built boats according to his instructions—sturdy, seaworthy arks of hemlock and fir—and ate the inner bark of trees to strengthen themselves for a long voyage. We call this the "Wailing time," because, each night, their wails struck the brazen hills like gongs. They walked the trails in procession, chanting martial hymns, completely mindless of the rain. One tinny dawn they departed: a tiny fleet lost on that vast expanse of gray, like a column of ants crossing the desert. We watched them crawl west through the downpour, then swing south on the track of Spanish galleons, then disappear. Cathy was with them.

I had watched her splash across our tiny meadow, skirt gathered about her waist, mud freckling white thighs above the waders, and guessed, wrongly, that they would go north—away from tropical sou'easters brewed in steaming equatorial baths, sent to us nose-to-tail like a string of cyclonic pearls. (I imagined Mr. Weather at his TV chalkboard sketching dropsical, grimacing warm fronts, pregnant with water. Maybe he conjures them, the bastard, and not the CIA—as the Cubans claim—or the nuclear waste dumps suspended like crab pots off the coast. What he refers to as "a big low-pressure system that just doesn't want to move" is really his own wizardry. I've never trusted weathermen.) At that moment, I could gladly have wrapped my fingers around The Messenger's throat.

Cathy has taken Little Noah, bundled snugly on her back. I have no good reason for remaining behind. But lack conviction to leave. If anything out there survives, why would it leave us alone? Why hasn't it come to collect taxes? I imagine their flotilla drifting from inhospitable Ararat to Ararat in search of palm trees, finally breaking up on some reborn volcano.

I am left with potatoes washed from the ground to rot in puddles on impermeable clay, springs sprouting from unexpected places. Even if there were food to cook, fire is undone. Nature will have the last word. We wonder when it will run out of fresh water and begin raining salt.

A friend visits from a neighboring peak. He hasn't eaten in days and is exhausted from swimming the saddle between us. I have nothing to offer him besides that moldy orange. He sighs as only the hungry can sigh and devours it without removing the rind. This before we discovered frogs. How—if one swallows quickly—they are not unlike a spoonful of Jello.

Actually, I have known about frogs since the day I introduced them to Little Noah. He seized the tiny, white-bellied creature I'd captured for him in his webbed hand and popped it in his mouth, swallowing it whole, snake fashion. I watched an amphibious foot dangle between his lips, then disappear, too fascinated by the momentary bulge in his throat to protest. Later, I amused myself by feeding him frogs when we had visitors, relishing the protests it brought from the cowled, androgynous followers of The German Measles. Although, in Little Noah's case, eating frogs did seem cannibalistic.

It has become our pastime, we survivors, to gather together and share tales of apocalypse. We sit on mossy logs, unmindful of the rain, which drips from every overhang and surface of us, except to occasionally empty an eye socket or squeegee a finger down a cheek, attempting to outdo one another in sheer outlandishness (as is perhaps the case with other mountain dwellers, of whom we hear rumors from passing fishermen, and those unfortunates still drifting about in nuclear subs). Our women have abandoned us. Who can imagine where they have gone: tropical atolls or a resort on the Black Sea?

Benson tells us about the time Hatfield the Rainmaker, under contract to make rain for San Diego in 1916, produced sixteen inches in two days, nearly flooding them out. That was nothing to the forty inches in three hours he conjured later in the Mojave Desert. He is loose again.

Walky-Talky tells us it's all due to nuclear testing; he heard it on the radio. Then reproduces, word for word, his own original newscast.

Our spirits lift. Someone may mention the 1876 China famine, when mothers sold off their children at market in lieu of poultry. Or give an account of the great Ethiopian famine of 1973, when speculators hoarded silos of grain in Addis Ababa, leaving thousands of people too weak from hunger to lift their heads off the street when the rains came, so they drowned in the gutters. "This world is one sorry model for fairness," says Benson. But, in truth, such accounts leave us feeling downright fortunate.

Tubercular mists drift, hogs grunt voraciously, attempting to uproot our stockades. Eventually they will succeed. They swim back and forth between peaks, devouring anything edible; we the only substantial animal life remaining. Early on, they rooted up our gardens and gutted cabins, while we huddled atop dead refrigerators in terror. They caught a few of the children out playing—I won't go into that—and loved to ambush our dogs, their lusty squeals echoing down canyons above the tremolo shrieks of their victims. Only Benson is unafraid of them. He leaps among them with an axe, downs a porker, and gleefully watches others circle in like sharks. We recoil at any thought of eating them, knowing what they have eaten. It would be a less forgivable cannibalism than Little Noah and his frogs.

"You hear about Old Lady Seward down the valley?" asks Spar. "Said she'd be damned if rain chased her out, and tied herself to the bed. Well, sir, water come in at the windows and under the door, right up to her chin. Then it took and lifted that ol' bed up and carried it through the roof, just like Lazaruth. They say she was bobbing right along good, cursing and waving her arms. Then—kabloop!—that ol' bed turned belly down."

Old Cory slaps his thigh and cackles dentureless laughter, tells us, yessir, 113 ships left their kindling on these rocks in them early days, though he couldn't recall no *Seward*. Was that a lumber schooner? Must'a been. He'd nearly married a girl named Seward once, old maid now, lived down to the valley.

"This ain't nothing to what it used to rain," he says. "Why, by golly, each winter'd take all the bridges out."

We laugh and slap his withered shoulders and try to convince ourselves we have only gathered for a smoke—though there hasn't been any tobacco in months. Finally return to our separate shelters, getting through the hogs by means of Spar's ruse, which is to drag a sack along behind by a rope; the hogs, remembering days when we had live chickens to put in the sacks, trample one another to get to them. Although Old Cory smells so bad that he can wade right through them without a sack, scratching their bristly heads as he goes.

Cory is a blessed man—chewing wood pulp and noticing nothing out of the ordinary but a persistent itch about his collar, where fungus forms a slimy emerald band. He looks joyfully up at the sky and proclaims, "Praise God, I b'lieve we'll get some rain yet, by golly. End this dangnabbed drought."

I dream of Cathy's return: Skipping up the hillside over meadows of daylily, and me running out to meet her, catching them both, tossing Little Noah in the air, his arms flapping delight. She is red-eyed, barefoot, only a few strands of moustache remain. I begin to ask if The Messenger ever received his final message, instead ask how things are out there.

"Wet," she says.

I tell her about the frogs. How Walky-Talky was ambushed and eaten by hogs one morning in the middle of a weather report. How Old Cory blames this drought on politicians. They're getting too old, he says; they think we all want to live in Florida.

Benson says he's closer to the truth than he knows.

We laugh together. Fall down in the mud and make wild love. While Little Noah happily stalks frogs.

It is becoming harder to separate dream from reality. Not only do I talk to her, but she replies.

We remain rooted like so many Old Lady Sewards, petulant and spiteful of fate, too tied to these stingy hills to try elsewhere. We have rejected false hopes. Although the Japanese current may have ferried Chinese raftsmen here in the Fifth Century, as The Messenger claimed, there's no reason to expect the inverse. Nor any reason to believe, even if we could reach it, that China—full two billion strong—hasn't drowned. Even the industrious Chinese couldn't build a large enough ark. But when we reasoned thus to the raft people, they snorted disdain and continued fashioning their crafts in the driving rain.

We thought them mad then, but now escape seems preferable to waiting. We build arks of our own. And argue over the command to carry two of every kind along with us.

"That's excluding hogs," reasons Spar.

"Did you write the book?" asks Benson. "Brother, there's a time to squawk and a time to follow orders."

But so little remains to take after the slaughter: a puppy or two, a wily tomcat, Lizzie the Lush, Walky-Talky's remains . . . pairs of absolutely nothing.

I watch water rising up an adjacent hillside, climbing branch by branch until it has devoured another tree. Then choosing a new mark. The rain is determined to drive mankind from the face of the land—to drift off like some new Noah seeking the Ararat of his destiny. Flake by flake, we carve redwood dugouts from great tree butts. Walls become thinner, and we leave a little knob at the prow as the Indians did—a *dau* for the Redwood Spirit.

We carve, the water rises.

To the Death

I need to tell you this. I need you to listen and not pass judgment. Can you do that? What can you do anymore but listen? It's the true item this time. They like me over there, they want me, they're rooting for me. Damn straight I need it. Twenty years, twenty opportunities ago I needed it. This is different. I need you to appreciate that. Do you think you can do that this once?

Nothing to it. We'd go swimming every summer afternoon. Well, the river was only a few blocks away. We walked over in congregation, the six of us, single file, like ducklings. Not Sundays, we didn't go Sundays. Mother and the six of us in descending rank, like mother hen and her ducklings. Hah!

Chicks. Mother hen and her *chicks*. Don't worry about it, it's only a word. I'd like you to pay attention. This job means a lot to me. I sense your negativity already. Pours off you in a foul sweat—ever since I was a kid. Sour smell of doubt—even in your condition. A glance, certain angle of the chin. You never had to say a word. Don't sneer. Don't you dare sneer. Jesus, I hate your sneer.

Me, Jimmy, Paul, Helen, Alice, Hester . . . not Petey. Petey was too small. We followed along like baby ducks. Lilly wasn't born yet. Remember Lil? Giggling. *Little Lil. You remember our Lil. Let's see: Jimmy-one, Helen-two, Alice-three, Hester-four, Jimmy-five, Me-six, Petey . . . not Petey. Jimmy-one . . .*

How many Jimmys does one family need? I can hear Dotty: "For heaven's sake, Don, give it a rest! You have said the exact same thing six times in a row." She never did get used to it. I believe she thought you repeated yourself to annoy her. Mind like a steel trap, that gal. No doubt it's why you married her. Some ironic nip there, huh? Fate's little mutt! Still, who can blame her? It gets old. Doesn't seem to bother you any. The thing is, it never did. Nothing new, more drastic maybe. You repeated the same tired fishing stories endlessly, like a professor rehearsing the same worn-out lecture. You insisted, "Hell, Will, people enjoy them."

All of us . . . except Petey. Petey wasn't born yet, Hester either. Did I say Helen? She's older. Imagine forgetting a thing like that? Who's born yet and who isn't. Hah! Nincompoop. Can't go swimming if you aren't born yet. That's the rule. Petey, Helen, Hester, Alice, Jimmy. Not Mother. Mother stood onshore. Dotty did. Did I say Lil? Not Petey. Mother? Did I say Dotty? Craning your head around, seeking her beyond the breakfast bar in the kitchen.

Dotty's your wife. Jesus, it's pathetic. Bury her one day, resurrect her the next. Move over J.C. I'd love to hear what she'd have to say about that. Tell me, what's the rule on aging infants? Sure, we have to forgive your slips now and then. Basic generosity. But I don't. I remember too well, while you don't remember zip—unless it suits you. That's the item. You ask me, they've mislabeled the thing. Not *memory loss* but *selective memory loss,* your lifelong condition. But that isn't the issue at hand. We should be able to bury the hatchet, condition you're in. I'm telling you about this new prospect, position, opportunity. I want you to hear me out. Can you manage that without sibling recitals? I put my bid in. Now we'll see. Look, I'm stoked about this.

Me! I was born yet. Still yam. Another item: laughing at your own bad jokes. *We went every summer afternoon, all six of us. We'd splash about while your mother stood onshore watching the current. No current to speak of that time of year. We'd pile out and dry ourselves, six ducklings in a row. We only had one towel.* Frowning, like I have a damn thing to do with it. *A minister's family couldn't afford luxury. Then we picked blackberries. Remember? Six little Indians covered in blackberry sap.* Hah! Not Petey, no. Five of us? Back to counting on fingers again. *Seven? Petey, Helen, Hester, Alice, Me . . . Hester wasn't born yet. Did I say Petey?*

You didn't say squat. Hardly ever. You'd pose incisive questions—as of "incisions," prosecutor's sharp knife—sit back, and watch me bleed. *Is this anything like that San Francisco deal?* You loved that one. Amazed you haven't asked me yet. What I'd like to ask your quacks: "Is paternal doubt another form of plaque fixed in the brain plasma? All the axons, dendrites, whatever, curled in the same direction?" *You need to settle down, Will, and think about your family.* Still saying it years after they split. Yeh, I think about them daily . . . hourly, if you want to know. I've made my share of bad choices, that's established. Bitch of it is, I believe you're forgetting which questions to ask. Blessings of memory deflation! Goes on long enough, you'll forget how we're programmed to relate. Me too. Old cat and dog finally lie down together side by side enjoying each other's warmth. Your doubt, my rage lost in the neural fog. Finally regarding each other across the moment: you sitting at edge of the couch, antsy as always, nubbly synthetic slacks hitched high-water up your ankles, no socks, one cheek stubbled, the other clean-shaven (proof shaving may be habitual but completing a shave isn't). Your shirt gone sour, I smell it from here. Dotty gave up. Something almost lovable in the way your hair dishevels to the left, as if to counterbalance the perpetual list of your head to the right. Artful asymmetry triumphs in dementia. What the hell! Freud thought all artists demented. What do you see when you look at me? Anything? I sit up straight as Straw Man on a posture fix, shoulders tense. Or throw my legs over the couch arm, determined to prove that I'm easy. Hey! You haven't brought up my stolen bike yet. You want to know the gospel truth after all these years? Bruce and I got rolled for our bikes. Some toughs knocked us off and walked away with them. I arrived home bikeless, busted elbows and knees, afraid to tell you what happened, knowing I'd let you down again. Nincompoop! getting my brand new birthday bike stolen. Still, I expected a little empathetic anger for the family team. You smugged chin to chest as now, eyes troubling over. Old Ledge Brow. The best marksmen have gray eyes, did you know? If I'd known as a kid I would've laid low, but kids aren't given to know these things. What was I talking about? Hah! Funny asking you.

So what are you up to these days? How's the family, Will? Where you working?

Jesus! Your left jab catches me with my guard down every time. All these years and I still don't know when it's coming.

Well, I've been trying to tell you—

My sister, Helen. Six sisters, three brothers. Not counting Hester. I don't believe she was born yet. Jimmy either. You puzzle over those many extended fingers, not knowing how to reel them in. *We went swimming every Saturday afternoon before church. Church was Sundays. Any nincompoop knows that. Daddy was upstairs working on his sermon, we'd go swimming to keep out of his hair. Daddy was the most patient man I have ever known—except Saturdays. "Look to the Lord on Saturday," he used to say, "and he'll appear on Sunday." Honor thy father. Hah! imagine needing a commandment for a thing like that. I didn't need any commandment; I loved Daddy dearly.* Chiding me a look.

Sure you did. Let me count the ways: his patience, ministerial aloofness, steward's expression when he sterned you, waxy jowls and chest welded together, gray eyes like God's own marksmen taking aim under brows. I know the drill, I see hints of it in the mirror. Jesus! Do I subject my son to that? I remember how you deadeyed opponents in court. When people ask me what my childhood was like, I tell them: eighteen years on the witness stand.

Well, Dotty worked Saturdays so she couldn't come. Daddy did. He swung us by the arms over the ripples, round and round, then he let go.

Hah. Kasplash. We loved that. Look at you! Gleeful boy resurrected. *Uncle Ragner did. Daddy couldn't come; he needed a nap after church. It's not easy wrestling the Holy Ghost every Sunday morning.*

Frankly, I don't buy into your holy daddy crap. Sure, I loved you fiercely—if awe is love. I couldn't so much as protest when you decided I'd left my new bike unchained outside the grocery store. Instant historical revision. You should know, you're the lawyer. What kind of nincompoop leaves his brand-new bike unlocked in front of the store? I wasn't mugged, no, I posted a notice on that bike inviting someone to steal it: "Please take this bike so my old man can tell me what a horse's ass I am for losing it. Here's the lock and combination number."

Combinations? I know all ten of them. You begin reciting.

No more recitals, Jesus! You can't blame Dotty for checking out. "I'm sorry, Willy," she said at hospital, "but there's just so much a person can take." You'll revise them, anyhow: *I am the Lord thy Father. Thou shalt not outperform me.* I've obeyed that one pretty well. *Thou shalt not kill thy wife.* How about that one? There are many ways to pull a trigger. You listening? Forget the sibling recital. The woman was ill . . . barely hanging on. She needed help. Didn't you realize? There were seven of you, by the by, not nine. Maybe the additional two are the kids you stalked in the park this morning. Did you see their mother's eyes? Screaming: pedophile freak. Jesus! Made me wonder, really did. I couldn't pull you away. You see them three blocks away, you're off and running, down on your knees, petting their knobby heads . . . Good Lord! If that's genetic, my balls go first sign. I've already made arrangements for the other business. You had—do you realize—a hand on the little girl's ass. Innocent? No doubt. Ask that bishop in Boston. Me insisting, "Let's go, Dad, we don't know these people." Instant outrage, like I'd pushed a button. Knocking my hand away and shouting like I wanted your wallet. Scared hell out of me. People gawking. Poor kids clinging to Mom's knees, afraid the Grinch had come to life and no stump-headed green sweetie either, but a nasty, stubble-cheeked, rheumy-eyed, squealing old fart. Dotty warned me about your episodes; I never believed her. You remember any of this? Listen! No selective disremembering.

Where are you working, Will? You had some kind of deal in San Francisco, sales work. How's the family? We don't see much of them anymore.

Here we go. Yeh, I'm selling leases on other people's children. We've got a good market share with brain-dead old men. Problem is, the commute's a bitch, since I'm living in LA. Look at you trying to puzzle it out. I work for Disney—okay? I hope to. I doubt you remember a damn thing about this morning, right? When I finally get you away, you're flushed, angry tears trickling through beard stubble, insisting, "That's my sister Helen. Don't I know my own sister?" Apparently not. Mom scurrying her kids away. "I love little Hester . . . always did." I'm afraid you'll chase after, but don't dare touch you. Then deus ex machina and thank God for it. Your attention caught by the towel they left behind. You coddle it against cheek, we're off to sibling recital again, your eyes longing off in the direction they've gone—for what you already can't remember. What's the fascination with kids? You say your sisters all died in the flu epidemic of 1918, with thousands of other innocent children—all doubtless named Hester and Petey. None of you were born in 1918, for crissake. So here I am with their towel, wondering how I'll get it back to them.

We better go. Dotty has lunch waiting. We always love a hearty lunch after swimming. Remember, Jimmy Boy? Don't you? We'd all five of us go in. Not much of a river, really. More a stream than a river. Maybe three-feet deep. You and Paul and Hester and Alice. Petey wasn't born yet. Ohhh— clapping hands in delight *—how he loved the little fish. Remember? Little bitty guppies. He would splash about on his belly and try to grab them in his hands. Remember that? Or was it Paul? . . . Petey? I went in first, anyhew. Always did. I ran down from the* road and splashed in—oldest, after all. Dotty shouting after me. Wasn't much of a river, more of a stream. Only one towel between us: red and blue stripes and green. I remember like it was yesterday. Trouble is, I can't remember a damn thing about yesterday. We didn't own swimsuits. Preacher's kids couldn't afford suits. We wore our skivvies. Yours always hung off your rear end. Hah! Remember? What kind of horse's ass goes about with undies hanging off his butt? The affection in your voice alarming. *Didn't own a suit between us . . . minister's kids.* Well, you wouldn't wear a coat and tie in the water anyhew. Any horse's ass knows that. You refused to go in; I never did know why. But you loved the little guppies. Remember?

Would you stop asking what I remember? I'm not the one with the memory issue. Not yet. Remember, Swiss cheesehead? Likely, I didn't go in because I wasn't born yet—not in real life beyond your cheesy memory. It used to be photographic. You recited precedents from case numbers, you recalled depositions word for word in court, spooked your opponents. "A fine mind like that," Dotty always said, "that's the tragedy. Such a fine mind." There you are squaring up like someone whispered in your ear, about to do one of your turnabouts of clarity. Spookier than the muddle.

I can't remember a damn thing anymore. My memory's all shot to hell. Not what it used to be. Can't hardly remember my own name. Imagine that.

Ephemera. That's all. What's more ephemeral than the organ which perceives ephemerality? This ephemera itself? Life and its cub reporter, consciousness? Maybe you're closer to knowing than the rest of us. And the human heart! What's more ephemeral than that? It isn't awe I'm feeling anymore, old man, it's something else. Pity almost. Affection. Give me time, I'll find a name for it.

To tell the truth, Daddy wasn't much fun weekends. He was tense. Mother—well she wasn't my mother, she was my stepmom. You knew Agnes didn't you, Will? She did her best. It wasn't easy. Eight children to care for, plus the congregation. A fine, upright woman. Good woman.

Not much fun. Who can understand a thing like that? Abruptly puzzled. *Standing right there making coffee, right there over the dining bar. Then she isn't.*

Momentarily, I see her collapse. Dotty? I ask. You had a good lucid run going a minute there. You do that. Momentary clarity, like the sun peeking through cloud cover. Maybe that's all there is: glimpses of clarity through vagrant cloud muddle. We can't accept it; we train ourselves to make cohesive sense where there isn't any. You're just ahead of the curve. Go on and wash up if you have to, but if Dotty's making lunch, heaven's chock full of surprises. Still, it's always an event when you acknowledge my existence, however vagrantly. Always was. Sure, you were formally aware of me, as a person is aware of their own shadow. At times, it even occurred to you I was your flesh and blood—like the time I got all As except a B in music appreciation. For a moment, anyway, before you launched into an oration about how, for Pete's sake, the family's gift for music must've passed me by. A pity. What gift? When did you ever listen to music? If Dotty turned on the radio, you barked, "Would you turn off that goldarned noise!"

I'm ready. The man arises.

For what? The county fair? An end to capital gains taxes? We're home—if that's where you're going.

Mother will have lunch waiting. How's about a short walk before we wash up?

How's about a dip in the river?

He looks puzzled a moment. *Either one. I'm easy to please.*

Yeh, you are. You killed her with easy to please. Easy to please, where's my lunch? Easy to please, where's dinner? (You'd finish one, she said, and want the other, or would go hungry all day and insist you'd eaten. One morning, you polished off a carton of bran bowl by bowl. Bound you up for days.) Easy to please, where'd I put my goldarned glasses? Wearing them, Don, you're wearing them. Easy to please, I'm off for a walk. Darn it, Donald, it's pouring out.

Refusing to easy-please yourself into a home where you belong. Give the old gal a break. Didn't it occur to you Dotty was sick, barely holding on? Heart disease, emphysema, and a three-year-old man to care for. Easy-pleased her to death is what you did. Don't stand gawking at me. It's rude. Cheek bristles reflecting patio light, scrappy patches of illumination, your fly open with your mouth. Better let me rebutton your shirt if we're going out. The Victorians were right: let appearances slide and we slide right in behind them. You keep staring at me like that, I'm outta here. I don't want you mistaking me for Petey or one of those damn kids.

Did we already go for a walk, or are we going? I can't remember a goldarned thing anymore. My memory is all shot to hell. You can't imagine what it's like. Embarrassing, for Pete's sake.

Sure I can. I've spent a lifetime embarrassed around you. Where do they come from, your brief lucidities—solid land in a universe of water? Weird. You know, I've been rethinking the bicycle theft thing. You're absolutely right: giving a new bike to a nincompoop son is like throwing it away. Absolutely correct, your little remake of history. What's history anyway but our own twisted perspective, constantly revised to our own ends? They should rename it "Allshuman's Disease," the tie that binds. Trouble is, history is all we have left in the end. Our own little turf of recollection. If that's wormed full of holes, what is there? Do you mind if I digress from our little tête-à-tête and get back to the main subject? Leave out stolen bicycles, San Francisco, afternoons at the river—which, given your penchant for revision, likely never existed. More likely the holy ghost writing sermons in the attic had you over polishing church pews with your tongues. Look back from tyranny in a family, you'll find previous tyranny every time, on back to Adam. Who needs infidels when we can hate each other?

How's the kids? I don't see half enough of them. We used to go swimming every day. You remember that, don't you? My grandkids loved it.

I'm telling you about my opportunity. True item this time; I sense it. They've had me in to talk, told me I should expect to do some traveling. No problem. Don't you dare tell me they say that to everyone. Bullshit. I'm stoked about this, I'm the man, I got OFFER written on my forehead. I've blown past opportunities. Absolutely. My memoir would be titled "Luck Saw Me Coming and Crossed the Street." Better yet: "Nincompoop." Hey, I know the score—unlike some present. I blew my marriage, okay. My single regret—I mean this, you old sack of worn out neurons—is that I told you about my affair. I can't imagine why. So I ball a girl at work, so what? What business is it of yours? Five years after, I could still see pews lined up in your eyes when you looked at me. I know how Bill Clinton felt. I still don't dare mention T's name. No doubt you never had an affair, not even with Mom. That's not my fault. Okay, that's unkind. But isn't all it's cracked up to be, I can tell you. What burns you up is you can't see your grandkids as much as you'd like. Those are my kids you can't see, pal. I hardly see them myself. God bless the day—yeah, I'm saying it—that you forget they exist. Hallelujah. All Petey and Helen to you. Jesus! But this thing! I've got my teeth sunk in so deep I've gone cross-eyed. I can taste the butter on my bread.

Hold your horses. She'll call us in a minute. Tiffany and her are probably talking about the new drapes. Her and Tiffany, I mean . . . Tiffany and she . . . she and Tiffany? Both of them, anyhew. Spooky the way you remember a name out of the blue.

My ex-wife and your dead one! Tiffany hasn't come with me for ten years, you realize. No, you don't. Blissful irrecollection. Things in place you wish to have there, forgotten if you don't. Better than religion. Talking to yourself again? Who needs testy listeners when you can converse with yourself? The garden again. I don't recall you growing a garden. To hear you tell it, you ran home between clients to weed onions. You fed the neighborhood, the state, hungry Africa. My kids helped you weed, even though they weren't born yet. What the hell. All your life you were mostly in conversation with yourself. Maybe we all are. Is that a precursor to the ailment? Solipsism? I live in this world alone, hiding out finally inside my head, kicking out a bigger and bigger hole in the brain 'til there's nothing left but a den for the self to squeeze in. I'm alerted, taking mental note to halt all self-dialogue. Can't hurt to take precautions. Still, it's ironic, I finally get my break, and you're too near brain zero to know it. Ah well, you wouldn't recognize me turned about on my axis anyway. Best I can hope for is to be tucked away as "Nincompoop" in the safe neighborhood of the past, gone on retreat with you into your mental cave. You rise and stretch.

Did Dotty go out? One of the girls must be making breakfast. Damned squirrels—looking out at planters on the patio—*they keep tearing up my rhodies.*

Squirrels don't eat rhododendrons, Dad.

Mine do.

What? Now you own the squirrels?

Mine are. Smiling at your little joke.

Who knows, maybe they're beyond us. They've assembled the populace of a lifetime together in the mind, and it's a busy, crowded, bustling place in there. Maybe the brain's capacity, which we use but a fraction of in earlier years, is fully tapped in its last gasp. Like that mythic instant before we die, whole lifetime packed in a moment number, only this stretched to span years. Within it, you reexperience every moment of your life. What leaks out is but a trifle of the entire progeny within, an anomalous hint. We can't begin to imagine. All people-time-places jammed together indivisibly in a splendid, fully engaging menage. Think of it! You move freely among them, through time, smiling, mumbling to yourself—agitated at times, sure. Who wouldn't be? It's from this last gleeful state of all-experiencing dementia that we have taken our notion of heaven.

When you turn, those marksmen's eyes seem to have taken aim at themselves and scored direct hits, shot through with blood. How to tell you Dotty is dead? We buried her yesterday. There will be no more lunches in the dining room facing the golf course. No one to button your shirt, or iron it, or explain you are already wearing two hats, you don't need a third. I can't bring myself to tell you. Do you think me that cruel and unforgiving? Jesus! How to explain if I don't get this job, there'll be no choice but to take you home to California with me? Live, the both of us, in my hole in Pomona on my part-time wages and what pittance you have left. Five siblings with Alzheimer's: Helen, Jimmy, Paul, Lilly, Alice . . . not Petey, he wasn't born yet, still isn't. You basically supporting them: forty-thousand bucks a year times five these past four years; who knows how much before. Stock market bust. A generous man. Except with me. Just a word now and then, pat on the back, good daddy hug. Why couldn't you bring yourself to do it? You had to follow in your daddy's footsteps? What's so fucking toxic about a son? Hey, it's not me bequeathing you the foul inheritance. But then I suppose you aren't bequeathing it to me either, having inherited it yourself. If only once someone could break the pattern.

> You stand nodding at me, a funny little smile growing on your lips, the dying light silvering your hair. Then befuddlement moves like a shadow across your face. So how's this supposed to work? How to manage the transition into Good Joe's Nursing Home without a straightjacket, needles, however they do it? How to manage the transition into my life without bloodshed? You preoccupied with shards of the past, me with its resentments. How do we keep from doing injury to each other, old man? How do we undo injuries already done? How do we learn to forget?

He totters, like a child, more loveable than I've ever known him. No judgment in his face at all as he looks at me. No bunched chin or lip curled up one side. Something like amusement or pleasure in his eyes as he appears to recognize me. "Whad say, Willy Boy, you ready for some lunch?"

How I Died

Tragedy, like the flu, slips up unexpectedly. That scratchiness deep in your throat, then it's all over you. Our car accident happened that way. Driving along the New York State Thruway, two o'clock AM, vague frozen world abstracted beyond windows. A warm, cozy nest inside the van, Sting singing low on the tape deck: "Fields of Gold." My wife had just gotten the promotion to supervisor at work, and we'd been down in Manhattan celebrating. Not drunk exactly, feeling good, until Sherry asked why it is every time something good happens she tightens up. "Beware the evil eye and all."

"Nonsense. You've anticipated this for years. You're just a little nervous."

"Still," she said.

"Still what? You have to believe good things can happen for you in life, or else—"

"Else what?"

"They don't."

"Oh rot."

I was about to get pissed off—she would have to spoil this thing for herself—when Wham! Like a pipe bomb went off in back of the van. Didn't see a thing, just the impact. Today, I'd think terrorists (illogical as that might be, driving through a frozen upstate night); back then I thought Fate had booby-trapped us. Sherry's anxiety fructified. Superb timing. Why not? Tragedy selects any old time it pleases. Wham. Actually, I was too busy driving to think. We were over on two wheels, way up off the ground, Sherry whimpering *Oh God Oh God Oh God*—like he was going to get involved in this sad shit—*Oh Shit Oh shit Oh shit* . . . so we canceled each other out. Down: whump. Careening on all four wheels, crouched tractionless as a bellyboarder over the road, doing something between drift, skid, and skedaddle. Mile marker posts coming at us from all sides—fast fast. Didn't even know I knew what to do: follow a skid toward the shoulder, saw-toothed black woods beyond—accepting Fate's itinerary—then ease away toward center line, finessing happenstance. That dance: accepting/resisting. *Oh Gods* . . . *Oh Shits* . . . whatever. My fingers clutching the wheel so hard plastic liquefied and fingernails dug right through into palms of my hands. Tires shrieking like small tortured animals caught in a snare, some vaguer sound beyond their squealing—flapping, could've been, of wing beats.

I had the sense I was not driving the van but standing over my own shoulder at a game console watching the road come at me on a video screen, throwing up obstacles: concrete center divider, mile posts, trees, icy patches. Somehow we slipped past. The van made peace with itself, asphalt turned from ice to frozen fossil tar. Grit and traction. What is the French word? *Frisson*. Oh yeah, the pleasure of friction. Life begins and is preserved in friction. We slowed to a stop on the shoulder, the van did. We kept catapulting forward, accelerated on Fate's motor. I couldn't do much, really, engine dead, wheel waxen in my hands. Sherry screaming about her legs, her back, my back, seat backs flattened behind us. We'd gone right back through them. Rather that missile that rear-ended us at something near one-hundred MPH had launched the van forward beneath us. In that Dracula glow of dash lights, green of demonic fireflies, Sherry and I regarded one another.

My wife's features momentarily blurred beyond recognition, digitally whited out, as newscasts will do when people don't wish to be recognized. Sherry saw me that way, too, I would learn later. Didn't prove anything. Likely just optical shock. Still, there was no reason to believe we weren't dead. That ghastly green glow seemed evidence of it. Moreover, I felt nothing: anesthesia numb. Two possibilities: either dead, yet somehow experiencing this as if I were not, or in deep shock (Death's younger brother). Cold damp sliced across the back of my neck, cutting ligaments, tendons. Blood? My occiput— I was alarmed to realize—rested against my shoulder blade, head collapsed to one side like a weary infant's. Or a penis after orgasm. Flopping about on loose gristle of the neck. Yet no pain. That worried me. We equate death with anesthesia—cold, maybe, but painless. No blood when I touched, just icy wind leaking in the ruined rear of the van. Sherry whimpering. The dead don't whimper. They may wail and shriek.

Then something snapped. Pop. My head solid up between my shoulders again. My neck doing the job it was designed to do. Aching like a sunnabitch. Pain and plenty of it. Thank God! Kidneys don't ache in death. Nor the tongue, where my teeth had chomped, swollen to the size of a small eggplant in my mouth.

Only after reaching stasis do you consider what has occurred, realize anything has happened at all. We are *Homo retrospectus*. No greater lie than the live-in-the-moment bullshit. The moment is gone before we register its passing, tragic moments in particular. We had been rear-ended, I decided by default. Though in the instant glance at the rearview after the big bang I'd seen nothing. I saw it now: an orange glow around a curve far back down the Thruway. Hellfire! People crackling, burning up in that inferno.

I was screaming, and it wasn't pretty, demanding to know if Sherry was hurt, when I might have asked or touched. Fear does that to me. Like the time she broke her leg skiing and a pearly white splinter of tibia jutted out through downy ski pants like a postmodern obscenity. I screamed at it. At her. *What had she done to herself, for crissake. How'd she managed that?* She had the delicate courtesy to pass out. But now both of us conscious and shouting at each other: *What did you do? Are you hurt? What did you hit, Larry? I think it hit us.* My neck. Her back. Her elbow. My kidneys. Her calves. Buzzing in my ears. Screaming may be therapeutic at such moments, burns off excess adrenalin. We were not crippled, it appeared, nor hemorrhaging (unless it's true that the soul hemorrhages slowly, the reluctant ghost bleeds away). Badly shaken. Judging from her reaction, my wife was psychologically intact. *I'm going to kill the bastard. I'll tear his nuts off and wrap them around his neck.* She had not yet seen that glow behind us. *I'll grind his eyeballs into the asphalt.* She was prying at the door with her fingers. Though it may violate the axiom that women are nurturing and men basic beasts, I wanted to go help the poor SOB back there, she wanted to throttle him.

"I'll tear his balls off."

"Would you calm down, please? We have enough—"

"Don't you tell me to calm down. Look at us. Look at me. Look what he did to us." There was blood on her hands.

Why assume it was a "he"? Though I did, too, of course. What woman would smack you out of nowhere like that? No warning? (Some I know at work maybe.) Still, we assumed. Sherry opened the door but didn't get out. *I think my feet are broken.*

I turned to look into the collapsed interior of the van behind us. Not that I could see much in the darkness, my neck doing its broken hinge thing again. Alarming. Then, like a dozen deep-root molar toothaches at once, I was blinded with pain. The engine coughed in an unsavory way and expired. Sherry threw open the door. *If you don't have the balls, I'll do it myself.* I seized her arm. No use. Fury has prodigious strength. She'd have gone for him, but her legs gave way under her, and she collapsed whimpering to the ground. I was good and scared then. She didn't care about the legs, was screaming at me to go back and finish the monster off, kick in his eyes. Sherry anneals under pressure. But the legs were fine, just cramped, since she managed to kick me solidly in the chest when I came around the van to help her up. Would surely have looked strange to a passerby: the two of us rolling about on the shoulder, beating each other up beside that ruined van. Leaking gas, engine releasing unsavory hisses, groans, metal fatigued and mourning.

But there were no passersby, that's the thing. Not a car.

"Jesus . . . Sherry." I had gotten her up. Likely she saw the glow of it on my face, as I did on hers: cheeks washed in pink, a little hellfire in eye whites. I was running then, best I could, for a car sideways across the road, burning with a kind of intestinal fury, belching flames from its guts. Dirty orange swirling smoke. All the way—perhaps three hundred yards—kept telling myself that cops see this kind of thing every night; I could handle whatever I found back there, could get a door open, maybe wrestle the poor bastard out and roll him in dirty snow. If only my head would remain upright.

For the second time that night I saw what I would come to know as "facial blurring." Existential fade-out. The driver seated still inside the car, glowing in the ambient blaze. His hair scattered as in sleep. I saw him clearly. But his face blurred beyond recognition. Next moment I realized the seat was empty, and he was standing perhaps fifty feet from the car, stunned, staring at it. Me at him, feeling a little cheated in some gothic way. And the odd thing, though the flames were in front rather than behind him, he was silhouetted, a shadowier figure than the one in the car. But no blurring.

"Are you okay," he asked, when I hobbled up.

"How about you, fella, are you okay? Jesus! look at your car."

"Totaled," he said. "Brand new."

"How did you . . . ?" How could anyone walk away from that mess? Front end compressed as if by a garbage compactor (what had become of the engine block?), windshield shattered, side mirrors folded back like wings. But the rear end perfectly intact. Spotless. Fancy little number: Acura. *Just bought it last week.* Freak hybrid:

the ruined/the intact joined at the waist. A motif I would come to appreciate.

"You okay, dude?"

"I think so. My neck . . . my wife," I motioned back at the van. *You're lucky she didn't get to you first.*

"I called," he said, displaying a cell phone. Still something of a novelty in those days. "Sorry. I'm real sorry. I fell asleep, I guess. Last thing I remember was: 'Rest Stop one mile.'"

"Maybe ten miles back." I stared at him.

"Yeh, I blew it. Sorry. I held my breath, opened the windows, I was singing to Van Halen. Like nothing worked. My fault, you know, dude. No problem."

Oh yeah there is, sure as hell there is. My wife—her legs, her back. Smacked her head real good. Lucky I got to you first.

He was shivering. Drugs I thought. Hyper, dancing about, telling me his life story: he didn't get enough sleep, worked in Albany and drove down to Manhattan three nights a week, his girlfriend chilling on him, he'd just been to see her, might be losing his job, and owed twenty grand on his Acura. *I'm not sleeping so good.*

Still, it's no reason—

No . . . really. Hey, you're right. What do you think? My fault, dude. I mean it. Totally. How's your wife? Maybe we should check it out.

I think you better sit down, fella. You're a little pale.

Yeah. Yeah. Maybe I better.

"I need to get back to my wife."

He waved a hand. How's the song go: lighter shade of pale? Funny thing is, his was a darker shade. Pale nonetheless. Spook pale. It was a miracle he lived through this, I said. Front end of his car peeled right back, engine—what you saw of it in the flames—like a corpse on a funeral pyre, split in half. Windshield oddly intact. I didn't know much then about symptoms of advanced cardiovascular shock, else I would have been more insistent, gotten him down and covered up. It was cold, ten degrees, the guy in shirt sleeves. Sweating and shivering at once, but wouldn't take my jacket. It's cool, he kept saying, dying of shock and brain concussion. His legs folded under him like a gateleg table.

———

My Uncle Paul was an insurance adjustor. As a boy, I remember him talking to my dad, his speech peppered with "fraudulent," "disingenuous," "deceptive," and "fatuous." When I looked the words up in the dictionary, I decided insurance adjusting wasn't any job I wanted. The adjustor called out to inspect our ruined van confirmed that notion. A frown had worked in permanently around his mouth and eyes, cheeks grayish-blue, cadaverous, as was a graven crease in his forehead. He smoked incessantly, lit one cigarette off another and crushed butts out against his left thumbnail. Impressive. The nail had thickened, cracked, and gone permanently black with a white weal dead center. Something familiar about him.

He circled the van. "What a heap of shit" (meaning pre-accident as much as post, I understood).

"I'm fond of it, anyway. I did the interior work myself. I'd like to salvage it."

"Yeh? I bet you did." He squatted and looked underneath with what seemed a painful craning of his neck (my own still on the blink), stood up, dusted off his hands. "Acura went right up your poop chute. That's why you're standing here today. Rode up under you. Half the impact went up—gas tank and transaxle." He was taking notes on a clipboard.

"Repairable you think?"

"Not this time, pal." *Total Loss.* I saw him write it. "Maybe $2,500 book. Tops."

True, the van looked a loss: collapsed over rear tires; stress lines and wrinkles in its metallic skin. Inanimate things, it occurred to me, age all at once. Wham. But who's to say a car is inanimate?

"That's preposterous, I've got five grand in the interior alone."

He smiled unpleasantly. "Sure you do."

"That's not counting labor, maybe two hundred hours. You don't believe me? I did the built-ins, appliances, and wiring myself."

"Heard you the first time. Total loss." He underlined it. "No insurance company I know about pays out for hobbies."

"Walnut cabinets, maybe five hundred dollars in fittings alone. Propane stove, fridge, and light fixtures. Take a look . . ." *Fraudulent*, I was thinking, *bogus . . . disingenuous*. But couldn't get rear doors open, they'd melded together. Sliding door on the side jammed. He shrugged and followed me over ruined front seats, flattened like operating tables. The adjustor whistled. "You got lucky."

He came across the lauan replacement door I'd slapped on a cupboard before the accident; original item had sprung. He worked thin wood between thumb and forefinger and chuckled, enjoying what he saw as my flimsy attempt at fraud. "Philippine trash mahogany, eight dollars a sheet at Home Depot. Good try, pal."

"Check the others. Go on."

"Time's up. You're not the only person trying to hype an insurance company today."

Something—maybe the tombish interior of the van—brought up a likeness. *I know you*, I said. *You're Kurt Feuerwahl. I went to high school with you.*

That's what they tell me.

An omen, though I didn't know it yet. Actually, the first sign was X-rays taken of Sherry's skull and spine the day after the accident. The technician couldn't get the camera positioned properly. He kept grinding its snout into her neck and lower back, tugging and yanking rudely at her. Finally, she slapped him. *That hurts!*

You keep moving. I can't get a clear image.

I am not moving.

Shaking maybe. It happens. Muscle tremors. All the prints are coming out blurry.

He showed us a take: edges clear—either end of a spooky spinal column—but the center where there might be a fracture blurred. I knew it was a portent at the time, but didn't know how to read it. We sat long in that waiting room after Sherry walked out, staring at a wall across the way. An idea beginning to take form.

Blurred . . . like that driver's face.
Don't do this. I don't want you doing this.

The cop arrived before I got back to the van that frozen Thruway night, as if he'd been waiting somewhere nearby. Sherry hobbled into the road to wave him down, his headlights flashing her off the highway. Though there hadn't been another car or interstate rig along that stretch. Strange. Four times, the cop asked if I was wearing my seatbelt. He kept nodding yes, but I didn't pick up on it. *Yes,* Sherry coaxed, *yes he was.*

I need to hear him say it, ma'am. Forms, he said, finally entering my answer. You know, it wasn't like me. In my line of work you have to be acute. Shock, I imagine. Sherry acute as ever; though couldn't walk, her head throbbing, hand trembling at her forehead.

Paramedics made no attempt to hide their concern—three AM on the slushy shoulder of a cruel interstate. Honesty time. *Acute cardiovascular shock,* muttering. The woman, quite young, kept saying, *He's hypo.* Poor dude's eyes trying to roll back in his head. We sat obediently awaiting our turn. I recall the girl looking in, parting Sherry's hair and clenching her teeth. I recall them talking it over with the cop, looking at the van. That's all. Can events blur, too? Time? They whisked our assailant away. We rode home fifty miles in the front cab of a tow truck. First light attempting its own futile truth when the driver wheeled into our drive. Finished the story he was telling about the worst accident he'd ever seen, where a father had been holding a finger to a hole in his son's neck to stop bleeding from the carotid artery. *Like that kid over there in Holland somewheres with his finger in the dyke. But the father passed under and the blood come squirting. Boy's mother pinned under the car maybe a foot too far away to reach him. When I arrived at the scene, she was still chewing at her leg to try and break free. She chewed half through it like you will hear about a wolf in a trap. Lain there in a lake of her boy's blood and chewed at herself. You know that's got to be hard, watching your kid bleed to death. You good people be careful now. You got real lucky tonight.*

Sherry seeming anything but lucky as I helped her out of the high cab. Not herself. Subdued. Nearly weightless. Seemed a contradiction. Once inside, we slept the sleep of the dead.

Weeks later we still didn't feel ourselves. *Bound to happen, a brush like that.* We would slip past each other in the house, both of us wondering why we should take so much time off work. Kurt Feuerwahl's client creams you like that, I suppose you owe it to yourself to take vacation time on his insurance company. Trauma leave.

Do you think he died?

What do you care? You wanted to throttle him with his own scrotum at the time, I recall.

That was then. I'm serious, Larry. You think he made it? He didn't look good.

We could check.

Typically, Sherry would go right to the phone. You don't make dispatch supervisor without having that go-ahead personality. But shook her head now. Death wasn't territory she wanted to trespass just then. Me neither.

I went for a walk one autumnal day mid-March, ragtags of dirty snow sucked up by unseasonable warmth. A balmy breeze blew off the Hudson, vaguely fishy. A bold posting on the front door of a house on the corner of Rhinebeck and Duvallier Streets: "Condemned by order of the Board of Health." I wondered what could condemn a house: raw sewage, infestations of maggots or rats? The last of fall's leaves rotting in ditches, along with a possum. Its skull eyes fixed on me as I passed. The Johannason's barn, set back off the old post road, freshly painted. Red with black hex signs up under the eaves. Sherry once complained about it to town council: "I don't appreciate being hexed every time I drive by." Sippy Kroener said it was part of our local heritage—Rensselaer Dutch and all—written up besides in *Architectural Digest*. Large enough to house 747s. I liked it, actually, but didn't dare tell Sherry. She mentioned a case where the Supreme Court decided students have a right to post hate messages inside their dorm rooms but not on doors other students must pass on their way to the john. "I can't reach my home without being hexed."

Sippy Kroener said they were meant to work opposite. "To keep off hexes. You ought to feel safer passing that way." But Sherry kept the heel of her hand planted on the horn every time she passed that barn, hexing the hexes.

Now, and oddly, hex signs blurred when I looked directly at them. Only stood bold in peripheral vision. Fresh paint, I told myself. A car passed, ancient station wagon, throwing up a cold, foul breath of wind from a roadside ditch which clung to my skin like a cobweb. Passengers in the car grinned back at me as children will, blessed with some secret knowing, but these weren't children. I could almost hear their goading chant: *Ha-ha, ha-ha-ha.* That instant the thought struck me: maybe we died in that accident and don't realize we are dead. We're walking dead, confused, undecided. That's something to ridicule.

I ran back to the house, burst in, and shared my revelation with Sherry. Her head shaking along with her hands. *No, no . . . don't. Larry . . . Don't you dare. Don't go there.* Not Sherry typical. Stricken, as if I'd spoken words she was thinking and had no defense against. We sat side by side on the couch until the room darkened, seeing little reason to turn on a light. Now and again we touched each other. Animal thing, but little reassurance in it. We might toss together on the rug and do violent orgasms. It wouldn't prove we were alive. The dead—in our waking state—surely fuck, they send e-mails, they wrap Christmas presents. No doubt they attend funerals and write corny odes to lost friends.

Finally I broke the spell, rose and turned on a lamp. In that swath of light, my wife's hair had bleached to apricot, straw dry as the hair I'd once seen on a mummy at the British Museum. Impossible. You don't dessicate so fast, not the walking dead. She was regarding me in little sips; I had no desire to know what she saw.

"But how's it work exactly?" I asked. "When I talked to Jody at work he responded as if I was alive. So did Mrs. Carpenter next door, the postman, your niece. Are they dead, too, and don't realize? All of us rushed forward—or sideways—into some purgatory where we go on living unawares? The dead world existing side-by-side with the living?"

"Would you stop, Larry! Jesus."

"Or maybe we slip back in secretly among the living after we die. They're no more aware we're dead than we are. *Death where is thy sting.* Comforting thought. Still, there may be telltale signs; we should watch for them. I've known people who seem half there; they return from a vacation and seem off. Maybe we're all dying and being born all the time. No big deal. Remember how Kennedy's assassination was reported in Thailand before he was shot. Maybe he'd already died, then he died again. They're more keen on these things over there. Or maybe we start dying the moment we're born, like they say. Some of us are just a bit more advanced—"

"Larry . . . please. Damn you."

"Look, something happened to us. We might as well be dead, we feel dead. That isn't going away. Then again," the thought struck me, "people do disappear after they die. They're gone. How's that work in? True, grieving wives sometimes report seeing their departed husbands standing in a doorway. They do make visits."

"You're losing it. Downright morbid. I want you to stop."

"That's the point. Don't you see? We are morbid. Maybe some of us slip through the cracks. Death doesn't quite nab us. That doesn't mean we're spooks or werewolves or anything. More like successful tax evaders. Common people missed by the auditor."

"Okay." She stood up. "I'm making dinner. You may be too morbid to eat but I'm starved."

"You're absolutely right. It's the kind of thing we should watch for: any change in eating habits. There's a chance, you know, there are multiple planes of being—of time. Life is just the starting point. You die out of it into a slightly jilted time frame: live people walking a mini-second ahead of us dead. We see them but they don't see us. We converse with them. Don't ask me how it works. They can't even explain schizophrenia, for crissake! Death is surely more complex. I'm only saying we should keep our eyes open, look for phenomena like talking out of lip sync, things like that."

Within days, Sherry was saying I'd grown philosophical since I died. And talkative.

I awoke the morning after my revelation living in the California high desert near Palm Springs. Hot wind licked through the bedroom window; I got up to close it, wondering aloud, "How can it be so hot in March? Why'd we pile on so many covers?"

You always do, Lar.

Turning at that voice, I found a strange woman lying in bed. Not possibly even Sherry reborn. This woman fleshier, broad-faced and jovial, skin the color and resonance of bronze. In time, I learn she is my second wife. Though I've given up chronological time since I died. What's the point of it? We can't decide whether my first wife died or I became too kooky for her. Sometimes I miss her. Then find Sherry asleep with her head in my lap, hair askew, straw dry when I run my fingers through it.

I've been studying the time physicists, Alan Lightman and others. I've tried on their theories, like the "echo effect" concept. Imagine one plane of time echoed by another, where the dead self and the living play tag with each other, one slightly ahead. Occasionally, we catch glimpses of our echo-selves; we call that "déjà vu." "Time's ocean" even more compelling. Past-present-future swim around us all at once—or we in it. We're all both living and dead at once, so it's easy to explain how the dead converse with the living and vice-versa. Think of it as time's pool, with eddies and currents working through, forward and backward. Sometimes little vortexes form within the broader water. That's when things get interesting. My new wife, Cora, Sherry, and my high school girlfriend all sit on my lap at once, flip past each other, rather, at slight intervals like one of those animated flip books. Very exciting. It no longer seems odd to me that Kennedy's death should be reported before he is shot. There's a mining town in Montana that just received word of his trip to Dallas on the wire services. I mourn their coming grief and Kennedy's assassination. No one should have to experience that twice, but that bullet keeps echoing. Important thing is not to get confused or distracted by any of this. Stay on track. Once you're dead it's easier. But then, likely, you are dead and haven't realized it. Only the pre-dead insist on linearity's sad traps. You see them scurrying about believing they'll get things finished before they die, believing there is some progression—winners and losers—all that rot. Existence is more like soccer than American football: you don't march straight on toward goal posts, you run round and round the field, sometimes get lucky. Try to envision linear sex and you'll catch my meaning.

We can look it up at the library. There's a new periodical database.

You look it up if you must, Larry. I'm sick and tired of the whole thing. I'd like to go on living again.

My guess is we can once we have a definite answer. It's disconcerting not to know whether you're living or dead.

I punch in date, place of accident. Pop! Up comes an article in the *Albany Journal*. Richard Henry Defrost died in the ambulance on the way to the hospital. May he rest in peace (at least be more happily agitated dead). *Acute cardiovascular shock . . . Driver and passenger in a Chevrolet van . . .* words blurred there. Existential whiteout. *At the scene . . .* I make out. *New York State troopers report both vehicles totaled.* Fate's censor has been at it. When I print out the article on an attendant printer, words fuzz as if it is running out of ink. A fidgety librarian offers help. Doubtless, I err in telling her I am trying to find out if I died in a recent car accident. She keeps glancing sideways at me, eyeballs walling white. When she pulls up the screen, the bottom of the newspaper page shears off. "Gracious." Something to do with scanning from the microfiche, she explains.

"Can you see how many were reported dead?"

"There's nothing there. Listen, sir, I really do think . . . Well, I'm not saying, of course . . . You're welcome to use library facilities—"

"The article was there when I looked." My eyes narrow at her, seeking telltale clues. "Ahhhh, I get it. If we're both dead, the blurring intensifies. Makes sense."

She doesn't cease looking back at me over a shoulder as she hurries away. I disappear into book stacks before she can summon security. Think how many misunderstandings occur just because people are dead and somewhat cranky.

Some days later I pull up Richard DeFrost's obit: twenty-six, an investment banker with an MBA from NYU, golf enthusiast. I remember him standing on the shoulder looking back at himself burning up in that brand-new Acura, shaking something awful. Third degree burns over eighty percent of his body. I might not have noticed the other two obits but for the blurring. The censor has been less conscientious here, no doubt assuming the living will not seek themselves among the dead. *Fatuous.* Has left clues: *Dispatch Supervisor . . . beloved wife of . . . known for her unflinching honesty . . . fatal head wound . . . Devoted gardener . . . tried his hand at short stories . . .* Might fit many people, but the blurring a dead giveaway.

I ask a stringy-haired college student if he can read the articles for me. *My eyesight!* I'd been studying him, not fooled by his air of cocky nihilism. The dead can pick out the virgin living like cocksmen pick out the undeflowered. Nothing but programmer's squiggles on the screen when we pull up the obits. "Wha'd you do, man? It's fucked."

"Be grateful you're living. You can tell your friends you talked to a dead man today."

"Freak! You should stay out on the street where you belong."

This morning Cora—Sherry more likely—left an announcement for my first Rensselaer High School Reunion open on my desk. I look out at mountains, happy that the dead rejoice in the glory of a mountain escarpment as much as the living do—perhaps more, recognizing as we do our affinity to the earth. We are simply another manifestation of the same minerals and elements, just as ephemeral, as permanent. She has circled the name: Kurt Feuerwahl (deceased—Vietnam). Dead years before he appraised my van. I regret that I didn't express my condolences at the time. I'd like to know how he died, but wouldn't have asked. You might think the dead would reminisce on circumstances of their deaths when they encounter one another. What could be more exciting? But death counsels circumspection. Nothing is tackier than living corpses one-upping each other in gruesomeness. We dead are studiedly civil, humbled by mysteries we don't comprehend. Tragedy, in itself, makes no sense. Why should it make sense? Just happens. Never conveniently. I make a mental note that if I ever meet Kurt again (maybe a vortex, a back-swirling eddy) I will express my regret. But, you know, we dead suffer amnesia at such moments. Confusion. We are all prone to Alzheimer's in death. The only cure is to live as vigorously as possible.

The remarkable thing, you know, years ago when I looked Kurt up in my yellowed yearbook, I found he was dead before his picture was taken. He looked it. Had been creamed on his motorcycle by a drunk driver his junior year in high school. No wonder he chose that profession. He didn't want anyone walking away from an accident with any less than he deserved—or any more.

"How many times can a person die before they stop dying?" I ask Cora.

"As many as they need to. Some get greedy." Cora winks at me.

"Does it ever end?"

Cora smiles vaguely off at an evening sky the blue of Rembrandt's dreams. We sit out front on the patio drinking beer; dusk like a cup of cool water dumped over the scalp on a scorching day. There is no cool without heat. No pleasure without pain. No life without death. She giggles as I talk, explaining some of time's wrinkles to her, outright guffaws when I stumble onto wiggier concepts. "Sometimes, time is like a postman who rings your doorbell and leaves a package which hasn't yet been sent. We call that 'intuition' or 'precognition.' Or like a thief who breaks in and steals the package before it's sent. That's a baffler—when all circumstances point in one direction, then what you expect to happen doesn't. But what baffles me most is how time can be an arrow and a circle and an echo all at once." Cora chuckles lustily, soon she will begin licking her lips. Such talk gets her hot. I never finish these dissertations before she throws the glass over her shoulder into the cactus garden and straddles me. "Not here in front," I insist.

"Why not, lover, we're the both of us dead."

True, it does make you less self-conscious.

I suspect Cora is long dead. Something pre-Columbian about her. The depth of her voice and texture of her skin. Impossible to determine her ancestry. Little of everything. Though her bronzed skin tone could be the buffing of time itself. It's while we are making love that I talk of serendipity. "Time jumps like a toad and fate with it. A chance meeting with someone who offers you a splendid job. Maybe she was your boss in some earlier life which you've forgotten. Traffic accidents are like that. Chance encounters with assailants who've been at us before." We both come then. Explosively. Right after, she whispers fragments of things which it has taken me years to piece together: names, as I take it, of our past incarnations, those many places where we've made love over the eons . . . Distinctly, one day, I hear her say "Sherry." Did I have to die to find Cora?

Fortunately, we living dead don't smell or putrefy in the heat. Which brings me to the final and irrevocable knowing. *Do we ever die? Completely? Dead gone completely out of this life?* Afraid so. Though I only came to know it recently, serendipitously. Or long ago following the accident? I'm working in the garden, anyhow. That's timeless.

The smell of a dead animal lingers about the place, growing ranker each day with annealing heat. Close but I can't find it. I find a hole, small burrow in the ground, but can't tell if the smell is coming from there. On a whim, I get the hose and pour water down (this several weeks after my revelation—did I mention it?), and I'm astonished when steam wafts out of the hole, coils creepily upward. "Gotcha!" I cry. Amazed. I've never seen anything like it. I run to get Sherry, thinking this will cheer her up. Death so hot down in its burrow it boils water. She stands looking down at it. Squats and holds a hand in rising vapor, rubs her fingers lustily together and looks slyly up at me (it's Cora, of course; Sherry would leap away in disgust).

"Don't do that." I grip her shoulder. "It could be diseased."

"Don't be silly. Its soul," she says, "that's its soul rising from the hole. Free now. We should rejoice for it." She rubs the hand over her face.

"Next you'll tell me it's Gandhi or Siddhartha finally released from the cycle."

She nods. "Sure. Could be. A very great event. And a commonplace one."

I regard her, awed. It's humbling to live with someone dead as long as Cora—her wisdom. She's right: a great and commonplace event. And I've never seen anything like it: an actual departing soul.

Could it be that from my new estate I envision what I could not see locked in corporeal time? Once it would have seemed preposterous: a dead ground squirrel's soul rising from its tomb in a vapor. Antimodern. Savage. Does death take you backwards? Does time finish its loop?

But I'm not dead, I would insist to Sherry. *We're not. It's some natural phenomenon easily explained by science.* She would agree, clinging hard as she could to life.

"Maybe it's my wife—my other wife," I say. "I can see her zooming along, living and dying on so many planes at once she can't keep track. Dispatching herself. She's capable of that."

Cora nods, then smells her fingers and shakes her head. "Not yet."

"How long?" I ask.

"It's a lot of work. You have to keep at it until you're ready to let go."

"Centuries?" I ask. "Eons? Seems you'd have enough of it."

"Then again, it's not really like that. You simply stop separating yourself and decide to blend in. No longer *you* but *us*."

"Part of the circling sea. Time itself." I nod.

"Do you want to make love? This kind of talk always makes me horny."

So we do—atop corn stalks, rolling in beds of lettuce, knocking heads off cabbage, crushing eggplant hearts. When we climax Cora evaporates. Just like that. Vapor rising upward, and I am clutching at it with my fingers.

ACKNOWLEDGMENTS

While it is true that writing is mostly a solitary task, the support and encouragement of others help keep it from becoming a lonely one. I wish to thank all those whose helpful comments on individual stories and enthusiasm for my work have informed this collection. Special thanks to my editor, Matt Bokovoy, for his tireless efforts, to Karen Wieder for her copyediting suggestions, to Pamela Uschuk and William Pitt Root, who generously read and commented on the manuscript, and to the editors at the magazines where these works first appeared, including Robert Fogarty at the *Antioch Review* for his editorial advice on the title story. Most of all, I want to thank my wife, Lucinda Luvaas, my first and most valued reader and my inspiration, who is giving my stories a new life in her splendid films.

The stories in this collection were originally published as follows:

"Original Sin" first appeared in the anthology *VeriTales: The First Anthology*, ed. Helen Wirth (Fall Creek, Ore.: Fall Creek Press, 1993), 97–121; reprinted in *The Sun: A Magazine of Ideas*, October 1994: 32–37.

"The Sexual Revolution" appeared in *Confrontation* 56–57 (Summer/Fall 1995): 87–92.

"Carpentry" appeared in the *American Fiction Anthology* 9 (Minneapolis: New Rivers Press, 1997): 198–208.

"Trespass" appeared in *Grain Magazine* 34.3 (Winter 2007): 49–58.

"The Woman Who Was Allergic to Herself" appeared in *Vignette* 2.2 (Summer 1996): 108–122.

"A Working Man's Apocrypha" appeared in *The Antioch Review* 62.3 (Summer 2004): 534–48. A film of "A Working Man's Apocrypha" was produced by A Wing 'n' a Prayer Productions and directed by Lucinda Luvaas.

"Yesterday After the Storm" appeared in *Glimmer Train* 12 (Fall 1994): 33–51.

"Season of Limb Fall" appeared in *Blackbird* 3.1 (Spring 2004), http://www.blackbird.vcu.edu/v3nl/fiction/luvaas w/season.html

"Hilltop (An American Story)" appeared in *The American Literary Review* 1.1 (Spring 1990): 91–102.

"Silver Thaw" appeared in *Oxford Magazine* 7.1 (Spring/Summer 1990): 100–106.

"Let It Snow" appeared in *Tamaqua* 3.1 (Spring 1992): 70–79.

"Rain" appeared in *Thema* 3.2 (Winter 1990/91): 129–52.

"To The Death" appeared in *Epiphany Magazine* (Fall 2004), http://www.eiphanyzine.com/archives/fiction_fall_2004/000007.html

"How I Died" appeared in *Pretext 10* (Autumn/Winter 2004): 3–19. (University of East Anglia, Norwich, Great Britain: Pen & Ink Press).

Northport - E. Northport Public Library
185 Larkfield Road
E. Northport, N.Y. 11731
261-2313